A MOST DEADLY GAME

We returned to the Green Room where we found the host of *Murder Game,* Peter Grover, holding court with the panelists, a glass of mineral water with a slice of lime in one hand. He smiled smugly at the group, then glanced to the door. Suddenly, his smile froze. The glass crashed to the floor.

Jayne and I stood in the doorway. The Allens back from the dead—which, I can assure you, had not been an easy journey.

"Good evening, ladies and germs. Are we all ready to play a little murder game?" I said.

The producer gasped. "You're not supposed to be here! You've been replaced!"

"Try it, and we'll see you in court," I told her pleasantly. "We've got a contract."

"Places, Mr. Grover," the stage manager said.

The show was about to begin. Consummate showman that he was, Peter recovered from his shock and quickly took charge. The producer spouted objections, but Peter's natural authority silenced her. Putting one arm around Jayne and the other around me, he smiled brightly. "Welcome back. I can't tell you how glad I am to see you. It would be a very dull *Murder Game* without my dear friends."

"Tonight, friends," I said, "the game is for keeps."

STEVE ALLEN

THE MURDER GAME

ZEBRA BOOKS
KENSINGTON PUBLISHING CORP.

ZEBRA BOOKS are published by

Kensington Publishing Corp.
475 Park Avenue South
New York, NY 10016

First Paperback Printing: January 1994

Printed in the United States of America

To my loved ones

Chapter 1

"Sorry," Jayne told the telephone. "On Thursday we have to be in Idaho, or Iowa—one of those states that begins with an *I.*"

"Albuquerque," I whispered from my side of the roll-away breakfast table.

"Steve, Albuquerque's *not* a state," Jayne whispered, putting her hand momentarily over the receiver. I smiled encouragingly at her grasp of American geography. Early morning sunshine was flooding our top floor suite, in a hotel that was located in Cincinnati . . . or were we in Cleveland?

This lack of knowing where we were or where we were going may seem strange to the average mortal not involved in the peripatetic world of show business, but for five weeks Jayne and I had been on a whirlwind coast-to-coast tour, sometimes in two cities a day, publicizing a new book, doing a play—A. J. Gurney's *Love Letters*—as well as making TV and radio appearances. I also did two symphony orchestra concerts, one lecture, and God knows what else. America was becoming a blur in my mind, a tapestry of theaters, restaurants, freeways, and shopping malls.

"Perhaps we can have lunch sometime in May or

June," Jayne was saying pleasantly into the telephone. She was talking with a pesky television producer, a woman not content to go through the usual channels (our agent or my office) and who had been leaving a trail of urgent telephone messages from Memphis to Minnesota, and clear down to this unknown city that began with the letter *C*.

Jayne was eating a peach, the telephone cradled against her well-formed and jewelry-bedecked right ear, saying, "Mmm . . . yes, I see . . . well, I'd be delighted to discuss this, my dear, but we're thirty minutes late already, and I—"

This business of waking up without having a clear fix on geographical location had started in my early years when I traveled a great deal with my vaudevillian mother. As a child herself, in keeping with a centuries-old custom among poor Irish families with large numbers of children, she had been more or less given away—loaned out?—to a pair of Irish women from the old neighborhood who had changed their name to the Watson Sisters and who worked as circus acrobats with a Mexican fellow named Zamora.

Under the general umbrella, or tent, of the Ringling Brothers Circus, she traveled through Europe and the U.S.A. between the ages of ten and thirteen. There must have been many a morning when she would awaken, probably having arrived in sleepy darkness the night before, without at first knowing where the new camp had been set down. I can still recall moments in my own childhood when I would awaken assuming that I was home, which itself had no fixed location but was a word that referred to a seemingly endless series of apartments in mostly poor sections of Chicago. It was usually the strange wallpaper that told me where I wasn't, though it gave no clue as to where I was.

In the present instance, I thought the time had come to do away with such a point of ignorance. I stood up and glanced out the window at a busy downtown city street some thirty floors below, but these days downtown city streets are nearly as interchangeable as hotel rooms. Then I remembered that a newspaper had arrived with our breakfast cart and, for a clever detective like me, should provide a vital clue. I unfolded the paper to discover the front page of *The Chicago Tribune*.

Ah, the old hometown. Of course. It was a relief to know where we were, but suddenly the whole show biz lifestyle struck me as crazy. Chicago was one of my favorite towns, and I hadn't even known I was here! I wondered if I should give up this life and get a *real* job. But I had been traveling for over fifty years, and it seemed a little late to start something new.

"Have you had your vitamin C?" Jayne asked, after hanging up the phone and looking at me with a worried expression.

"E, C, and B," I muttered, stepping cautiously back to the hotel window. I was experiencing a new difficulty, perhaps even a mental breakdown. The problem I was having was that the view out my window, upon further consideration, simply didn't *look* like Chicago. I could find no sign of the river, Lake Michigan, or the neighborhood around the Ambassador East, where we usually stayed in Chicago.

"Columbus, Ohio," said Jayne, coming to the rescue.

"But the newspaper . . ."

"I asked the concierge to send the Chicago paper up with breakfast. There was a review I wanted to see.

Don't worry, dear. Columbus didn't know where he was, either, and they named a town after him."

Jayne and I had a good laugh. Then she told me about *The Murder Game*.

Chapter 2

The overly persistent producer who had been on the phone had an actual name—Phoebe North. During the few moments my attention had lapsed and Jayne had finished her conversation, she had agreed to meet with Ms. North for exactly fifteen minutes at the Dallas-Fort Worth airport. We had a short layover there the following Thursday, en route from St. Louis to Albuquerque, and apparently by lucky coincidence, Phoebe North would also be in Dallas at just that time. She would pop into a limousine, meet us at the airport, and pitch her proposal to Jayne while we changed planes.

I wouldn't want anyone to think that Jayne and I ordinarily do business like this. As I've indicated, when someone wants either of our services, separately or as a husband-wife combo, they go through our agent or speak to my secretary at the office. They lay out the proposal, and we say yes, no, maybe, or let's find out more details. In show business, however, unusual things happen all the time. Movies, plays, television shows, recordings—all these projects occasionally germinate from chance meetings at airports, restaurants, parties, sometimes even a shared restroom. In this case, Jayne consented to the unusual meeting for two reasons: She was curious what this Phoebe North individual could be like, and the lady producer was trying to put together a revival of the TV game show, *The Murder Game,* of which Jayne had once been so successfully a part.

Perhaps I should explain that, in those early TV days, game shows telecast during the evening hours had a certain glamour, which God knows they don't have now. There was *What's My Line?,* on which I served as a regular panelist, working with Arlene Francis, Dorothy Kilgallen, Bennett Cerf, and our host, John Daly.

The other most prestigious show of that same sort was *I've Got a Secret,* in which Jayne appeared as a panelist, along with Henry Morgan, Bill Cullen, and the actress Faye Emerson. The program's host was Garry Moore. We lived in New York in those days, and since that was where most of the main game-show action took place, Jayne also had time to work on *The Murder Game* once a week. Programs of that sort, you see, are not rehearsed, so there's really nothing for panelists to do but show up at the studio, do thirty minutes of on-camera work, and then go home. With the possible exception of hosting a talk show, which is really stealing money, serving as a panelist on a game show is the easiest gig in show business.

And so on a Thursday in early April—two days after getting lost and found in Columbus, Ohio—Jayne and I flew through an unseasonably early thunderstorm in a jet plane which was tossed about in the dark clouds, causing Jayne's airline lunch to remain untouched. Nothing kills my appetite. The sky was so black I don't know how the pilot ever found Texas. At the last moment, we dropped out of a cloud onto the runway, bounced a couple of times, and then lumbered toward a rain-soaked terminal as everyone on board applauded.

As I was leaving the plane, I noticed that the stewardess, who had assumed the duty of saying goodbye to every passenger, had a sweet, rich deep-Southern accent. Instead of saying *bye,* what she was actually saying was *bah,* to each of about one hundred fifty travelers. She sounded exactly like a sheep.

"Bah, humbug," I said to her when I reached the exit door.

"Stop flirting," said my wife. I grinned sheepishly.

We walked up the ramp and into the terminal, where huge families were meeting long-lost grandmothers, and uncles in cowboy hats. Then I noticed a young woman cutting through the crowd, smiling at us with a thousand watts of energy. She couldn't have been over five feet three, but this young woman was a dynamo.

"Mr. Allen! Miss Meadows! Thank you so much for letting me meet you here. I'm Phoebe North. Your plane was seven minutes late, so I'd better get right down to business."

Phoebe took hold of Jayne possessively by one arm and walked between us, guiding us down the terminal corridor toward our connecting flight to Albuquerque. I'm always surprised how young some of these new generation Hollywood executives are. Ms. North had a mischievous, round freckly face and looked rather like a naughty seventeen-year-old girl. Presumably she was older, although at my age everyone under thirty looks like a high schooler. As we walked, the lady producer talked in short staccato bursts of nervous energy.

"First of all, I have to tell you how fabulously excited everyone at the network is about the show. I mean, we grew up on this show. What was Sunday night without *The Murder Game?* Jayne, let me tell you honestly, for me this is a lot more than a chance to produce just another television show. This is like . . . well, a piece of my childhood."

"I was almost a child myself then," remarked Jayne with only a touch of sarcasm. But it had been twenty years since the show had gone off the air, and Phoebe North must have been in diapers at the time.

As the young producer gushed on about the network's plans, I found myself a little surprised. *The Murder Game,* after all, belonged to an earlier era when conversation was an art and wit a more gentle thing. Peter Grover, creator of the show—and most urbane host—had dreamed up the game a quarter of a century ago, and it had made him a rich man. The idea was that each week the permanent celebrity panel would compete against a guest panel to solve a fictitious murder, the general plot of which was acted out in a brief skit at the start of the show. I suppose there was a bloodthirsty element in all this, but the point was to be as clever and witty as possible and make logical deductions to solve the crime and therefore win the game. As in the case of *What's My Line?* and *I've Got a Secret,* it was the wit and sophisticated banter between host and panelists that made the show a hit; there were no flashing lights, buzzers, or electronic boards to distract the audience. In a sense, the show was only once removed from the type of parlor game like charades, which people used to play when they still possessed the simple ability to amuse themselves, before television turned us into sofa-spuds.

"The network really thinks the show could work again?" I asked Phoebe, interrupting her flow of

14

hyperbole. She turned to me with her mouth agape, as though I had questioned the traditions of my people.

"Mr. Allen! All over the country there are mystery weekends and mystery cruises—this sort of thing is really big now. Anyway, America's in the mood for nostalgia," she told me firmly. "In fact, we're going to give *The Murder Game* its old Sunday night time slot. And we're not going to tape the show, we're going to broadcast *live* each week!"

"No kidding!" I said. Live television was an entirely different creature than the canned variety—more fun, more tension, more highs, more lows, more everything, including problems. If you made a goofola in live TV, it was broadcast into the living rooms of America. Naturally, this created an excitement that was quite different from what you find on the set of a taped program. To tell the truth, live television was a lot of fun, and much of that fun and sense of immediacy got through to the audience.

"Isn't the network taking a gamble on this?" I asked.

Phoebe shrugged. "Well, they've given us an order for ten shows. If it works—as I'm *sure* it will—we get picked up for a year."

"Have you talked to the others?" asked Jayne, referring to the old gang who had made the show such a hit.

"Oh, yes! Peter's going to be the host, and we have Sylvia, Dominic, and Susan for the panel, just like the old days. Even Amaretta has agreed to do her old shtick. So you see, Jayne, you absolutely *must* be on the panel, too. The show wouldn't be the same without you!"

"You're keeping the same format?" Jayne asked.

"Jayne, I wouldn't dare change a thing. We're only going to change the set a little, make the game a bit more visual for today's audience. Perhaps eventually we'll add one or two young faces. But basically the show is going to be *exactly* what it was twenty years ago."

Personally, I was a little worried by Phoebe's comment of changing "the set a little" and adding "one or two young faces." My suspicion was that there would be flashing lights and a big, glitzy game board, and by the time Phoebe and the network got through updating the show for the nineties, it would bear little resemblance to the original hit. Jayne, however, let this pass.

"So why isn't Abe Brautigan producing the show?" she asked instead.

Abe was the original producer, a wiry, fast-talking New Yorker who could be pretty gruff if you didn't know him, but who had the heart of a teddy bear. Phoebe sighed. "I'm sure he was a fabulous guy, Jayne. He's like a legend to me."

"Was a fabulous guy?"

"Didn't you hear? He died a few months ago. There was some sort of accident involving a golf cart at his retirement community in Palm Springs. I don't know the details, but I *do* know it's going to be hard to follow in the footsteps of such a man. But I want you to know, Jayne, that you can count on me to give the show the same love and attention to detail that made Abe such a giant in the business. So you'll say yes?"

Phoebe looked so young and hopeful, I could tell that Jayne was loath to disappoint her. My wife is a real softy for such childlike hopefulness.

"I'll think about it," Jayne said. "It's a commitment of time, of course, and frankly I've been wishing for a vacation. You know, Phoebe, I loved doing the show all those years ago, but I've often found in life that it's best to leave the past alone."

16

"But at least you'll think about it!" Impulsively, she gave Jayne a big hug and kiss on the cheek, and then she gave me the same, just out of general enthusiasm, I suppose.

We had arrived at our new gate, and it was time to board the plane to Albuquerque.

"I'll give you a call next week," said Jayne.

"I'll keep my fingers crossed."

As we disappeared down the ramp, Phoebe added, "I love you guys." Strangely enough, I felt she did love us . . . for this one moment, at least, when Jayne could help her career. I had almost forgotten people could be so young and full of self-interest.

I held Jayne's hand as we climbed back into the dark and thunderous heavens, leaving such matters as TV game shows far behind.

Chapter 3

A week and three cities later, Jayne and I descended from the clouds one final time, arriving at Los Angeles International Airport close to the bewitching hour of midnight. After all the travel of the past few months, it was a comfort to see the familiar sprawl of yellowish lights spreading out beneath our plane.

When the cabin door opened, I inhaled the scent of smoggy air and knew I was home. Inside the terminal we saw our chauffeur, Jimmy Cassidy, asleep in an orange plastic bucket chair with a Hollywood Park race form open across his lap.

"Morning, Cass," I said gently. He came awake with a lazy smile and a yawn. Maybe he was still dreaming of some sweet pony coming down the final stretch at 20-to-1 odds. Cass is a born optimist, even though he loses time and time again.

"Steve! Mrs. Allen! Holy cow, what time is it?"

"Time to go home," I told him.

Cass stood up and took Jayne's carry-on bag, seeming momentarily shocked by the weight. Jayne doesn't quite carry the kitchen sink around the country with her, but almost. When Cass had recovered his balance, we headed down the airport hallways, joining a shuffle of late-night passengers, most of whom looked as if they were walking in their sleep. Large air terminals never sleep, of course, they simply slumber in a strange half-life neon glow. Despite the late hour, there were strains of Muzak floating from hidden speakers, playing Les Brown's old recording of "Sentimental Journey." Personally, I'd had enough journeys, sentimental or otherwise. I just wanted to get home to bed.

"Hey, I heard a joke while you were gone," Cass said brightly, coming wide awake. "It's about a new Korean cookbook—*Twenty Ways to Wok Your Dog.*"

Jayne rolled her eyes.

Cass didn't care. He kept chortling to himself and repeating the punch line. *"Twenty Ways to Wok Your Dog! . . .* Hey, are you guys hungry? If you want, we can stop at this all-night Korean barbecue I know on La Cienega."

"Not while I'm eating," I said.

Cass chuckled. The guy is a wiry leprechaun, an old Irish cowboy from Wyoming who originally came to Hollywood to be an actor in westerns. Unfortunately, with Cass's luck, he arrived just about the time westerns were going out of style, so he ended up being my driver instead. But Cass isn't the sort to be bitter about a mere historical accident. He lives on his dreams, holding a near-religious belief that westerns will one day return to fashion and he will become a star. I often think that for guys like Cass, the dream is better than the real thing.

Jayne and I waited briefly at the curb while Cass hustled across the street to retrieve his car. The limo is not exactly inconspicuous; it's a vintage 1965 burgundy-colored Cadillac, built when gas was cheap and Detroit was riding high. I used to feel a little embarrassed riding about in such a gaudy crate, but having

Cass as a chauffeur you get used to a certain level of eccentricity. At least it's a very comfortable car, and it has all the conveniences—car phone, stereo, TV, VCR, ice bucket, the works. I once told Cass I was planning to put a piano in the back. He actually took me seriously, got a dreamy look in his eye, and said, "Yeah! Wouldn't that be swell?" I have since learned that it's better not to give Cass any wild ideas. He comes up with enough on his own.

Anyway, it was into this glitzy burgundy machine that Jayne and I climbed. We sat back into the soft upholstery with a contented sigh as Cass floated through the traffic, telling us about all the basketball games we had missed and some of the funny things that had happened to him in the weeks we'd been gone. Cass is one of those people to whom a lot of funny things happen.

"Oh, yeah, and there was this chick I met at the supermarket the other day. Did I tell you about her yet?"

"No, Cass," I replied, yawning.

"Hey, look, are you guys tired? Should I just shut up?"

"Well—"

"Personally, I'm *dying* to hear all about the young lady," Jayne interrupted.

"Okay. Well, our shopping carts sort of collided in the aisle between the ice cream and the pantyhose. I mean, it was one of those classic situations. Whammy! And there I am with this sweet young thing, both of us apologizing like crazy. And then she says to me, 'Say, aren't you Jimmy Cassidy? Jayne Meadows' driver?' "

"Not Steve Allen's driver, huh?" I said grumpily.

"She said she remembered my picture from some magazine where I was driving Mrs. Allen to an open-

21

ing. Hey, I was impressed. Most people, they don't notice the chauffeur in celebrity photographs. We sort of fade into the background. Don't people ever stop to consider how celebrities *get* places?"

Actually, Cass was overrating the degree of our dependence on him. Most of the time I drive myself about, and so does Jayne. But there are occasions— premieres, big show biz parties or benefits—where it's much more convenient to have Cass drive us than to stand in line for thirty or forty minutes at the end of an evening waiting for our car.

"Anyway, the lady says it's a funny coincidence, but she was just thinking about Jayne Meadows and this TV game show she's trying to produce—"

"No!" Jayne shouted.

"Anyway, this lady turned out to be a television producer, and you'll never guess what she was trying to produce? You remember *The Murder Game,* Mrs. Allen?"

"Oh, yes."

"Well, it seems the network is all set to put the show on again, and this lady starts telling me that I could be a real big help to her if I let her know what would tempt you, Mrs. Allen, to be on the panel again."

"Tempt me?"

"Yeah. She knows you're not hurting for money, but she said maybe there was some gift you'd like—a boat, a car, maybe a nice trip—something that would be a token of her great esteem for you, you see, and maybe—"

"A bribe," I muttered.

"What did you tell her, Cass?"

"I said I thought you had all the boats and cars and nice trips to Europe you'd ever need; that wasn't the way to get to you at all."

Jayne was interested. "So what *is* the way to get to me?" she asked.

I saw Cass smile into the rearview mirror. "I suggested she set up a scholarship deal for some poor kids from the wrong part of town. That was the kind of thing that would impress you."

"Not bad, Cass. And what did she offer you for your help and time?" I asked.

Cass looked uncomfortable, which is rare for him.

"Come on, 'fess up," I said cheerfully. And then I felt bad when he told us what it was.

"She said the network was going to do a western in the fall," Cass said flatly, his eyes on the road. "She said that if I found a way to convince Mrs. Allen to take up her old spot on the panel of *The Murder Game,* she'd use her influence to see if she could get me at least a small part on the series. She mentioned the role of some ornery old cook at this ranch where all these teenage cowboys live."

For a moment I was angry enough to endanger my blood pressure. Phoebe North had done her homework in a big way. It just wasn't fair to play with the man in such a way.

"Well, are you going to talk me into doing the show, Cass?" Jayne asked gently.

"Naw," Cass said. "Hell with it. You know what I think? I think that meeting at the supermarket wasn't an accident at all. I think she arranged to bump into me with her cart, and it makes me sort of mad to be used like that."

"But, Cass, it's the chance you've been waiting for," Jayne reminded him. "You'd have a role in a western."

"Maybe," Cass said. "But the show sounded kinda dumb, if you wanna know the truth. And anyway, I'm getting too old to be a TV star. I mean, hell with it. I'll just stick to drivin' this old Cadillac . . . as long as you guys are willin' to put up with me."

"I think we could put up with you for a long, long time," Jayne said.

Sensing how angry I was, Jayne took my hand. I didn't trust myself to speak until we were safely home, sitting on the familiar sides of our bed. Then I exploded. "This is really too much, tempting poor Cass like that! Playing with his dreams. I hate it when high-powered people try to manipulate someone as vulnerable as Cass."

"She's not a monster. She's probably vulnerable, too."

"Jayne, the woman makes Mata Hari look like a schoolgirl. She's a pushy, conniving—"

Jayne interrupted my tirade. "She's a woman, dear, and television is still a man's world. All that aggression is probably just a bluff. She's running scared. She feels she has to come on twice as strong as everyone else just to keep her job."

"She's not going to keep it long if she tries a stunt like that again," I grumbled.

Jayne came over and rubbed the tension from the back of my neck. "There, there," she said. "Cass will survive. And as for Phoebe North . . . for a young woman like that, it's absolute *murder* to get ahead in this town."

Chapter 4

The Murder Game wouldn't go away. I was brushing my teeth in the bathroom—a reasonable choice of location, I think—when Jayne wandered in, holding in her hand a long list of phone messages that had come to the house while we were gone.

"Well, that's strange," she declared. "Sylvia Van Martinson phoned three times yesterday saying I should call her back the moment I got in, no matter what time it was."

"The reason for the strangeness-factor of your account is not apparent."

"I can't understand what you're saying when you talk while brushing your teeth," Jayne said.

"Then permit me to go *pitooey* without at the same time engaging my pituitary gland," I said.

"Can't you take anything seriously?"

"Of course," I said. "I take medicine very seriously. If you take it casually, you can get into a lot of trouble. But really, what's so strange about hearing from Sylvia Van Martinson?"

"Because," Jayne said, "I don't think I've seen her for almost ten years."

I glanced at the clock. "Well, it's too late to return her call now."

"Yes. I'll try her first thing in the morning. Do you suppose it has to do with *The Murder Game?*"

Sylvia Van Martinson is the very successful publisher of *Sophistication* magazine, one of those glossy rags that tells a large segment of American womanhood what to wear, how to diet, how to catch a husband, and a dozen time-tested ways to tell if your husband's cheating on you. Sylvia inherited the magazine from her father—she comes from an old Brahmin East Coast family—but she was the one who turned the publication into a raging success, some say by sheer ruthlessness. Personally, I've always liked Sylvia. She does and says exactly what she likes and has that easygoing eccentricity that often comes with old money. Twenty years ago we saw a lot of her, for she was one of the original panelists on *The Murder Game,* along with Jayne. But over the years we'd gradually lost touch.

A lot of that goes on in show business—touch-losing, I mean. And if you happen to live in or near the two chief celebrity centers—Los Angeles and New York—you can lose contact with literally thousands of people.

"How old do you think Bobo is now?" Jayne asked when I came into the bedroom. Bobo was Sylvia's daughter.

"Twelve?" I suggested.

Jayne looked at me in exasperation. "Darling, Bobo was twelve last time we saw her."

"Good. All you have to do is remember when that was, subtract the year from the present year, add your results to the number twelve, and you'll have her current age. It's an extremely logical deduction," I assured my wife with a German accent.

"Go to sleep, Steve." That seemed like a splendid idea. I curled up beneath the covers on my side of the bed and was soon dreaming about sitting in with the Basie band, which I've actually done a few times over the years on TV.

But dreams—my dreams, at least—always seem to have a frustrating element to them, and the problem in this one was that before I could get to the piano bench, which Bill Basie vacated to accommodate me, he had kicked off the tempo and the band had started to play. For the life of me, I couldn't figure out either the key or the tune.

That, too, actually happened to me, thankfully only once, when I presented an award years ago to Lionel Hampton at the Paramount Theater in Los Angeles. The proceedings had been completed and I was walking off stage, when suddenly Hamp said, "Hey, folks, how about having Steverino play something with the band?"

The fact that this suggestion was greeted by thunderous applause has nothing whatsoever to do with my prowess at the instrument, such as it is. The point is that audiences always accept with riotous applause and cheers any such proposal from an entertainer.

"Say, ladies and gentleman, I've just noticed that Adolf Hitler is sitting right out here in the third row tonight. Don't ask me how he got here, but watta ya say? Let's get old Ade up here and have him do that cute little soft-shoe we all remember from his days at Berchtesgaden."

Applause and cheers!

Anyway, before I could get seated, the band was off and wailing. There was music available at the piano, but since I don't read it was of no use to me. If I'd been able to hear the instrument, I could have, very quickly, picked out the key, but the rest of the band was playing so loudly that there was literally no sound whatsoever apparent to me from the piano.

Since nobody could hear me, I suppose I could have sneaked through the entire arrangement playing in every wrong key in the book, except I suddenly realized from reading words on the arrangement, that a brief piano solo was coming up. At that point, of course, I could hear myself all too clearly, and it took only about two beats to realize that I was considerably wide of the key-mark. Fortunately, the bass player looked at me, smiled in a fatherly way, and held up four fingers, so I jumped into A-flat and thereafter did not disgrace myself.

Because of my syncopated snoring, Jayne could not sleep. She tried reading for a while and had just turned off the light when the unlisted phone line on our bedside table rang. I woke briefly, long enough to put my pillow over my head; so Jayne, by default, was the one to answer. Even with my ears covered, I could hear the voice on the phone.

"Jayne, thank God! Where have you been? Steve's office said someplace like Iowa or Uruguay. I don't know how you do all that traveling. Somehow, the older I get, the less faith I have in airplanes!"

There was no doubt about the identity of the caller. Jayne immediately recognized the throaty Brahmin sound of Sylvia Van Martinson.

"Sylvia! Do you have any idea what time it is?" Jayne peered past the telephone to the bedside clock. "It's two thirty-five. I hope this is important."

"Good God, Jayne, don't be such a stick-in-the-mud. Who sleeps anymore? Hold on a sec while I freshen my scotch and soda."

"Sylvia . . . Sylvia!" Jayne was stunned by the colossal rudeness of the woman to call at two-thirty in the morning and then put her on hold. Was she drunk? Was she crazy? Jayne was about to hang up when Sylvia came back on the line.

"That's better," Sylvia said. "Look, darling, I have to ask you something. Have they been after you, too?"

"They?"

"You know. Those people. That horrible woman."

"Phoebe North?"

"You got it, sweetheart. And everyone used to say that I was aggressive. Did you hear about poor Abe Brautigan?"

Jayne was actually in the process of lowering the phone back onto its cradle, but she paused at the mention of *The Murder Game's* original producer.

"Yes. I was sorry to hear about Abe," she said. "He died recently—in a golf cart accident, wasn't it?"

"Humpft!" snorted Sylvia. "Look, I found out something, but I can't tell you on the phone. Why don't I pick you up in half an hour?"

"Sylvia, at this hour I'm going nowhere but to bed. Perhaps we might have lunch tomorrow, and you can tell me what this is all about then."

"Splendid! Have you ever tried Abdul's? It's a darling little falafel cart at the Third Street Promenade in Santa Monica. All the trendy people go there. You have to find him, of course, because he moves his cart around like a gypsy, but that's part of Abdul's esoteric appeal. I'll meet you there at noon sharp."

"Sylvia . . . Sylvia!" Jayne tried to object that she was not about to waste her time searching for some trendy but movable food cart, but the phone had already gone dead.

"She's nuts," Jayne said thoughtfully. "Really sideways, as you put it."

"Are you addressing me?" I muttered, coming out momentarily from beneath my pillow.

"Do you remember hearing those crazy stories about Howard Hughes during his Hollywood days? The poor man finally checked into a bungalow at the Beverly Hills Hotel and left messages for people in a nearby tree. Well, I think our dear Sylvia is heading down that same path."

I was awake now, so Jayne recounted the details of her strange conversation with Sylvia and their plans to meet for lunch.

"Just don't go," I advised her.

"I won't."

"Life is too short to accept lunch invitations from crazy people," I told her. "An occasional dinner, yes. But lunch should be reserved for the sane."

"Absolutely," Jayne said. "And besides, I've been gone for months. Tomorrow I just want to unpack, read my mail, and say hello to my geraniums and poor Mr. T."

Mr. T was not the whilom actor of the same name, but rather our goofy, lovable springer spaniel, so named by our son Bill, his original owner, because he has a T-shaped marking on his back. The dog, not Bill. Both Jayne and I apparently have some modest gifts for the training and management of human beings, but we've never had much success at doing the same with our dogs. I don't know whether we love them too much, spoil them, or just what the problem is, but all of them, over the years, have seemed to quickly realize that they—not one of us—were the boss.

The next day, despite her stated intentions of the night before, Jayne went to lunch anyway, naturally curious as to what Sylvia had to tell her.

Chapter 5

By morning, fog had drifted in from the Pacific, covering the Los Angeles basin with a soft blanket of gray. It was Sunday, and the moody hues of the sky made everything seem sleepy and fuzzy and still, like a Japanese watercolor. In southern California, you can never be certain what April weather will bring.

Jayne sat next to Cass in the front seat of the burgundy limousine—it was easier to talk that way—as they drove from our house in the hills above the Valley along the San Diego Freeway and then into Santa Monica.

"Santa Monica sure has become full of fashionable young folk," remarked Cass as they made their way down a street lined with boutiques and little restaurants. "A bunch of Yippies, I guess."

"Yuppies," corrected Jayne.

Santa Monica is a once-fashionable part of Los Angeles that faded into a gentle neglect, for a time, and is now being reborn in a new and trendy incarnation. The Third Street Promenade was part of this rebirth—a once-derelict downtown street near the beach that was now closed to traffic and transformed, with cute little stores, kiosks, and cafes, into a gathering spot for the young with money to spend.

The fog lifted suddenly, creating a dazzling display of sunshine, as Cass let Jayne out of the car near a sushi bar on Santa Monica Boulevard. She wandered past a group of street musicians and into the pedestrian mall. Closing a street to automobiles was a revolutionary idea in southern California; it brought people out in full force. There was a carnival atmosphere in the air. Jayne walked past jugglers, acrobats, and a young black man playing a soulful saxophone in a doorway, sans accompaniment. He had a hat in front of him to receive any money he might charm from passing wallets. The young musician played with such lyrical virtuosity that Jayne stopped to put a few dollars into the hat.

"Many thanks," said the sax player, lowering his instrument.

"Perhaps you can help me," said Jayne. "I'm looking for Abdul's falafel cart."

"Abdul? He usually parks down towards Broadway. You should find him there—if he's back from Tahiti."

"Tahiti?"

"His yearly vacation, you know."

"Ah, I see."

Jayne wandered on through the milling Sunday crowd, wondering about a street vendor who could afford a yearly vacation in the South Seas.

On the corner of Broadway and Third, she saw a large pushcart with a multicolored umbrella overhead and a menu that indicated Abdul's basic "Falafel Nouvelle" could be purchased at a starting price of $9.95, going up to $29.95 with various additions such as caviar and Maine lobster. Standing behind the cart

34

was a young man with a ponytail, dressed in jeans, a Hawaiian shirt, and Birkenstock sandals. He was dispensing falafels as fast as he could to a line of hungry people that stretched down the block. Jayne, having the old-fashioned idea that street vendors were people who sold hot dogs for fifty cents, was flabbergasted at such a phenomenon.

She peered about the crowd, looking for Sylvia Van Martinson but seeing only a host of faces, mostly under the age of thirty. Jayne recognized a screenwriter, two agents, a famous set designer, and a cinematographer waiting in line, but she saw no sign of her old friend. She glanced at her watch, noting that it was ten minutes past noon. She was late. Had Sylvia come and gone? It didn't seem likely.

Jayne waited near Abdul's cart in a position that allowed her to scan the crowd. She shifted from one foot to the other, becoming annoyed that Sylvia would leave her waiting. After another five minutes Jayne approached Abdul, whose hands seemed to be in perpetual motion stuffing falafels and pocketing money.

"Excuse me, but do you know Sylvia Van Martinson? I was supposed to meet her here at noon."

Abdul glanced at Jayne with annoyance and started to tell her to wait in line like everyone else. But then he recognized her—more or less. "Aren't you Jayne Meadows? *The Honeymooners* was . . . like . . . my all-time favorite show. I used to love it the way you'd say to Jackie Gleason—"

"That was my sister Audrey," Jayne corrected for perhaps the zillionth time in her life.

It works the other way, too, of course. Fans are constantly addressing Audrey as Jayne, asking her what it's like to be married to a comedian, etc.

Once they had gotten all this straight, Jayne knew

she had the young man's full attention, except for his hands, which kept up a steady pace of give-and-take. Like most restauranteurs, Abdul perceived that celebrities were good for business.

"Sylvia Van Martinson is a tall woman . . . gray hair, I imagine, though I haven't seen her for a few years. She has a very autocratic manner."

"Oh, sure. Sylvia. The magazine publisher," said Abdul, serving falafels as fast as his hands could work. "I once catered her office Christmas party. She comes by a couple times a week, though I don't think I've seen her since before my trip to Tahiti."

"You haven't seen her today?"

"Nope. She was supposed to meet you here, was she? That's really very flattering to my business. But I gotta tell you, the lady is a little out to lunch—no pun intended. Maybe she just forgot."

Jayne thanked Abdul and moved aside. The man was probably right; Sylvia had simply forgotten. Perhaps she had been drunk when she called and had awoken with no recollection of the conversation and a hangover to keep her abed.

At twelve-twenty, feeling angry and silly for having come, Jayne approached Abdul one more time. "If you see Sylvia, will you tell her I was here?"

"Sure thing. Hey, look, would you like to try today's special? I call it the Baghdad Bash. For my friends, I do a deal where you buy nine falafels and get the tenth one free."

"Perhaps another time," said Jayne with a vague smile, moving away. She was irritated at having wasted such a large part of her first day home. Most likely Sylvia's hint that Abe Brautigan's accidental death was not accidental was only the raving of a rich, egocentric old woman who had lost touch with reality.

Cass stepped out of the car to open the door for Jayne when he saw her coming. "You look kinda put-off, Mrs. Allen," he said. "Didn't lunch agree with you?"

"She stood me up!" Jayne fumed. "Wait till I give her a piece of my mind!"

"Why wait?" Cass handed her the cellular car phone.

Sylvia had lived for years in a big old-fashioned mansion on the Santa Monica beach. Jayne had to call our house to get me to look in her address book for the private number. Then she sat in the limo, dialed the number, and waited grimly.

But a man answered the phone, and he was not a butler. He was a detective. The body of Sylvia Van Martinson had been found by a fisherman an hour earlier, washed up on the beach.

Chapter 6

Sylvia Van Martinson's house was a rambling two-story white frame albatross sitting on a long though narrow beach lot. The shape of the lot limited the architecture and made the house look a little like a railway train about to roll into the ocean, with the living room as the engine in front and the two-car garage on the Pacific Coast Highway as the caboose. The entire property was surrounded by a high white picket fence; from the outside you could see only the tall eccentric gables of the upper story and a profusion of treetops. The grounds, once elaborately planted, now grew wild with neglect. Vines of bougainvillea had a choke-hold on the house, and Jayne found an unsettling air of age and decay wherever she looked.

A uniformed policeman answered the door and led her through a living room crowded with furniture. They walked out a sliding glass door to a swimming pool in the ocean-front yard. Near the pool, a Japanese man wearing tan slacks and a loud sports shirt was talking with a pale young woman.

"You say she swam in the ocean every day? Rain or shine?" the Japanese man was asking.

"Yes," muttered the woman, almost inaudibly.

"My mother believed it kept her in good health. She swam all year round."

"Well, it killed her in the end," the man said, and then glanced to Jayne. "I'm Oshi Okimodo. From the coroner's office. And you?"

"Jayne Meadows Allen. I was supposed to meet Sylvia for lunch today." Jayne turned her attention to the young woman. "You must be Bobo, dear. I haven't seen you since you were twelve. I'm so very sorry to hear about your mother. You'll have to tell me if there's anything I can do."

Bobo did not look healthy; her face was still soft with baby fat, as though she had never completely matured, and there were dark circles beneath her eyes. She gazed at Jayne curiously.

"You gave me a doll once," she said. "For my ninth birthday. She had a little gingham dress, and I called her Samantha."

"That's right," said Jayne. "How sweet that you remember."

Bobo turned her gaze toward the waves breaking on the beach. "I used to pretend Samantha was an orphan, so she could do anything she liked. Once she was kidnapped by white slavers, and I had to rescue her from a harem."

The young woman spoke in a flat, unemotional tone. It occurred to Jayne that Bobo was in a state of shock, unable to assimilate the tragedy of her mother's death. When she told me about it later, I recognized the emotional state since I had experienced it some years earlier when my own mother died. At the time, my mother had been living in a cheap rooming house in Hollywood—being an old vaudevillian, she preferred such quarters to the more comfortable apartment I would have been glad to provide—had apparently

40

put up water to boil two eggs for her breakfast, stretched out on her studio couch, and suffered a heart attack. The building's manager smelled the eggs burning when, probably half an hour later, the water had boiled away.

I felt the normal shock when I arrived at her quarters and saw her body, but immediately thereafter became emotionally numb and was, for several days, literally incapable of weeping or even feeling any emotion strong enough to give rise to tears. And then, one evening as I was going through some of my mother's papers, I came across a little note she had written, and suddenly the dam burst. I wept like a child for quite a long time.

"Why don't you sit down inside, my dear," said Jayne gently. "I want to have a few words with the coroner, and then I'll come in for a chat."

Without a word Bobo obeyed, drifting in a daze toward the house. Jayne watched her with concern. "Oh, how desperately sad to lose your mother!"

"What about her father?" asked Oshi Okimodo.

"Let's see, that was Sylvia's third husband. I believe he owned a New York advertising agency and died of a heart attack in the early eighties. Bobo's an orphan now."

"A damn rich orphan, I guess," said the coroner, looking with a critical eye at the house. "I bet you could get a coupla mil for a big old place like this, on the beach."

Jayne turned to the man. "Will you please tell me what happened to Mrs. Van Martinson? She was an old friend."

"There isn't much to tell. The victim was sixty-four years old and should have stayed out of the surf this time of year. Those waves are pretty big down there;

we've had fifteen-foot swells today. And the water's still cold enough to get hypothermia if you stay in too long. Most likely the old lady got pounded by a wave she didn't see coming and simply drowned."

"But you heard her daughter. Sylvia swam every day of the year. She was an expert swimmer, and she knew these waters well."

The coroner shrugged. "All it takes is one big wave. You know, the lady wasn't as young as she used to be. She should have been using her nice heated swimming pool instead."

"Did anyone see her in the water?"

"No. The fog was pretty thick this morning. Another reason the old lady should have skipped her daily swim."

"Will you please stop calling her 'the old lady'!" Jayne snapped. "Mrs. Van Martinson was a very fit and athletic woman."

"You . . . uh . . . saw a lot of her, then?"

"Well, not for some time."

"What's it been? A few weeks? Months?"

"Years, actually," Jayne said unhappily. The coroner raised an eyebrow and did not pursue the obvious conclusion that Jayne really had no idea as to Sylvia's current fitness to swim in the often-rough Pacific Ocean.

"Who's in charge of the police investigation?" Jayne asked.

"What police investigation?"

Jayne stared at the coroner in surprise. "You mean the police are not going to investigate this extremely suspicious death?"

"Mrs. Allen, I know she was an old friend and all, but these accidental drownings happen all the time around here. The problem is, you see, a lot of people in California grew up on Frankie Avalon movies—

Beach Blanket Bingo, stuff like that. As a result, they just don't have the proper respect for the ocean."

"Mrs. Van Martinson did *not* grow up on *Beach Blanket Bingo,*" Jayne said. "Has the body—"

"It's already been taken to the morgue. Look, Mrs. Allen, we're going to do an autopsy, and if there's any indication of things not being quite right, we'll automatically refer the matter to the police. But offhand, I'd say this is just one of those unfortunate accidents that could have been avoided if the old lady—excuse me—if Mrs. Van Martinson had paid a little more attention to her age and her limitations."

Jayne felt a wave of depression. *Age and limitations!* She was annoyed with herself that she had let ten years pass without seeing her friend and also upset she had not let Sylvia come over the previous evening, to say whatever had been on her mind. Now Jayne would never know.

"When I called earlier, a policeman mentioned a fisherman had found her," Jayne prodded. "If he was on the shore, perhaps he saw her struggling in the water."

The coroner shook his head. "I told you about the fog. Anyway, the body had been in the water at least forty-five minutes. The current had washed it down the beach, almost to the pier."

Jayne glanced down the beach a half mile to where the Santa Monica pier jutted out into the ocean. Everything now basked in brilliant April sunshine, the fog dispelled. It was hard to believe in death on such a lovely spring day.

"The fisherman . . . he was a poor Vietnamese trying to feed his family," said the coroner with an inappropriate chuckle. "I guess he sure had a shock when a corpse washed up at his feet!"

"When do you estimate to be the time of death?"

"According to the daughter, Mrs. Van Martinson left the front yard here with a towel at about nine A.M. The fisherman found the body at ten-forty-five. We're estimating the time of death to be nine-forty-five."

"Then she swam for nearly forty-five minutes? Isn't that a rather long time?"

The coroner shrugged. "Well, we'll have a more accurate time of death after we do the autopsy."

"And what about the towel?" pressed Jayne. "You said she left here with a towel. Did anyone find the towel on the beach?"

The coroner shrugged again. He was very good at it. "I don't believe anyone looked. You think it's important?"

Jayne was too frustrated to answer. As far as she was concerned, the investigation into Sylvia's death was being handled very carelessly. So far, there was no investigation at all.

"You know, I had another death not far from here just a week ago . . . a famous rock star," the coroner said. "Actually, a lot of famous people die in Santa Monica. It makes my job very interesting."

Jayne glared at the man. Then a movement in the living room window caught her eye and she glanced toward the big rambling beach house. The pale face of Bobo Van Martinson appeared briefly from behind a curtain, gazing out at her. When the girl saw Jayne looking back, her face retreated quickly into the shadows.

"Thank you, Mr. Okimodo. I'll be in touch," Jayne said.

"Sure thing," replied the coroner vaguely.

Jayne walked purposely into the deep shadows of the old house to seek the orphaned daughter.

Chapter 7

"Bobo? Is that you?" Jayne called, moving through the dark, heavily furnished living room, with bric-a-brac on seemingly every surface. Despite the sunlight outside, the interior was cloying, gloomy. Jayne told me later that as she said the name Bobo aloud, she recalled my having theorized a good many years ago that young women with odd nicknames—the kind you read in New York gossip columns: Bobo, Bee-Bee, Boo-Boo, Mousie—probably inadvertently created the names themselves, at the age of three or four, by simply mispronouncing Barbara, Mary, or something as conventional.

"Bobo?"

The girl spun around on a large swivel rocker. She was eating a chocolate truffle, which had left a brown smear at one side of her lips.

"My mother said I shouldn't eat chocolate, but now I can do anything I like," the girl said simply.

Jayne sat on the sofa facing her. "How old are you now, dear? Twenty-two?"

"Twenty-three. My mother had me when she was old. Personally, I'm never going to have children. I think sex is icky."

"Do you have a boyfriend?" Jayne asked.

"Not now. Used to. But he just stopped calling me one day. Mother would have made me break up with him anyway, because he didn't have any money."

Jayne decided it might be best to steer clear of what had obviously been a thorny mother-daughter relationship. "Bobo, your mother called me very late last night. There was something she wanted to talk to me about, but she wouldn't say over the phone. I believe it had to do with Abe Brautigan—the man who used to produce our show. Do you have any idea what it was your mother wanted to tell me?"

Bobo had been sucking on her truffle as though it were a hard candy. She popped it into her mouth now and bit down with a soft crunch. "Nope," she said. "What time did she call? Between two and three?"

"Yes. How did you know?"

"In the last few years, no matter what time she went to bed, my mother always woke up around two and made phone calls until she got sleepy again. Usually took about an hour. It was her crazy time, she used to say. Somehow she found it soothing to talk to people over the phone. It was the only thing that would help her fall back to sleep.

"I see." Jayne sought a polite way to phrase her next question. "Your mother, then, was she . . . well, had she gone a little? . . ."

"Bonkers? Oh, yeah. I think it runs in the family. Mother said I shouldn't worry, though, because being a little crazy was a big help in running a magazine."

"Do you plan to run the magazine now that your mother has passed away?"

Bobo shook her head slowly. "I'm not *that* nuts! What do I know about anything like that? Tell me something. Do you think I'm homely?"

46

"Why, no, dear. Not at all."

"It's okay. You can tell me the truth. I mean, I know I'm not exactly Michelle Pfeiffer or anything. Mother said the only men who would want to marry me would be after my money. I suppose I'll have a lot of that now that she's dead."

"I suppose you will," said Jayne, still struggling to find some logic to this conversation. Perhaps Sylvia's late night phone call meant nothing; it certainly seemed that the woman had been a little mad. Her young daughter was, too, somewhat.

"Bobo, tell me about this morning. Your mother went to the beach at nine?"

"Yeah. She always swam at nine o'clock on the weekend, seven during the week—before leaving for her office downtown."

"By any chance, did she have an appointment to meet someone this morning?"

"On the beach you mean? I doubt it, but she . . . like . . . never told *me* anything, you know."

"What about her health? Do you know if she had any . . . problems?"

"Nah, she was healthy as a horse." The girl smiled slyly. "Mom always said she'd outlive me, so I shouldn't count on an inheritance. I guess she was wrong about that one, huh?"

"This morning . . . did you actually see her walk to the beach?"

"I didn't see her at all. I was in the darkroom most of the morning."

"Darkroom?"

"Photography's my hobby. Would you like to see?"

Jayne said she would and Bobo led the way to the back of the house, where an old walk-in pantry had been converted to a darkroom. Trays of sharp-smell-

47

ing chemicals stood next to an enlarger. Piles of contact sheets and enlargements were stacked everywhere.

"I like to hide out on the beach with my zoom lens," said the girl. "It's loads of fun. I sneak around and take pictures of people—and they never even know it."

Jayne glanced through a stack of photographs, trying to make appropriate sounds of approval. Most of the photos were of young lovers, kissing and lying in each other's arms on various beach blankets, blissfully unaware that they were being photographed. Some of the pictures verged on the obscene. Jayne found it rather spooky to imagine a lonely rich girl creeping from her big house onto the public beach to capture these moments of passionate embrace.

"So what do you think?"

"Well, I think you have considerable promise as a photographer," Jayne said tactfully. "Perhaps you might get around a bit more and take pictures of mountains and flowers, sunsets . . . maybe even people standing up. Do you have a car?"

"I flunked my driving test three times," Bobo said cheerfully. "Mom always said I was too high-strung to drive a car. What do you think?"

"I think you should decide these things for yourself, Bobo. Tell me something, dear. Does your mother have an office here at home?"

"Sure. Upstairs next to her bedroom."

"Do you think it would be all right if I looked around a bit? Perhaps there's something on her desk that would give me some . . . well . . . clue as to what she wanted to say to me."

"I don't mind. And my mother won't mind, either, because she's dead. So I suppose it's all right. But

48

you'll probably find she just wanted to talk to someone who would help her go back to sleep."

"But she left a number of messages for me during the day as well."

"Perhaps she was trying to take a nap? That's a joke! Mother never napped during the day. That's *my* escape. Sometimes I sleep all afternoon."

Jayne sighed. She was relieved when Bobo gave her directions to the upstairs office but remained behind in the darkroom to develop more film.

Sylvia's home office was a large, sunny room sumptuously furnished with country antiques. Unfortunately, like the rest of the house, there seemed to be too much furniture and too many objects. Sylvia obviously had had trouble throwing anything away. Jayne somehow felt like an intruder in her old friend's inner sanctum. There are few things sadder than the cast-off belongings of someone recently dead: a pair of old eyeglasses, an opened book, a half-empty can of roasted cashew nuts. All these struck Jayne with a gloomy finality.

"There's no sense getting depressed. Better just get on with this," Jayne told herself, speaking aloud to chase away the shadows of death. Sitting at Sylvia's huge desk, she forced herself to go through the drawers. She found check stubs, business records, and letters from the IRS. In the third drawer from the top, Jayne discovered a half-eaten golden box of Godiva chocolates; apparently, a sweet tooth ran in the family. There were also envelopes, paper clips, and various office supplies. On a side table adjacent to the desk, there was an IBM personal computer. Jayne and I are of the generation that has never felt entirely comfortable with computers, but she knew how to turn the thing on and was pleased to find Sylvia used WordPerfect, the one software program about which Jayne had some slight knowledge.

She called several files up on the screen. The majority seemed to be story ideas for the magazine. Others pertained to business matters. On the surface, at least, none of them concerned *The Murder Game*. The problem was there were hundreds of files, some thirty or forty pages long with strange computer names like IXPRS-5, JANDOC, and MAGFIX, which did not reveal their meaning. Jayne quickly realized she could spend weeks in this office exploring Sylvia Van Martinson's life.

She shut the computer down and told herself this whole thing was silly. She should accept Bobo's explanation that the late night phone call had meant nothing. Jayne decided she would spend five more minutes in the room, and if a cursory search yielded no clues . . . well, she would just give up. She glanced over at Sylvia's wastebasket, which was overflowing with envelopes and scraps of paper. It seemed as good a place as any to seek the remnants of a person's life.

Going through the discarded papers, Jayne learned that Sylvia had recently sent the Sierra Club one hundred dollars and was a generous supporter of public radio. There were torn envelopes that had once contained bills from Southern California Gas and U.S. Sprint. There were candy wrappers, a safety pin, and a small ball of Scotch tape. Finally, near the bottom, was a crumpled piece of paper with a cryptic message. Jayne recognized Sylvia's handwriting at once. The message said: "VERDI. 10 AM UNDER THE PIER. MASTER C."

It was the phrase *under the pier* that caught Jayne's attention and made all her dormant suspicions return. Could this be a rendezvous with someone called Verdi under the Santa Monica pier, near where her body had been found? Ten A.M. certainly was dangerously close to the time of Sylvia's death. But who was Master C? None of it made a great deal of sense, and of course the note could have been several days old and therefore have nothing to do with the morning's events. Still, Jayne slipped the wrinkled paper into her handbag.

For a moment she felt guilty removing "evidence," but then reminded herself that this wasn't evidence if the police weren't investigating Sylvia's death as a crime, so there didn't seem any harm. Besides, the note had been in the wastebasket, and by tomorrow the maid would probably have cleaned the room and then nobody would have the message, evidence or not.

As Jayne was justifying her small theft, she heard a sound on the landing outside the closed office door. A cat perhaps? A person? She stood up quickly from the desk, crossed the room, and pulled open the door—startling Phoebe North.

"Oh! Well, hello," said Phoebe, trying to regain her poise. "I just heard about Sylvia's death on the radio. Isn't it a terrible thing? I came as soon as I could."

Jayne studied the young producer's guilt-ridden face. There was something strange going on, and Jayne was determined to get to the bottom of it.

"I believe I've made up my mind about *The Murder Game*," she said.

"You'll do it?"

"Darling, you couldn't keep me away with a gun."

Chapter 8

You may well be asking how did I, absent at the time, know all these particulars about my wife's adventures? The answer is simple: She eventually described it all to me. Several times. In detail.

At the time, however, I was distracted by my own obligations. I was concentrating on jazz, arranging for recordings of some of my new songs with singers Frankie Randall and David Silverman, and rehearsing with a band of old friends, including vibraphonist Terry Gibbs, pianist Paul Smith, and drummer Frank Capp.

Having been married to me for thirty-eight years, Jayne knew this, so I was surprised one afternoon a few weeks later when she came into the living room with plans to separate me from my Steinway.

"Darling, do you think if I dressed in black and white, like piano keys, I might lure you out for the evening?"

I grinned at her, with only about one third of my attention.

"Does this mean you'll escort me to the party to-night?"

"Party? A birthday party? Anniversary? A damn-the-diet dinner?"

"A little of all that," she said vaguely. It wasn't until we were safely ensconced in the back of Cass's limo, on our way to Beverly Hills, that she divulged our destination.

"You remember Phoebe North, dear? That funny young woman you liked so much when we met her in the Dallas-Fort Worth airport?"

"You mean that aggressive producer who tracked Cass down in the supermarket?"

"Well, we're going to her home, so be nice. She's throwing a little press party to celebrate *The Murder Game*'s going back on the air."

"Oh, no!"

Jayne squeezed my hand in a comforting way. "Don't be grumpy, darling. You'll have some old friends to chat with. Peter Grover and all the old panelists from twenty years ago will be there. Even dear, gaudy Amaretta will be there with her new husband."

"But why are *you* going to be there?"

"Well, I've decided to do the show again. I told you weeks ago. You were playing the piano at the time."

"Who's taking Sylvia's place on the panel?" I asked.

"There's a lovely young TV actress, Shadow Bennington, taking over the spot. She's supposed to be very sweet."

"Shadow Bennington? Sounds like a heroine from a soap opera."

"She is. And more people watch her than Peter Jennings, Dan Rather, and MacNeil/Lehrer combined."

We rode for a moment in silence, then Jayne suddenly and mysteriously said, "Darling, I want to show you something."

She handed me a piece of paper that had once been crumpled but was now neatly folded into a square. I turned on the light in the back of the limo, adjusted my glasses, and read the message: "VERDI. 10 AM UNDER THE PIER. MASTER C."

I smiled. All of a sudden I understood why Jayne was doing the show. "You think there's some foul play here, don't you? You're doing *The Murder Game* so you can nose about and catch the killer!"

"Don't laugh, Steve. Sylvia's death seems *very* suspicious to me, particularly after she called me the night before with something important to say about poor Abe. At any rate, I had more or less decided to do the show anyway. This was simply the clincher. You know, if you'd been listening to me the past few weeks, you'd be suspicious, too."

"Well, what did the coroner say?" I asked, curious in spite of myself.

"Accidental drowning. Apparently, the ocean was rough that morning, and Sylvia was rather old to be swimming by herself. But doesn't it seem suspicious to you that she had a ten o'clock meeting under the pier? What if Verdi or Master C met her there and held her head under water long enough for her to drown?"

"But this note could mean anything at all, and for all you know it could be months old."

"Steve, I found it in her wastebasket. And I checked. . . . The maid emptied that basket every day."

"Maybe Sylvia just got around to throwing it out. It seems like an awfully thin piece of evidence to establish that a murder has—"

"You've started with less."

"But the Santa Monica beach is a pretty crowded place, particularly near the pier. If two people were struggling in the water, there would have been an eye-witness."

I saw Cass glance in the rearview mirror and exchange a conspiratorial look with Jayne. I suddenly understood why he had been missing the past few days and why I'd been driving myself around town.

"Let me guess," I said with a knowing smile. "Cass has been lurking around the pier trying to dredge up a witness." I looked at Cass. "Any luck?"

"Naw," he said. "I've been talking to surfers, fishermen, street people, the carnies who work the pier and snack bars. Nobody saw nothing unusual that morning."

"But it was foggy," Jayne said quickly. "For most of the morning you could hardly see more than a few feet in front of you, and the fog didn't lift until eleven-thirty. I told you all that."

"I guess I was playing the piano." Jayne didn't smile. "Sylvia went swimming in the fog?"

"Sylvia swam every day, summer or winter, rain or shine."

"I imagine the tricky currents finally caught up with your eccentric friend. Maybe you should reserve your detective skills for *The Murder Game,* dear."

Jayne glared. "But this isn't a game! This is murder!"

Chapter 9

In the flats of Beverly Hills, the hierarchy of wealth begins north of Santa Monica Boulevard with smallish houses in the 500 block, quite grand houses in the 600 block, mansions in the 700's, and then, crossing north of Sunset Boulevard, glamorous estates where among the owners these days are perhaps Saudi princes or ex-dictators of Third World nations who managed to steal half the national treasury on their way out of town.

Phoebe North lived in the 500 block of North Foothill Drive, in a cute little gingerbread house that looked as if a witch might live inside. There was a steeply sloped roof that seemed vaguely Bavarian and could be architecturally practical if southern California ever found itself on the receiving end of a mountain snowstorm. The bottom part of the house was more generic California-Spanish: stucco walls, red tile steps to the front door, and wrought iron bars around the lower windows. In Beverly Hills everyone knows that nothing is real except the movies, so you might as well mix and match your styles to whatever is your fancy.

Phoebe was at the front door to greet us, wearing a

black cocktail dress that showed rather a lot of shoulder and more leg. I guess she was trying to be a vamp, but with her round, freckly face she managed to look more like some feminist version of Dennis the Menace. She gave Jayne and me the show-biz cheek-kiss and acted as if we were all the closest of friends. I put on my best party smile and entered the living room, where I saw a few network and studio executives I knew, a number of PR people, a few reporters from publications like *TV Guide, Daily Variety, Hollywood Reporter,* and *Time,* and a camera crew from *Entertainment Tonight.* This was the type of party where you didn't want to drop an hors d'oeuvre down the front of your shirt, lest you later find a photograph of yourself looking less than glamorous on the magazine racks near the supermarket checkout stands.

To parties of this general sort, one invites not just the media people but also assorted creative and/or famous folk who, though they have no particular personal interest in the project being promoted, attend such events simply as a way of seeing their friends in the business. The first ones I spied were the lovely Anne Jeffreys, whom I perhaps too invariably address as Miss Beautiful; the still-aristocratic Cesar Romero, who was talking to the eternally boyish and likable Roddy McDowall; and comedian Jack Carter, who at that moment was eliciting uproarious laughter from Steve Lawrence and Eydie Gorme, our old friends from the original *Tonight* show days. From the distance I couldn't quite make out what Jack was saying, but the words *putz* and *schmuck* were distinguishable.

Not long after we arrived, Jayne was whisked away to pose for a photograph with the other surviving members of *The Murder Game.* She stood between Peter Grover, the host and creator of the show, and

Dominic Carrow, one of the panelists. Peter was dapper and smiling, quite a bit shorter than he appeared on television but every bit as charming. Dominic, on the other hand, was a bit of a snake. He had gained weight over the years, and with his slick black hair and round figure, he looked like a cross between Luciano Pavarotti and Lucifer. When he wasn't in the spotlight on various game shows, Dominic wielded a poisonous pen as a syndicated columnist for nearly a hundred newspapers coast to coast. His barbed social commentary generally helped define who was considered well-dressed, chic, and attending the right sort of parties, and who was not. I'd never liked the man, possibly because I'd never made his Ten Best Dressed List, but there were hostesses from Manhattan to Santa Barbara who would just about kill to be mentioned in his column.

Also in the photograph—standing to the left of Grover—were Susan Fitzgerald, grande dame of the New York stage now diminished with age; the ever-glamorous Amaretta, whose job on the original show had been to turn over the game cards, present the prizes, and smile; and finally, a pretty young woman I assumed was Shadow Bennington, the soap opera star who was replacing Sylvia Van Martinson on the panel. Everyone from the original show had aged in twenty years, as mortals must, except for Amaretta. Her hair was more blond than ever, and when she smiled there was a tightness around her chin and mouth that hinted at the surgeon's knife. It had always astonished me that this creature of no discernible talent had managed to promote herself into becoming a major celebrity. After *The Murder Game* had gone off the air, she had married a string of rich men and had come out of each short union with a hefty divorce settlement, the size of which was invariably reported on the front pages of the tabloids. It was a surprise to everyone that the woman's latest husband—number eight—was a good-looking but penniless young fellow in his mid-twenties, nearly young enough to be her son, though I'm sure she would scratch out the eyes of anyone who said so to her face. The young man went by a single name, Christo, just as she did. If they had ever had real names or real backgrounds, they were long forgotten. Hollywood is a place where people like Amaretta and Christo can reinvent themselves and get away with it.

This is partly because both a good many Americans and most of the entertainment community have surprisingly little interest in talent but an almost morbid fascination with success. If you are merely the best young violinist in Ohio, the finest actress in Boston, or the funniest stand-up comic currently working in the San Francisco area, you have an excellent chance of going to your grave no better known.

There are, of course, directors and producers who are exceptions to this insensitivity, but the situation is far from perfect. Most studio and network executives are quite readily bowled over by the factor of celebrity, and God help the truly gifted young artist who is "up for" a film role but in competition with a celebrity with only one third of the artist's ability.

I stood by myself during the photography session, enjoying the fact that this was Jayne's scene and not mine, and that I could be a quiet spectator. After the photographers had finished their work, I was dismayed to see Dominic Carrow heading my way. I tried to hide my face in a tray of hors d'oeuvres being circulated by a waiter, but Dominic came at me anyway.

"Steve, you're looking mah-vellous," he said. "Isn't

it fabulous to see everyone together again? All our old friends from days gone by!"

"Fabulous," I agreed. Despite his somewhat feminine tone of voice, Carrow was not gay. Well, come to think of it, he was rather gay; what I mean is he was not homosexual. I would not be the least bit surprised to learn that he made it with giraffes with the aid of a stepladder; if you can be sexually straight and weird at the same time, he was both.

He lowered his voice. "Have you met Christo, Amaretta's new hubby? Don't look, but he's standing behind me with a glass of champagne. The other night at Spago, she threw an artichoke across the room at an actress she thought was flirting with him. I give that marriage six months."

I glanced over Dominic's shoulder. Christo was standing by himself with a sullen expression on his face, looking as though he would rather be with people his own age.

"And doesn't Susan look old as the hills?" Dominic asked, jarring into my thoughts. I glanced over at the aging Broadway actress, Susan Fitzgerald. "Frankly, she's senile and utterly broke. A friend told me she tried to film a commercial last week but couldn't remember her lines, poor thing. But she has this lovely secretary, Lance—a fabulous boy. He does more than sharpen her pencils, I'll bet."

I covered my ears with my hands and said, "No, no! I won't listen to this! Dom, you'll rot my mind."

He giggled. "Oh, you funny man!" he said, and then, to my gratitude, wandered off.

"Had your fill of gossip?" came a cultured voice to my left. I turned to find Peter Grover, who was impeccably dressed, as always, in a British-looking suit of dark tweed.

"Peter! How's the world been treating you?"

"Better than I deserve, I'm sure," he said. And then he went on to talk about his various business enterprises. Peter had become truly rich from creating *The Murder Game,* as well as its various spin-offs, including the successful board game of the show. Apparently, he had invested well and had diversified. He owned a shopping mall in Hawaii, a hotel in Carmel, a string of radio stations in the Southwest, and now told me he had just ventured into dietetic, low-fat pizza that he was hoping would sweep the nation. "All boring stuff," he confided in his self-mocking manner. "But it keeps me busy. Actually, I'm thrilled at the prospect of getting out of the stuffy boardroom and in front of the camera again. I'm only sorry Abe isn't around to enjoy all this."

"I was sorry to hear about his death," I said. Then, recalling Jayne's suspicions, I pried a little. "He died in some sort of accident?"

"I warned him not to retire," Peter said. "Retirement often kills active people. Abe moved into this absurd golf-only community outside of Palm Springs, the kind of place where everyone buggies about in these dumb little electric carts. Unfortunately, that's what did him in."

"What do you mean?"

"Well, apparently his condo was on a small hill. One morning he got into his cart to go to play Bingo at the community center, and the brakes failed on the damned thing. He went down the hill, out of control, and slammed into the side of a house. I'm told he was killed instantly."

"What a strange accident."

"Yes, but people don't maintain carts as well as they might automobiles. They're toys to them."

"When did this happen?"

"About six weeks ago. But I doubt if poor Abe would have lived that long, anyway. Retirement was boring him to death. When he found out the network was planning to revive the show, he tried to get his old job as producer back. They wouldn't have him. Said he was too old. They wanted young blood."

Peter sneered the last words, and my eyes followed his narrowed gaze across the room . . . to where the young-blooded Phoebe North was bearing down on us, followed by a seedy young man who seemed out of place in this chic gathering.

Grover was probably right in reporting the network's reaction to rehiring Brautigan. There actually is such a thing as gray-listing in today's youth-dominated entertainment industry. Sometimes it makes sense, often it doesn't. Nature being partly cruel, there will come that inevitable day when all the handsome young actors and actresses, blessed with more beauty than talent, must face the fact they're unhirable because they've lost their looks, and they must "retire" as gracefully as possible. But for an "unhirable" like Abe Brautigan, looks had nothing to do with it, and a graceful retirement had never been an easy or satisfactory alternative.

Phoebe began speaking when she was about five feet away. "Are you having a wonderful time, Steve? Isn't this fabulous, Peter? It's nearly time for the cake. Wait till you see it! It's shaped like a giant dagger, with twenty candles, one for each year *The Murder Game* has been off the air."

"Well, then, you'd better turn off the lights so the cake can make a grand entrance," said Peter.

"Great idea!" She turned to the young man following her. "Did you hear that, Ernie?"

"I'll be carrying the cake," Ernie said petulantly, "so how can I get the lights at the same time?" The fellow appeared to be a production assistant, the sort who might be some more important person's relative or lover. I am not hesitant to reveal a personal bias by saying that my reaction to the young man began several yards behind the normal starting line, simply because of his hairstyle.

I do not refer, as some readers might assume, to length. Indeed there are circumstances when I would judge the very style he sported as appealing and attractive, but only if it was encountered on young boys below the age of nine. In this particular coiffure, the hair was not combed backward but was styled so as to sprout out in a 360-degree free-fall from a central polar top, in a double layer of two deliberately distinct colors. The top layer was dyed an unnatural shade of blond and was trimmed off about halfway down the head, as if the hairstylist had been guided by a kitchen bowl placed over the cranium. The bottom layer was a considerably darker shade of brown. The desired effect, I suppose, was the look that was Hollywood's version of the hairstyle of English schoolboys.

"Let Steve get the lights," Peter suggested.

"Glad to," I assured them.

Phoebe showed me a place in the hall, just off the living room, where a set of four light switches was mounted on the wall. The assignment was complicated by the fact that from where I was standing there was not a clear line of vision to the kitchen, from which the cake would be brought. We worked it out, however, so that at the right moment Phoebe would give a hand-signal to Peter, who would be standing in the living room, and then Peter would signal me.

Standing patiently in the hallway, I glanced at

64

Jayne, who was across the living room talking with Brandon Tartikoff, head of Paramount Pictures, a bright and likable young man, not at all like a character in *The Player*. Phoebe and her assistant bustled into the kitchen, and Peter took his position midway into the living room.

While I waited for my cue, Susan Fitzgerald came toward me. "Excuse me, but by any chance have you noticed the location of the little girls' room?" she asked in a slow alcoholic drawl. Her voice was shaky, her figure shrunken by age. The sight of her saddened me. I thought about how she had looked thirty years earlier in a production of *The Cherry Orchard*. Her presence had been electrifying. It was depressing to find her so reduced and befuddled, with the heavy smell of scotch on her breath. Though we had met many times in the past, I wasn't sure she recognized me.

"I believe it's down the hallway, second door on the left," I said.

"What?"

"Second door on the left," I repeated more loudly, and pointed. I had seen Shadow Bennington emerge from there a few minutes earlier.

"But have you seen Lance, my secretary? He's not supposed to leave me alone like this."

"I'm sorry. I don't know him."

"What?"

"I'VE NEVER MET HIM," I said slowly, and loudly enough that a few people nearby gave me a look.

"Well, you don't have to shout. I'm not deaf." With a dignified turn of her aging body, the actress made her way down the hall. Instead of going where I had indicated, however, she began walking up the stairs to the second floor. I wondered how the poor soul was going to hold up on the panel of *The Murder Game.* It was hard to imagine her solving imaginary crimes with the verve and quick thinking required on live TV.

I turned back toward the living room, where Peter flashed an amused smile my way and shrugged in a what-the-hell manner. I smiled back weakly. At that moment, he gave me the signal to kill the lights.

I hit the switches, and the house was plunged into darkness. Then, accompanied by various oohs and aahs, the massive cake emerged from the kitchen, the twenty candles sending out a warm, flickering glow. I was surprised to see that it was Phoebe, not her assistant, who carried the cake.

She set it down on the buffet table in the living room and stood back admiringly. "I think Peter should blow out the candles," she announced. "Peter, where are you?"

Just at that moment, the French doors leading to the backyard flew open and a gust of wind blew out the candles, plunging the living room into darkness a second time.

"Well, *that's* a sign from heaven," I heard someone say. There was laughter in the dark.

"Turn on the lights, Steve," Phoebe called through the blackness.

I had stepped a few feet beyond the hall into the edge of the living room to watch the arrival of the cake. Walking back toward the light switch, I tripped over a low side table I had not remembered was there. The darkness of the house was total.

"Ow!" I said.

"Are you all right, dear?" Jayne's voice came from somewhere across the living room.

"Having a wonderful time. Wish you were here," I called back.

It wasn't easy finding a light switch in a dark, unfamiliar house. After my encounter with the side table I moved more cautiously, walking with arms stretched out in front of me. I found the wall and then felt with my fingertips, searching for the switch. My hand touched a small framed painting, which crashed to the floor. Oh, I was having a great time.

"What are you doing? Playing Blind Man's Bluff?" someone asked. There was laughter and then, out of the blackness, came a high-pitched scream. The laughter stopped dead.

My hand was shaking as it at last closed on the switch. The light was startling and sudden, revealing a group of frightened faces.

"That was a terrible joke," said Peter. "Which of you screamed? I bet it was you, Dominic."

"Not I," said the columnist.

Something made me turn back toward the hall. Susan Fitzgerald, grande dame of the New York stage, was sprawled at the bottom of the stairs, her neck twisted at an unnatural angle and her eyes staring at the ceiling. It didn't take a doctor to know she was dead.

Chapter 10

The press was calling this "the jinxed reunion." Jayne was calling it murder, though she couldn't say how the deed had been done or why. As far as I was concerned, it did seem strange to have three accidental deaths of people connected to *The Murder Game* in such a short period of time: Abe Brautigan, Sylvia Van Martinson, and Susan Fitzgerald. If you looked at each death individually, however, there didn't seem much doubt they were all nothing more than unfortunate accidents.

"You're wrong, dear," my wife said.

"Jayne, I am *occasionally* wrong, but I don't think so in this instance. Abe, Sylvia, and Susan were all getting on in years. I'm not saying they were *addled* exactly, but they certainly weren't paying enough attention to what they were about."

"Your toast is burning," Jayne remarked, for we were having this particular conversation in our breakfast room. A small plume of black smoke was circling toward the ceiling. I popped the toast up.

"Jayne, you have to face the facts," I said with an indulgent smile. "Abe was a little out of it. The brakes on his golf cart could have been wearing out for months, and he probably wouldn't have noticed or done anything about it until it was too late. Sylvia was no spring chicken, either. She was definitely sideways, and she shouldn't have gone swimming by herself in the ocean in the fog. And as for poor Susan . . . well, you should have seen her. She smelled of liquor and hardly seemed to know where she was. It doesn't surprise me at all that a befuddled old woman might fall down the stairs in an unfamiliar darkened house and break her neck."

"Do you think *we're* getting old?" Jayne asked.

"Of course not. Just the rest of the world."

"Well, I could agree with you if each of these deaths was separate. But all three together? Isn't that stretching coincidence a bit far?"

"Lady Luck has no memory," I said. "They know that in Vegas. Each time you throw the dice, you have precisely the same chance of winning or losing."

"It's murder," Jayne said stubbornly. "I don't know how or why, but I'm going to find out."

So there we were, two separate points of view, the yin and the yang of the Allen family. I did a soft-shoe around the breakfast table, singing, "You say tomato and I say to-mah-to. . . ." Jayne stuck her tongue out at me.

I realized I now had a personal stake in this TV game show reunion, jinxed or otherwise. After Susan's accidental death, the network had asked if I would take her place on the panel. I agreed, though I had to reschedule a couple of concerts—one a week-long engagement at the Jazz Alley club in Seattle and the other a weekend with the Cleveland symphony orchestra. I didn't tell Jayne this, but I was, in fact, hedging my bet somewhat. I knew the idea of murder was absurd, but just in case I was wrong, I thought I'd better be around to keep an eye on my wife. If a knight in armor was required, I didn't want to be too far away.

Over the next few weeks, there was a fair amount of coverage in the press regarding the upcoming show. I think Phoebe North was ghoulishly pushing the jinxed-reunion angle, including the who-will-die-next question. The woman, shamelessly hungry for a hit, didn't seem to care how she got her publicity. Whenever I saw her, she seemed happy as a clam—if indeed clams are happy, which may be just another PR hoax.

In any event there was building excitement, and on a Sunday evening less than a month after Susan's death at Phoebe's party, we all gathered in a theater near Universal City in the San Fernando Valley, from where *The Murder Game* would be broadcast. There had been no further accidents that month.

I've mentioned that *The Murder Game* was to be broadcast live. This is not entirely accurate; as we all know, planet earth is a strange and irrational place, and time is relative. The show aired coast to coast in the eight to eight-thirty time slot, but for this miracle to occur, we actually began our broadcast in Los Angeles at five o'clock. The program thereby would appear live on the East Coast at just that moment, where it was eight, and then be played on tape in California three hours later, with appropriate adjustments for Central and Mountain Time.

Jayne and I arrived at the theater at three and went at once into makeup. At about four-thirty, the studio audience was admitted and guided to their seats by young men and women in beige uniforms, generally kids starting up the long ladder of a career in television.

At about a quarter to five, a stand-up comic came

onstage and began warming up the audience. After a few laughs, he got down to the nitty-gritty of what was expected of them in exchange for their free tickets: They were here to applaud and laugh, and in case there was any doubt about it, there was a big electric sign above the stage that would light up with the word *APPLAUSE* whenever that activity was necessary. "The laughter you can do on your own . . . or else!" said the comic.

To make sure the audience was in good form, they were given a few chances to rehearse while the applause light flashed its message and the comic waved his hands about and shouted things like, "More! Come on, people, you can do better than that!"

A few minutes before five, the warm-up man introduced "your favorite host . . . the charming, the witty, the fantabulous . . . Peter Grover!" At which point Peter walked on stage and in his own soft way worked the audience himself for a few minutes. Then he took his place behind his podium and waited for the countdown to begin.

Nerves were taut both in the control booth and backstage. Thirty seconds before the start of a live TV broadcast is always a tense time, but tonight was more so than usual. The crew had never worked together before, and even the old-timers had opening-night jitters. I saw Phoebe North backstage at 4:59. She was biting her fingernails and looking close to collapse.

"Easy does it," I said.

She gazed at me in what appeared to be terror. Poor, ambitious Phoebe. Her entire career was riding on this experiment, and she had momentarily run out of her usual self-confidence.

"Relax," I told her. "It's just a show."

"For you maybe," she said with surprising frankness. "For me it's everything I've been dreaming about since I was a kid."

The cameras were ready. The lights dimmed in the theater as they rose on the stage. The floor manager, earphones on his head, stood between camera one and camera two and began his countdown.

"Ten . . . nine . . . eight . . . seven . . . six . . . five . . . four . . ."

The last three seconds he indicated only with the fingers of his right hand.

Suddenly, after a twenty-year absence, *The Murder Game* was once more on the airwaves.

Chapter 11

As Peter Grover introduced the celebrity panelists one by one, we came onstage to thunderous applause, whether we deserved it or not, and took our places beneath the bright wash of lights.

A dreadful thing has happened to the once simple matter of applause on television: It has become inflated and exaggerated beyond all rational bounds. I am myself first to applaud wholeheartedly—even to leap to my feet—when something truly exceptional takes place onstage. As a number of my fellow comedians have told me, they love to have me in an audience because I laugh readily and applaud vigorously. A couple of decades or so back, there was a direct correlation between the volume and duration of applause and the merits of the person for whom it was intended. Alas, not so anymore.

Jayne was first to enter. Peter kissed her cheek and then passed her on to Amaretta, our all-purpose bimbo, who was standing with her usual brilliant smile in a shimmering white above-the-knee cocktail dress. Amaretta applauded along with the audience; part of her job was to look perky and act as if *The Murder Game* were great fun. She gave Jayne a sisterly embrace, being careful not to muss their makeup, and then ushered her to a seat behind a long table at stage right.

I was next. I shook hands with Peter, kissed Amaretta's offered cheek, which was warm, moist, and florid, and took my seat to Jayne's left. Shadow Bennington followed me, sitting to my left, and finally Dominic Carrow, at the end of the table.

"And now let's meet tonight's challengers. Sign in, please!" said Peter, and one by one the four guest challengers filed out from the wings, signed their names on a blackboard, shook hands with Peter, and were then ushered by Amaretta to a table stage left.

The guest panelists for this first show included a famous alleged psychic who claimed to have worked with the police on real-life murders, a criminal attorney, a private eye, and a woman journalist who covered the crime beat for the L.A. *Daily News.* I should mention that all the challengers had had a chance to rehearse the game backstage. In theory, the celebrity panel would have an advantage, since we would be doing the show every week, but the guests were familiar with criminal investigation, and given the rehearsal, the odds were probably shifted in their favor—though not if *I* could help it. I smiled across the stage at our four opponents, but inside I was motivated to win. When it comes to solving mysteries, I liked to think I had at least moderate gifts.

"Remember, this is only a game," Jayne whispered in my ear during the first commercial.

Phoebe had assured us that *The Murder Game* would be exactly as it had been twenty years earlier. Not to my surprise, this turned out to be nonsense. In the old days, the set had been very simple; like John Daly during my days as a panelist on *What's My*

76

Line?, Peter had kept score by using flash cards that he flipped over by hand. Now all this was done on a huge computerized game board that occupied the entire rear of the stage. The board was lit up with hundreds of flashing colored lights and shone as brightly as the marquee of a Las Vegas hotel. Studying its visual barrage of bright reds, lavenders, yellows, blues, and greens, I was reminded of G. K. Chesterton's marvelous line upon being introduced to the giant lighted advertisements of New York's Times Square back in the 1920s: "What a beautiful sight for a man who couldn't read."

In the old days, the crime to be solved had been acted out in a live skit at the start of each show by a few obliging semi-celebrities. Tonight, the stage turned dark, and accompanied by dramatic music, the game board transformed itself into an enormous video screen. We watched a brief, pretaped clip, keeping a sharp eye glued for clues. The skit was tongue-in-cheek, a murder mystery played for laughs, but it contained all the information we would need to solve the crime.

Twenty years earlier, the skits had been narrated by Peter. I was surprised to find Amaretta providing this service on the new version. Now that she was a celebrity, I suppose they had had to offer her a bigger part. The only holdover from the past was that the skit was still acted out by various TV celebrities, mostly from sitcoms and adventure shows the network was trying to publicize. In any event, the crime was played out as follows:

Accompanied by Amaretta's thin, childlike voice, we entered the household of John Mertz, a slick and unscrupulous millionaire, owner of The Mertz Department Store. We soon met Margaret Mertz, John's wife of thirty years, an unhappy woman who was forced to clean the Mertz mansion from top to bottom by herself every day, because John liked it immaculate but was too cheap to hire a maid. (The studio audience had been encouraged to hiss at such revelations.)

Then there was John, Jr., a son treated badly by his father and not permitted to live his own life. His sister Annabel, on the other hand, was the apple of her father's eye. Unfortunately, Annabel had married a ne'er-do-well, Bruce Babbit, a handsome lad who had been given a job as assistant manager at the family store.

In the brief video, we watched John Mertz accuse his son-in-law of embezzling ten thousand dollars from the store. Bruce insisted he was innocent and accused John, Jr. of stealing the money to pay off gambling debts. A family quarrel erupted and Bruce stormed out of the house, announcing loudly that he was going to his club.

And now entered a final suspect, George Bezelman, head accountant of The Mertz Department Store. We watched George meet privately with Margaret Mertz, whispering something into her ear. Unfortunately, we could not hear what he was telling her.

The action jumped forward to the middle of the night. We heard a horrifying scream in the dark and then discovered Mertz, Sr. dead on the floor of his bedroom with a knife in his back.

This was the end of the clip. The lights came on, the video screen became a game board again, and we were ready to play. The whole scene had lasted less than three minutes, briefer than it has taken me to recount the action.

We now had to decide between five suspects in the murder of John Mertz: Margaret, the wife; John, Jr., the son; Annabel, the daughter; Bruce, the son-in-law; and George, the head accountant.

Peter stood beneath the game board, smiling mysteriously. He seemed to delight in throwing the puzzle out to us. "I'll remind you, panelists," he said, "you are allowed to make only *one* accusation—so you'll need to win as many clues as possible. . . . Amaretta, start the clock!"

Amaretta did exactly that, pressing a button to set the clock in motion, which began the game. The clock was almost at the top of the game board, showing digital seconds and minutes flying by. Above the clock, the grand figure of $100,000 appeared in flashing red lights on the board. This was the prize the guest panelists would share if they correctly guessed the identity of the murderer. Unfortunately, time was of the essence, and the amount of money began to decrease immediately at the exact rate of $83.33 a second, or $5,000 per minute—to be reduced all the way to zero if neither team made the correct guess during the twenty minutes of actual game time. To watch the money disappearing at such a rate induced a dismal sensation, similar to watching the sign above the Hard Rock Cafe in Beverly Hills second by second recording the depletion of the world's rain-forest acreage.

The guest team was tossed the first question. In the old days, Peter would simply read the question from a card, but now the game board did a little song and dance and announced the question without visible human assistance: "WHERE DID BRUCE BABBIT SAY HE WAS GOING WHEN HE LEFT THE HOUSE?"

This was pretty easy, but it was only the beginning of the game.

The guest team briefly conferred among themselves,

and then the criminal lawyer, in a rather self-satisfied voice, announced their answer: "To his club."

"That is . . ." Peter paused for dramatic effect, " . . . absolutely correct!"

The guest panelists smiled as Peter continued. "And now you may choose a clue category."

The game board lit up with various squares, each of which contained a different clue category: Old Secret, Motive, Police Files, Time of Death, Alibi, Forensic Lab, Blind Luck, and Misc. The guest team chose Police Files, and Amaretta handed them an envelope to open and examine among themselves. We on the opposing team were not allowed to see this clue, although it was flashed to home viewers and the studio audience, who chuckled appropriately and emitted a few oohs and aahs. (Later that night, while watching a replay of the show, I learned that this first clue read: "$10,000 CASH WAS FOUND UNDER THE MATTRESS OF THE VICTIM'S BED.")

But I had no idea what the clue was as the guest team looked at each other in comic dismay, not certain what it meant, and the game board flashed a new question for them to answer: "WHAT WAS THE COLOR OF GEORGE BEZELMAN'S NECKTIE?"

As long as they continued to answer questions correctly, the game would remain with them and they could compile clues. Fortunately for our side, the guest panel had apparently not paid attention to small sartorial details. They answered "gray"—incorrectly —and the question passed to our side.

"Light green," I whispered to my colleagues, but my fellow panelists insisted the necktie was light brown, and they were right. Our team had won a clue, and I tried not to care that I personally was not off to a good start. I felt certain I would have the important answers when they were needed.

I wanted to select the Old Secret category for our clue but again was outvoted by the others, who wanted to go for Motive. I shrugged, even though I thought my teammates were underestimating the power of an old secret to cause a crime. Still, the Motive clue was interesting: "JOHN MERTZ WAS ABOUT TO DIS-INHERIT HIS CHILDREN AND LEAVE THE MAJORITY OF HIS MONEY TO FOUND A TOWN PARK THAT WOULD BEAR HIS NAME."

During the twenty seconds we were given to consult amongst ourselves and decide if we wanted to make an accusation based on our clue, dramatic music played a sort of countdown motif.

"What a nasty man," whispered Jayne, who tends to take such things personally and emotionally.

"This means the whole damn family had a motive!" said Dominic, leaning my way.

"Only the children," I corrected. "It says Mertz was going to disinherit his children, not his wife, and leave the *majority* of his money for the park. We can there-fore deduce that Margaret still had a stake in the inheritance."

"So she's innocent?" asked Shadow.

"Perhaps," I said.

Peter informed us our time for discussion was up, and we were thrown the next question: "BRUCE CLAIMED IT WAS HIS BROTHER-IN-LAW, JOHN, JR., WHO EMBEZZLED THE $10,000. WHAT MOTIVE DID HE GIVE FOR THIS THEFT?"

We all agreed immediately that Bruce claimed John, Jr. desperately needed the money to pay off his gambling debts. Since we were right, we received another clue. This time the others went along with my desire to see the category Old Secret. The clue informed us that Margaret had once hoped her daughter Annabel might be able to study ballet in New York City, but daddy John had nixed the idea.

This didn't seem such a deep, dark secret, but I supposed it was necessary information.

We missed the next question, and the game was passed back to the guest team.

By the time the next commercial arrived, the prize money was down to $47,385.39, and we had earned a few more clues. We now knew that John, Jr. had originally had his heart set on becoming a doctor, but as with his sister's ballet plans, the ambition had been overruled by the old man.

We next learned that John, Jr. had once been arrested for drunk driving and that son-in-law Bruce was having an affair with a saleswoman from the lingerie department. We discovered that George, the head accountant, was secretly in love with Margaret, and that for thirty years she had been fantasizing about an ocean voyage around the world, a plan her husband had vetoed each time it was brought up. None of it added up to a lot, but of course we had no idea what clues the other team was getting.

Finally, with $27,322.74 left on the clock, the guest team made an accusation, the attorney acting as their spokesman. The fellow was tall and good-looking, and he took a vaguely condescending attitude toward the game. "The killer is Annabel," he said firmly.

"And the motive?" asked Peter. (The winning team was required to guess both the identity of the killer and his or her motive, as an insurance against wild-guessing.)

"Annabel killed her father to keep Bruce from going to prison. You see, she had discovered that it was her father himself who had embezzled the ten thousand dollars from the store, arranging the whole thing so that it would seem as if his son-in-law had committed the crime. John Mertz had always hated Bruce, of course, and was trying to break up his daughter's marriage."

Peter smiled and asked Amaretta to pass him the important envelope, which he opened. After skimming the contents, he said, "I'm afraid that is . . . the wrong answer!"

The criminal lawyer looked as if he couldn't quite believe his ears. For a moment I thought he was going to ask for an appeal, but instead he sank back into his chair with a deflated sigh.

Now that the guest team had made their one allowable accusation, their only hope was to keep us from winning. They could do this best by guessing all the answers to the various questions and keeping us from collecting any more clues. If neither team won, a tie would be declared and the guests would be invited back the following week for another chance. If *we* won, however, the guest team's TV days would be over, and new challengers would take their place.

We played another five minutes, and the clock ticked down to a mere $2,298.15. Suddenly, I had an inspiration!

"It was Margaret!" I cried, to the surprise of my teammates. Of course I should have conferred with them before making the all-important accusation, but since the game was nearly over, there hadn't seemed time.

"This is your official accusation?" asked Peter, sensing disunity in our ranks.

We took a moment to confer. "It's *not* Margaret," Dominic said heatedly. "It absolutely cannot be."

"No, I think Steve may be right," Shadow Bennington countered. "Let's trust him on this." A bright young woman.

"What do *you* say, Jayne?" Dominic asked, leaning down the table.

"I say we're running out of time and Steve's guess is probably our last chance."

So Dominic was outvoted, which left him slightly grumpy.

"Our answer is Margaret," I repeated to Peter and the TV audience, hoping I was right.

"And the motive?"

"She was tired of watching her husband destroy her children's lives. When she found out it was her husband who had embezzled the ten thousand in order to wreck Annabel's marriage, it was the last straw. She decided to act."

Peter Grover's smile was neutral, neither confirming nor denying the guess. "And how did Margaret know her husband had embezzled the money?" he asked.

It wasn't necessary to correctly answer that question to win the game, but I was on a roll so I took a wild guess. "George told her when he whispered in her ear."

Peter knew who the killer was, of course, but he pretended to consult his piece of paper. Finally, he smiled broadly and announced that we were correct.

So there it was.

I don't like to brag, but there really was a lot of applause—and I don't think all of it was due to the flashing applause sign.

To fill up the last few moments of the show, the actors who had appeared in the murder video came out from backstage, and we all got to meet John Mertz and family in person. The $2,298.15 remaining on the clock would be added to the next week's game, creating an ever-increasing prize as long as the celebrity panel continued to win.

Finally, the theme music came on and the credits began to roll, taking us off the air. When our microphones were dead, Jayne turned to me and said, "Well done, darling. Now if you could only help me solve the *real* mystery!"

I smiled indulgently at Jayne's suspicions as I took her arm and led her out of the studio.

Chapter 12

I half woke to the sound of a man's voice in our bedroom. "The jinx continues," said the voice—one of those too-perfect public-speaking voices—"as death once again strikes the panel of a popular game show. More on that story in a moment."

"Steve, dear," Jayne cooed into my left ear, gently shaking me awake.

I had been deep in a dream, and it took me a moment to come fully awake. Sunlight was pouring into our bedroom, a cheerful beginning for a new day. I groped for my glasses on the bedside table. The clock read 7:36. It was the morning after the broadcast of *The Murder Game,* and Jayne had turned on our bedroom television set.

I groggily observed an attractive young woman on the screen discussing a new cure for allergies and sinus headaches.

"I heard this in the kitchen on NPR," Jayne said. "I thought we should listen to what the networks have to say."

"About sinus headaches?"

"Shush," she said.

After sinus pain, we were treated to a short discourse on acid indigestion. It's peculiar, and not entirely coincidental, that news broadcasts are often sponsored by remedies for various body disorders brought on by stress.

"I'd rather be dreaming," I told my wife.

"Here we go," she assured me, just as the TV screen filled with the image of an earnest young man. The young man began speaking in a too-perfect masculine voice.

"Columnist Dominic Carrow was killed late last night in a freak accident at his Laurel Canyon home," the anchorman said. My heart did a small skip. I had never particularly cared for Carrow, but the news of his death was a shock.

"What do you have to say now?" Jayne asked.

"Just a moment. Let me listen."

The anchorman explained that the death of the celebrated columnist had occurred when his electric garage door had lowered upon his head. For a moment we were treated to a view of the deadly door. And then the screen changed to Lt. Benjamin Washington of the L.A. County Sheriff's Department, a distinguished-looking African American in a dark suit. The lieutenant told the viewers that a full investigation was in progress. At the moment, however, it appeared that Carrow's death was nothing more than an unfortunate household accident. Thousands of Americans die in such mishaps every year.

The anchorman reappeared and summarized Lieutenant Washington's speculation that Mr. Carrow, returning from the broadcast of *The Murder Game* and parking his late-model Mercedes in the garage, had perhaps heard a phone ringing in his house and in his hurry to answer it had not noticed the closing door. The report concluded by saying that this was the third accidental death in recent weeks among those associated with the hit TV game show from the early seventies, the other two victims being Susan Fitzgerald and publisher Sylvia Van Martinson. The thought crossed my mind that there were really *four* accidents associated with the show, if Abe Brautigan were to be included.

"Well?" Jayne said.

"Well what? Household accidents happen all the time."

Jayne glared at me and made a grand exit from the bedroom, flinging back over her shoulder, "Don't choke on your toothbrush, dear."

I thought about the news I had just heard. The series of deaths was definitely becoming alarming, and yet I still felt Jayne's judgment was premature. There was no *factual* evidence to indicate a killer was doing everyone in. What motive would anyone have for murdering all these individuals? I wondered how in the world the sheriff's department had thought Dominic was hurrying to answer a ringing telephone. As far as I knew, he lived alone. So who had been around to hear the ringing? Was there a secret witness the police weren't identifying?

I sat upright in bed, staring hypnotically at a pine tree outside the window, telling myself one minute that I was foolish to get involved with this, then the next that I would be foolish *not* to, since Jayne and I were among the ever smaller circle to whom these freak accidents were occurring.

In the end, I decided I'd better investigate. What if there really *was* a killer out there? I should at least protect my wife from danger.

I picked up the bedside phone and dialed Cass at his apartment above our garage.

"What's up, boss?"

"Are you dressed?"

"Sure."

"Good. I'd like you to bring the car around front."

"Where're we goin'?"

"A little trip to Laurel Canyon . . . and, Cass, I want to be discreet, so be as quiet as you can, okay?"

"Discreet. You mean you don't want Jayne to know, huh?" He paused for a moment, thinking. "You're on the trail of whoever killed Dominic Carrow, aren't you?"

"I just want to poke around a little, that's all. Just bring the car." I hung up the phone and started for the front door. Jayne loomed up out of the den as I walked by.

"And where are *you* going, darling?"

"Oh, I thought I'd take a drive with Cass to the Farmer's Market. Maybe buy a bag of oranges or something."

"Are you going by way of Laurel Canyon, by any chance?"

"What for?"

Jayne smiled her knowing smile. I know I could have just confessed, but there's a certain amount of competition between Jayne and me when it comes to solving mysteries. I didn't want her to know I had almost changed my mind about the deaths being accidental. At least not until I had taken a closer look at the facts. It didn't really matter, anyway; I was sure she knew what was going on in my mind.

I sat next to Cass in the front seat of the Caddy as he headed onto the Ventura Freeway, going south toward Laurel Canyon.

On the car radio, which Cass had playing softly in the background, Ken Minyard of station KABC's

"Ken and Barkley Show" referred to a "bumper-thumper" on the 405 freeway. "I get a kick," Cass said, "at the casual way radio people here in L.A. talk about car accidents. They're usually described as bumper-thumpers or fender-benders—as if it was a joke that some poor guy has to have his car hauled away from the scene, won't get it back for two weeks, and will probably have to pay sixteen hundred dollars for something my old man used to fix with a hammer back when he drove an old Ford Model-A. Jeez, fender-benders. Any day now I expect one of these guys to say, '. . . and on the Ventura Freeway this afternoon, a little murder-wurder seems to have popped up.'"

I suddenly had an idea. Dominic Carrow's society and gossip column was syndicated in about two hundred papers around the country through a New York wire service known as the World Newspaper Syndication Corporation, or WNSC. The chief editor of WNSC was a man named Jeffrey Brattle, who had once briefly worked as a writer on my old Sunday night show. We weren't close friends, but I enjoyed his company and ran into him from time to time on trips back east. Jeffrey knew Dominic better than anyone, and it occurred to me that he might have some information the papers had left out.

I used the car phone to dial New York City information and got the number of Jeffrey's West Fifty-seventh Street office. It was late morning in New York, and I reached Jeff just as he was about to step out for lunch.

We spent a few minutes in polite conversation, mentioned our mutual shock over Dominic's death, and then Jeff said, in his gravelly smoker's voice and streetwise New York manner, "Let's not kid ourselves. Dominic was a schmuck. But I'm gonna miss him. He used to make me laugh."

"Jeff, do you know any reason somebody might have had it in for him?"

"You think this was murder?"

"You were probably closer to him than anybody else. What do *you* think?"

"What I think is that we don't have automatic garage doors in New York City, we just got muggers and crazy taxi drivers. . . . So what the hell do I know about it? Right? But a funny thing happened last night. An hour or two after Dominic finished doing *The Murder Game,* he phoned me from some restaurant. He said he had a big scoop for his column and that he'd be faxing me some pages in the morning. He wanted me to substitute the new material for a column he had written last week and try to get the copy into the afternoon papers."

"Did he say what the scoop was all about?"

"Not a hint. I asked him, but he only chuckled and said it would knock my socks off."

"Was he excited? Frightened?"

"No, laughing. Really enjoying himself. I had the impression he had the goods on someone. You know how Dominic was about sticking it to people. He enjoyed being nasty."

"Maybe the person he was going to stick it to stuck it to him first."

"I'm amazed one of those society matrons he voted worst dressed of the year didn't do him in years ago."

When I hung up the phone, Cass was guiding the burgundy limo off the freeway and onto Laurel Canyon Boulevard.

"Cass! Look out!" A silver Porsche suddenly emerged from a driveway, and I grabbed the dashboard as Cass narrowly avoided it. Then we continued on to the house of death.

Chapter 13

The road to Laurel Canyon ascends from the San Fernando Valley to Mulholland Drive at the very top of the Hollywood Hills, then winds its way down through a long green canopy of trees to Sunset Boulevard on the other side. For several idyllic miles you almost have the illusion that you are in the country. Charming little hillside homes are hidden away beneath great spreading oaks with Porsches and BMW convertibles in the driveways. There is a smell of eucalyptus in the air, and the harsh urban sprawl of Greater Los Angeles seems far away.

Dominic Carrow lived on a treacherously winding road that made its way up from Laurel Canyon Boulevard back toward the top of the hills. The house was so quaintly rustic you'd think Goldilocks had lived there rather than a columnist with a poison pen. The little cabin was covered with rough redwood shingles and, seen from the rear, seemed engulfed in a tangle of luxuriant rosebushes.

When Cass and I got out of the limo and began to explore, we soon discovered the cabin was built on an extremely steep embankment, the front end dangling out over empty space, with a sun deck held up by long pylons anchored in the hillside some thirty feet below. It all looked very precarious. You had to have a certain California optimism to live in such a place, especially in earthquake country.

Now that I was here, I wasn't at all certain what I was looking for. The house seemed dismal, empty of life. Cass and I tried a side door and found it locked. We walked around the bungalow, peering into various windows. I had a glimpse of a pine-paneled bedroom with a canopied bed. As Cass strained to peer over my shoulder, he suddenly slipped on the steep incline and landed in a manzanita bush. I helped him up, and we returned to more solid ground.

"This sure is a fun way to spend a morning," he remarked sarcastically.

"Cass, I'm sorry I dragged you out here."

"Hey, I wouldn't miss it, man."

As a matter of fact, I was feeling fairly foolish. There wasn't anything to be seen other than an uninhabited Laurel Canyon cabin lazing in the late morning sun. I'm not sure what I expected. . . . Maybe bloody footprints in the grass with a sign saying: THE MURDERER WENT THIS WAY.

I led Cass to the two-car garage, the fatal electronic door of which was firmly shut and locked. There wasn't anything to be seen here, either.

"You finding all kinds of wonderful clues?"

"I'm getting *ideas*," I told him. "A lot of detective work is just walking around like this and getting a feel of things. For instance, right now I'm trying to imagine if there is any way this garage door could have closed on Dominic's head accidentally. What do you think?"

Cass squinted at the garage door from several angles. "You asking my expert opinion as a chauffeur and someone familiar with garage doors?"

"Yeah."

Cass scratched his head and made a big production out of thinking things over.

"We-el, Dominic probably had a gizmo underneath his dash to open the garage door from his car, see? A garage-door clicker. These things open the door while you're approaching in your car. After you're parked, you either take the thing with you and close the door behind you, or you hit the button on your way out. I guess a real dummy *could* get himself conked on the head as the door was coming down."

I was staring at the killer door, trying to imagine the scenario. Could someone else with a clicker have used it as a murder weapon?

The sound of Cass's snapping fingers jarred me out of my reverie. "I've got it!" he said. "Dominic arranged all this, I'll bet. He committed suicide!"

"With a garage door?"

"This is clever," Cass assured me. "His life insurance policy wouldn't pay off for a suicide, so he makes it look like a freak accident—and his wife and kiddies live happily ever after on all the dough."

"Only he didn't *have* a wife and kiddies," I mentioned.

"He didn't have life insurance, either," said a voice from behind us. Cass and I spun around to see a large black man standing in the driveway behind us. I have no idea how long the fellow had been watching us or where he had come from. He was staring at us curiously, and we stared back. He was forty-something, with a pear-shaped head that was wider at the jowls than on the balding top. What hair he had was rather gray and distinguished. The man wore a navy blue suit, white shirt, and dark tie. His black shoes were shined to a high gloss. I recognized him from my TV screen earlier in the morning.

"Lieutenant Washington," he said. "L.A. County Sheriff's Department."

I smiled as pleasantly and innocently as a trespasser might manage while facing the law. "Pleased to meet you. I'm Steve Allen, and this is my driver—"

"I know who you are," he interrupted. "The question is, what are you doing here?"

"That's simple," I assured him. "My wife has this crazy idea that all these people are being murdered— first Abe Brautigan, then Sylvia Van Martinson, Susan Fitzgerald, and now poor Dominic. So I thought I'd better come over here and look into it a little. Put her mind at ease."

The lieutenant raised a skeptical eyebrow. "And what is your conclusion, Mr. Allen?"

"I don't have the foggiest," I admitted cheerfully. "But it seems a bit hard to imagine how Dominic could have been so careless as to be standing in the garage doorway when the door was coming down."

"Stand back," said the lieutenant.

"I beg your pardon?"

"Move out of the way." Lieutenant Washington had a proper tone of authority and a badge to back him up, so Cass and I moved a few steps away from the garage. The lieutenant took something from his right-hand pocket and I saw it was a garage-door opener. He pressed it and the garage door began swinging open, revealing a bright yellow two-seater Mercedes sports car inside. The garage door, I noticed, opened outward, with the bottom moving up toward us in the driveway.

"The victim had this in his hand when we found

him," the lieutenant said. "We think he parked his car inside the garage, got out, pressed the button, perhaps accidentally, and walked right into the closing door as he was hurrying out of the garage to get into his house to answer the ringing telephone."

Lieutenant Washington pressed the button on the opener to illustrate his point. The garage door began closing with a small electric whir. A person walking quickly from inside the garage could get a very nasty crack indeed if his head collided with the massive moving door.

"Wait a minute," I said. "I have two objections. First of all, Dominic wouldn't press the button to close the door until he was *out* of the garage."

"Yes, but you have to remember he's opened and closed this garage door a thousand times," said the officer. "It was the sort of automatic gesture he didn't even think about anymore. Anyway, it was dark, the victim was upset, the phone was ringing; he just wasn't thinking clearly. As a result, he pressed the button too soon."

"Why do you say he was upset? I had just done a TV show with Dominic, and he seemed fine."

The lieutenant stared at me and didn't answer. Police generally prefer to be on the other side of the question-asking.

"What's your second objection, Mr. Allen? No, let me guess. It has to do with the ringing telephone."

"That's right. Dominic lived alone, so unless you have some secret witness stashed away, there's no way to know if the phone was ringing while he was parking his car."

The lieutenant smiled ever so slightly. This was a man with a deadpan face, but he could not resist letting us know how clever he was.

99

"Come this way, please," he said, leading Cass and me inside the house, using a key from a key chain to open the front door.

Carrow's house was full of wood and hanging plants, with sliding glass doors looking out onto the sun deck and a hillside view of smoggy L.A. spreading out to the horizon. The kitchen was open to the living room, with a bar separating the two areas. On top of the bar was a telephone answering machine. Lieutenant Washington pressed the button marked MESSAGES. I heard a familiar male voice: "Dominic . . . I thought you'd still be awake. I was just calling to say how sorry I am about everything, but that's show biz, I guess. Look, let's have lunch next week and talk this over. Give me a call in the morning."

The voice stopped, and then I heard the flat monotone of the answering machine's robotic tongue: "Sunday, 11:52 P.M. End of messages."

"Do you recognize the caller's voice?" asked the lieutenant.

"Of course. It's Peter Grover."

The lieutenant nodded. "Mr. Grover has already verified that he made this call late last night from his house in Bel Air. He was calling to console the victim from being fired from the panel of your TV show."

"Fired! From *The Murder Game?* That's nonsense!"

"Not at all. Apparently, Carrow was considered too old to cut the mustard. The sponsor and the show's producer—a Ms. North—decided to replace him with someone more appealing to today's audience. I believe they have a rock star in mind."

I was stunned. I could now well accept the lieutenant's theory that Dominic had been upset as he arrived home. "So you think Dominic was rushing to answer this phone call. But how can you be so sure?"

"Because of the time. You see, the victim's wrist slapped the pavement as he fell to his death and his Rolex broke at just that moment—11:52."

"But it's still conjecture," I insisted. "You're only guessing that Dominic was rushing to the phone and that he was preoccupied and that he pushed his door-closer button too soon. You don't know any of these things for an absolute fact. So it's still possible he was murdered."

"Yes, it's possible," said the lieutenant, his small ironic smile fading. "However, murder seems most unlikely."

"Who found the body?" I asked.

"The private security patrol most of the people up here hire to keep them safe 'n' sound. The patrol car was making its rounds last night about half past twelve and happened to notice the victim's legs protruding from the closed door. They investigated and gave us a call."

"I see," I said gloomily. The image of Dominic Carrow lying with the door closed on his head was not a pretty one.

The lieutenant guided us out of the house and carefully locked the front door. "Well, these accidents happen," he said. "Just the other day the wife of one of my friends blew herself up lighting the pilot of her gas water heater. There was a gas leak."

I couldn't take any more. Grabbing Cass firmly by the arm, I led him back to our limo. "Come on," I muttered, "let's do something safe . . . like drive home on the freeway."

Chapter 14

I had kept from Lieutenant Washington the not-so-insignificant tidbit that Dominic Carrow had apparently been working on a hot scoop at the time of his death. Could this have had anything to do with his "accident?" It seemed a distinct possibility, particularly with Carrow's penchant for nasty revelations. Perhaps someone had not wanted his or her dirty laundry aired in public. I was determined to find out what the scoop was all about—before the police muddied the waters.

Unfortunately, I didn't know where to begin. Unlike most important columnists, Dominic had always worked alone. He didn't have a legman, so there was no one I could ask. I was tempted to break into his house and look through his desk for any clues he might have left behind. Wednesday morning, in fact, I had Cass drive me by the Laurel Canyon home a second time, but we saw two squad cars in the driveway and decided not to stop.

At Mulholland and Laurel Canyon Boulevard, I had Cass pull over. Looking out over Los Angeles, spread at our feet, I realized the City of Angels seemed very peaceful from these heights. The serenity allowed me to think. I decided Peter Grover might be able to help, so I used the cellular phone to reach him at the offices of Grover Enterprises, from where he ran his small empire of hotels and radio stations—his "straight gig," as he liked to call it, with his usual self-deprecating humor.

"Hey, Steverino, glad you called," he said. "What's up?"

"I wanted to ask you a few questions about Dominic. Do you have a moment?"

Peter chuckled. "Ah-ha, so the comedian is playing private detective again! You can't resist the challenge, can you, Steve? You always have to solve the puzzle."

"Well, it *is* puzzling," I admitted. "Not only Dominic, but Abe, Sylvia, and Susan are gone, too—and all of them . . . well . . . mysteriously."

"I can't argue with you about that."

"I understand you phoned Dominic the night he died. . . . As a matter of fact, the police think he was hurrying to answer your call when he hit his head against the closing garage door."

"Believe me, I've been asking myself why I couldn't have called just five minutes earlier—or later. Perhaps Dom'd still be alive if I'd stopped to pour myself a drink. And the irony is that I was trying to be helpful." Peter sighed. "I guess you've heard that Dominic had been fired." He chuckled sadly. "Definitely not his lucky day . . ."

"He was told Sunday night about being fired?"

"Immediately after the broadcast. Phoebe, with enormous lack of tact, taste, and simple human kindness, came up to him in the Green Room and just blurted out that his services would no longer be required. No warning. No 'I'm sorry.' It was the network's decision; she was simply the hatchet. They've hired this Neanderthal with long hair. Some idiot by the name of Tommy Blue."

"The rock star."

"Right. The idea, of course, is to update the show for a younger audience. We're getting old, man."

"Like everyone else on earth," I said. "So how did Dominic take the news?"

"Very well, actually. He pretended to be amused about the whole affair. He was sitting with Shadow Bennington, probably trying to impress her."

"You were there?"

"I was passing by on the way to my dressing room."

"And Dominic seemed okay about all of it?"

"Yeah. But then, driving home, I started thinking that he might be more upset than he was letting on, so I got the idea of offering him a job. I thought he might do a fifteen-minute or half-hour show each week for my string of TV stations in the Southwest. A scandal-of-the-week-type thing. It probably would've been a hit. From Dominic's point of view, of course, it wouldn't compare to *The Murder Game,* but it was an offer at least. He'd feel wanted again."

"That was very thoughtful of you, Peter. But wasn't it rather late to be calling?"

"Nah. I knew Dom rarely went to bed before two. Frankly, I was worried about him. Despite his show of bravado, it couldn't have been pleasant to learn he was about to be replaced, especially by a dodo like Tommy Blue."

"Phoebe actually told him who his replacement would be?"

"Cold turkey."

"Look, Peter, did you by any chance hear Dominic talking about a big scoop for his column?"

"Not that I remember. Of course, he was always

onto some story or other, digging the old dirt. It was what he lived for."

"And possibly died for."

"Well, I suppose anything is possible," Peter said. "You might ask Shadow. She was there. I believe they were heading out for Chinese dinner somewhere. An odd friendship between those two, but I suppose it's understandable. He spared her the usual romantic advances, and she looked decorative walking into a restaurant on his arm."

After hanging up with Peter, I used the car phone to make a series of calls in which I was finally able to locate Ms. Bennington—on the set of the soap opera *Nights of Passion*. I rarely watch daytime television, so I was unaware of her fame and notoriety as the character of Amanda Laslow. Apparently, this was a show that went as far into X-rated situations as daytime television would permit. Amanda Laslow was what they used to call a vamp, stealing husbands right and left, the sort of character housewives love to hate.

I told Cass to drive to the soundstage in the Valley, where I found Shadow, as Amanda, repelling the advances of a handsome middle-aged man who wouldn't take no for an answer.

"It's over, Michael," she was telling him. "You just have to accept that you don't thrill me anymore."

"You can't dispose of me like this!" cried the man. "Why, I left Carolyn for you! I left my children!"

"Tough," Amanda said. "You should have realized I only play with men like you."

Amanda/Shadow turned to leave, as three television cameras followed her movements. The man tried to stop her, pulling at her blouse, which ripped partially open to reveal a black lace slip underneath—the allotted amount of quasi-nudity allowed in daytime television. Unfortunately, there was a problem with the blouse, which did not rip as far as the director wanted. The wardrobe woman was called, a new blouse was supplied, and the scene was taped a second time. When it was finished, Shadow stepped out from behind the lights and came my way.

"Steve! What brings you here?" She offered her cheek to kiss.

"I was hoping to ask you a few questions about Dominic. Do you have a moment?"

"Ten minutes, to be exact. And then Amanda seduces a new victim. Why don't you come to my dressing room—that is, if you dare." She laughed a soft, breathy laugh.

I laughed with her, happy to see she had a sense of humor about her profession.

Her dressing room was a trailer in the narrow alley between soundstages. Inside, she cleared a small stack of books from a chair so I could sit down. I caught a few titles. There was Carl Jung's *Memories, Dreams and Reflections,* a John Updike novel, the collected short stories of Dorothy Parker, and a survey of the labor movement in the 1930s.

Shadow Bennington—as I hope I've made clear—was an extremely beautiful young woman. She had rich chestnut hair, smoldering brown eyes, and just a hint of freckles beneath her TV makeup, which gave her an appealing earthiness. But Hollywood has always had more than its share of pretty young women. It was her choice of books that made me regard her more closely.

"I imagine you want to go on from the soaps to do serious films with social messages?" I asked, with only a small twinkle.

She laughed merrily. "Not at all! I don't really want to be an actress at all."

"You don't? Then what are you doing here?"

"Working my way through college, actually. I'm in my third year at UCLA. I keep that a deep, dark secret, by the way, since it doesn't exactly jibe with the character of Amanda Laslow. Some people wait tables to pay their tuition. I do this."

"You must manage to pay for more than the tuition," I suggested.

"Well, I'm saving for grad school and maybe a small ranch in Montana. My dream is to raise horses and be a vet."

"That sounds like a very sensible dream. Are you a country girl originally?"

She laughed. "Not really. Unless you consider West Covina the country."

"Is that where your parents are?"

Shadow's smile faded.

Perhaps it was just that she had grown up watching me put questions to guests on television talk shows and therefore felt she was somehow obliged to give me straight answers. The suddenly somber look on her face made me think her parents might not be living.

"Are your folks still alive?"

"My mother is," she said. "My father died when I was seven. My mother married again—unfortunately."

"Why unfortunately?"

She paused for a moment, bit her lip, and then surprised me by saying, "Well, I think it's unfortunate when an adult sexually molests a child, don't you? It disgusted me so much I almost got sick every time I looked at the man. I was too terrified of him to tell my mother, so when I was fifteen I just . . . ran away."

"At fifteen life can be pretty hard on the streets."

"That's for sure. Fortunately, I didn't want to waste my life; I wanted something more. So I got through high school with a G.E.D., and then I was accepted at UCLA. Someday, when I'm on my ranch in Montana, I'll be able to look back on all this and have a good laugh."

When you first see a beautiful woman that's about all you see. Being pretty is a kind of archetype, a mask. And then the layers begin to fall off, and you find the individual beneath. With Shadow, there were a lot of layers. I could sense toughness and determination, but also a fawnlike vulnerability.

"So what made you decide on acting as a career, however temporary?"

"There was a man," Shadow said. "He was quite a bit older than I was, and he had money and power. He took care of me for a period of time and helped me get this job. You'd know his name if I told you—which I won't."

At that point she seemed to read my mind. "You think less of me for that, don't you?"

"Why? Should I?"

"If I was only sleeping with him because I wanted what he could do for me, yes, you should."

"But you loved him?"

"Very much. Against my better judgment."

"Why so?"

"He was married."

"Oh." I took her hand. "I'm sorry," I said. Personally, I was unable to judge harshly such a bright young woman who, though sexually abused by her stepfather, had worked her way into college and a glamorous job as an actress, and who dreamed of going further still—to a ranch in Montana where she could be clean and free. I felt certain Shadow would have her ranch one day. One had to be at least a little desperate to work so hard, and this young woman's journey could not have been an easy one.

It seemed time to change the subject. "About Dominic," I said. "I understand you had dinner with him Sunday night."

"Yes. He invited me. We went to Mr. Chow's in Beverly Hills."

"You'll have to excuse me, but I have trouble picturing you sharing a meal with an old gossip like Dominic. I'm surprised you accepted."

"So am I, really," Shadow said with a shrug. "I think I felt a little sorry for him, getting the ax like that. I tend to identify with outcasts. Anyway, I was full of adrenaline from the show—I've never done live TV before—there wasn't anybody waiting for me back at my apartment, and Carrow was a harmless old coot. So we had dinner. Do you think it was wrong?"

"Of course not."

She smiled. "To tell the truth, I rarely turn down an invitation for a free meal. It goes back to my days of being poor on the street."

"Did Dominic talk about himself?"

"Not much. He wanted to talk about me, actually."

"About anything in particular?"

"My childhood. Career. My plans for the future. That sort of thing."

"By any chance did he mention a big story he was planning for his column? Something he had just found out?"

Shadow thought for a moment, then shook her head with a small smile.

"Funny," I said, "his editor in New York said he

called Sunday night to hold his column for something new. Something really hot."

Shadow's smile suddenly froze. "My God! Why, that son of a bitch!"

"What?"

The girl stood up angrily and began to pace about her trailer. "When will I ever learn not to trust everybody I meet? It's *me,* for God's sake. *I* was his goddamn scoop, and I didn't even know it."

"You mean about your being molested and running away from home?"

"Unfortunately, there's more," Shadow said, shaking her head in exasperation. She seemed undecided whether to tell me or not, but after a moment she sat down again and spoke in a voice that was weary beyond her years. "When I was fifteen . . . when I was on my own on the streets, I supported myself for a while doing the one thing for which I was qualified. My stepfather taught me to have a very low opinion of myself. It was only for a six-month period; at the time it seemed better than starvation or going home."

I suddenly felt very sad. "And you told Dominic all this?"

She nodded. "I've never particularly kept it a secret. I'm pretty proud that I had the strength to survive it all. Are you going to be ashamed to sit next to me on the panel next Sunday?"

She was smiling, holding her breath and staring at me with hopeful eyes.

"No problem," I told her. And I meant it.

"Thank you." Her eyes moved away from mine and studied her hands clasped tightly in her lap.

An assistant director came by the trailer to call Shadow back to the set. At least I now knew what Dominic's exclusive story was all about. The fact that a popular soap opera star had once been reduced to working as a teenage hooker was just the sort of thing to explode onto the front pages of the tabloids.

For a moment I was so angry at Dominic for planning to expose this sweet young woman that if the garage door had not killed him, I would have been tempted to do so myself.

Chapter 15

A curious thing happened on Friday. Jayne had given me a shopping list of various items, from avocados to zucchini, that Cass and I were to pick up on my way home from a recording session in Hollywood. We stopped at a huge supermarket on Sunset Boulevard, one of those places that brings home the unpleasant statistic that Americans consume forty percent of the world's resources though we are only six percent of the global population. Everything was for sale here, from beach umbrellas to imported beer, rump roasts to deodorants. Aisle after aisle of glittering packages that would soon overflow landfills.

Cass and I were both tired. We filled up our cart mostly in silence, arguing occasionally about the merits of one brand over another, whether it was a savings to buy the giant economy size, and what Jayne would choose if she were here to guide us.

While we waited at one of the ten checkout lines, our fixed stares accepted the temporary amusement of the tabloid headlines positioned amid the chewing gum and razor blades. I read a few depressing tidbits about Princess Di's disintegrated marriage to Prince Charles, noted the claim that live dinosaurs had been discovered in Texas, and scanned a picture of a 447-pound woman who had crushed her mate to death on their wedding night. Suddenly, one of the more lurid scandal papers caught my eye. In the upper right-hand corner of the tabloid's cover, along with snapshots of Shadow Bennington, Peter Grover, Amaretta, and the long-haired rock star Tommy Blue, was an old photo of Jayne and me walking into a theater for some long-forgotten premiere. The headline read: "WHO WILL BE THE NEXT TO DIE ON JINXED GAME SHOW?" And then, in smaller letters, "PANIC HITS DEATH PANEL. STORY ON P. 13."

I couldn't resist opening the newspaper to lucky page 13. There were more photos, including Amaretta in a revealing bathing suit, as well as Sylvia Van Martinson, Susan Fitzgerald, and Dominic Carrow, victims of the "deadly jinx." The article quoted Phoebe North, who spoke about the growing panic among the surviving panelists but insisted that the show would go on. The sleazier tabloids often invent quotes, but I could tell that in this instance someone had actually spoken to Ms. North. "We're all terrified," she was quoted as saying. "I only hope no one will die before next Sunday—particularly now that our numbers have gone through the roof and the network has picked us up for a full year."

"She's exploiting this!" I whispered.

"It's a ghost from the past," said a strange voice, breaking into my thoughts. "If I were you, Mr. Allen, I'd take your wife on a nice long vacation and forget all about that game show."

I looked up sharply. I was slightly disguised behind dark glasses and a Chicago Cubs cap, so I was surprised someone had "made" me, as we say in the police business.

"It's a ghost from the past," the voice repeated. "That's the source of your jinx, you mark my words."

The voice belonged to a wrinkled woman behind the cash register. I had become so engrossed in the tabloid article that I had not noticed we had arrived at the front of the line and that this wraithlike creature was ringing up our purchases. She had unnaturally red hair and leathery skin from too many years in the southern California sun. Her voice was raspy, witchlike. Her hands moved quickly, sliding fruit and vegetables across the scanner.

"Sometimes in these cases you gotta find yourself a good exorcist," she continued.

I smiled indulgently. "There's no jinx on *The Murder Game*. That's just superstitious nonsense."

The old crone cackled. "Nonsense? Well, a few years back I was working in a store that was jinxed. A woman had died on aisle twelve, and she came back to haunt the place—vegetables mysteriously spoiled, cans fell off shelves for no reason at all. Finally, there was a big fire and the whole store burned to the ground."

The cashier glared, challenging me to rationalize such phenomena. I handed her the appropriate cash for my groceries. "Well, there are many things under Heaven and earth, Horatio, which we cannot explain," I paraphrased. "But as for *The Murder Game*—"

"It's a ghost from the past," the woman insisted, not allowing me to finish my thought. The woman was convinced she was right. "And the name ain't Horatio, it's Hannah. You mark my words now. And watch your back."

With a smile and a wave, Cass and I escaped. This

115

was probably a fairly typical exchange for southern California, but the funny thing was, I *did* mark her words. I remembered them very well indeed—for some time thereafter.

Chapter 16

On Sunday night, as the time for the live broadcast of *The Murder Game* approached, I had a feeling of vague dread.

"What do you say we break our contract?" I suggested to Jayne. "It'll cost us a few dollars, but what the hell. After all, murder is serious business."

Her eyes widened. "I thought you didn't believe in the—"

"It's not a belief, just an assumption."

I met Tommy Blue in the Green Room a few minutes before the start of the show. He was wearing a flamboyant shirt that was unbuttoned nearly to his navel; there was a large gold cross on a chain around his neck, an earring in his left ear, and his long hair was perfectly coiffed up from his rather apelike forehead in a series of curls. At the moment I noticed him, he was hovering over Shadow Bennington, inviting her to his concert the following week at Radio City Music Hall.

"Unfortunately," Shadow said, "doing two shows out here, I can't leave Los Angeles."

"Hey, I'll fly you in my private jet," Tommy said, leaning close to her.

"Oh, Steve, Jayne!" Shadow cried, obviously relieved when she saw us enter. "Have you met Tommy? Tommy, this is Steve Allen . . . and Jayne Meadows."

"Pleased to meet ya," said Tommy, offering his hand for a shake but hardly taking his eyes off Shadow. As if we had never interrupted, he continued his pitch. "Look, babe, if you can't make Radio City, no problem. Maybe we can go to Cabo San Lucas when I get back."

Shadow smiled dangerously. "The answer is no. I'm going to the ladies' room before we go on the air. Jayne, will you join me?"

"Certainly, dear." The two disappeared down the hall.

"Chicks!" Tommy said. He shook his head, catching sight of himself in a mirror. "Hey, does my hair look all right?" He patted his curls and gazed at himself in part profile. "I hate it when my hair gets messed up."

I was saved from replying by Peter Grover's entrance into the Green Room and, shortly afterwards, the return of Shadow and Jayne. It was time to play *The Murder Game,* and we marched one by one from backstage out in front of the cameras, to the well-rehearsed applause of the studio audience. It seemed a little strange and more than a bit sad to have Tommy Blue in the seat so recently vacated by Dominic Carrow. Still, I tried to forget everything but the playing of the game.

Tonight's mystery was centered around a modeling agency. As had happened the first week, we met the various suspects in the tape at the beginning of the show: Ted Lund, a silent partner in the agency, the man with the money; Dora Adams, the agency's top model; Steve Sharp, a fashionable photographer;

118

Melinda Cross, the agency's second most popular model, who naturally aspired to be number one; and finally Agnes Thompson, an overweight receptionist recently hired from Office Temps when the regular receptionist was hurt in a car accident.

Daphne Dobs, the owner of the agency, was found dead in a darkroom, facedown in a tray of chemicals. It wasn't a nice death, and it was our job to find her killer, competing against a guest panel that tonight consisted of an actual homicide detective from the L.A.P.D. (a woman), a mystery novelist (also a woman), a professor of law from U.S.C., and an investigative reporter from the *San Francisco Chronicle*. It seemed an imposing panel to take on. Before we had to do so, however, the show paused for commercials.

"Take your goddamn hand off my leg!" I heard Shadow say through clenched teeth. We were seated behind a desk that revealed only the top halves of our bodies, and apparently Tommy Blue had been taking advantage of this fact to "hit" on Shadow.

"Hey, babe, I just can't help myself. You do things to me I can't understand."

"Well, if you don't keep your hands to yourself, I'm going to do something you *will* understand," Shadow promised.

"Hey, can I help it if I'm young and passionate? Look, I think my hair is out of place. Where's the goddamn makeup girl?"

The "goddamn makeup girl" appeared almost magically and held up a mirror for Tommy to adorn his curls. After turning this way and that, he decided to tuck one of the curls behind his right ear. The makeup girl was dismissed only seconds before we went back on the air.

The guest panel answered several questions correctly, won a few clues, and then it was our turn. We had to recall what Steve Sharp, the photographer, claimed he was doing at the time of the murder. The answer was simple: His alibi was centered around a supposed romantic tryst with Melinda Cross, model number two. I was about to give this answer when Tommy Blue spoke first. "Hey, I got it!" he said. "The dude was getting it on with Dora!"

"That is . . . *not* correct," said Peter.

"No, I meant the other one. What's the other broad's name?"

"Melinda Cross," I said, trying to smile. "This is a team game, pops. Why don't you try consulting with the rest of us before you answer any more questions."

"Hey, no sweat. Actually, that's who I meant. Melinda what's-her-name."

"Cross," I repeated crossly.

It was looking as if this would not be our night. The guest panel dominated the game and kept winning one point after another. We just couldn't get going. It was frustrating. And then I got a crazy feeling. I *knew* the answer. It didn't come to me from the clues, though there were a few that helped, and I had managed to gather some information from the opposing team's correct answers. Mostly, though, the answer just came, almost mystically, due in part to Hannah, the wrinkled old crone from the supermarket.

But we had to answer a question correctly for me to make the accusation. It took two more questions before the opposing team finally missed an answer and the action returned to our court.

"I know who the killer is," I announced.

"Wait a minute," objected Tommy. "We gotta confer on this, man."

120

Peter gave us fifteen seconds for an off-microphone conference.

"I know the answer," I repeated.

"I think we should gather some more clues," Tommy insisted.

"I think we should trust Steve's intuition," Shadow said.

"I second the motion," said Jayne. "I'm afraid you've been outvoted, Mr. Blue."

And that was that. I told Peter I was ready. "The killer is Agnes Thompson, the temporary receptionist. No one recognized her because she had gained weight and her looks were gone, but years before she had been top model with the agency. Daphne had fired her after discovering she was having a romance with Ted Lund, and Agnes was blackballed from the business."

"So her motive for killing Daphne Dobs?" prodded Peter.

"Revenge," I said.

"You're absolutely . . . correct!" Peter said. There was applause and much hoopla in the studio. Jayne and Shadow kissed me on different cheeks, and I guess I was grinning from ear to ear. Even Tommy reached over to shake hands and congratulate me, but as he did so, the creep took advantage of leaning over Shadow to put his free hand squarely in her satin-clad lap. Shadow didn't move. She didn't so much as look at the offending hand but only sat there smiling. I think Tommy momentarily believed he had triumphed, that Shadow had succumbed to his advances. As for myself, I suspected differently. There was something unnaturally bright about her smile.

The moment passed. We went into a final commercial and then came back again, live and on the air.

Peter thanked the guest panelists and then thanked us, and the closing credits began to roll.

That's when Shadow made her move. The camera with the red eye was pointed our way, the credits rolling, when she simply reached over to Tommy's perfectly coiffed hair and apparently pulled his scalp right off his head. Beneath the artificial locks of the wig, Tommy Blue was nearly bald.

The audience gasped, then burst into thunderous laughter. Tommy was too shocked to move. He sat there, mouth agape and eyes bulging, as Shadow let the wig fall askew on his head. The gorgeous locks covered his eyes and the laughter increased in volume. Seconds later we were off the air.

Tommy stood up, incoherent with rage. "You've got to stop anyone from seeing this!" he screamed at Peter. "You've got to keep it from going on the air!"

"Sorry, but we were live," said Peter.

Tommy whirled toward Shadow. "You bitch!" he said hoarsely.

"You idiot," she hurled back at him. "I hope that will teach you to keep your hands to yourself."

It was only when we were getting ready for bed that Jayne thought to ask me how I had guessed the killer was Agnes Thompson.

"Easy," I told her. "She was the ghost from the past." I smiled mysteriously.

"Well, you're awfully good with games," Jayne said with a mysterious smile of her own. "Now you must guess what *I've* done."

"I can't imagine."

She smiled again. "I've figured out who the *real* killer is," she said.

Chapter 17

Apparently, my wife had been busy the preceding few days. She brought me a cup of camomile tea from the kitchen, then sat on the edge of the bed and told me of her adventure.

On Monday, about the time Cass and I were meeting Lieutenant Washington, Jayne took her bright red Lazer out of the garage, rolled down the windows, and drove herself to Palm Springs. She was still troubled by Sylvia Van Martinson's late night phone call, particularly the mention of Abe Brautigan and the hint that Sylvia had found out something about him. Of course, Sylvia had not been entirely coherent that night. Even her daughter had admitted she was slightly sideways most of the time, so perhaps this had meaning; perhaps it did not. But Jayne had to know, and it seemed something might be gained from a visit to Abe's final home in the desert.

In the old days—when Jayne and I were young and foolish and recently arrived in southern California from New York—the drive to Palm Springs took you on a narrow two-lane highway through mile after mile of farms, desert, and romantically sweet-smelling orange groves. Eventually you arrived in the full desert, where the air was so clear you could see every detail of the nearby mountains as though they were etched with a knife. Needless to say, smog and L.A.'s middle-aged spread have changed all this. The orange groves are gone, replaced by instant suburbs and identical shopping malls. Jayne drove along Interstate 10, a huge multi-lane freeway, her senses assaulted by the exhaust of diesel trucks and screaming radios from passing cars. She thought about rolling up her windows and turning on the air conditioning to block out the noise and air pollution, but there was a cooling breeze that felt too pleasant to shut out.

After the town of Redlands, the traffic began to ease. A few miles later, Jayne pulled off the interstate onto Highway 111 and followed the road down into the Mojave Desert, a great dry basin bordered by brown craggy mountains. Only occasional crevices from earthquakes new and old marred the landscape. Wildflowers were in bloom and the air was only slightly polluted, a vaguely yellow haze obscuring the once-clear sunlight.

Jayne could hardly believe all the changes in the thirty years since she had first come here; she wondered what the desert would be like thirty years hence. Probably just another suburb of Los Angeles. Palm Springs, once a small and sleepy village, now had high-rise buildings and a major airport. Once a year, on Spring Break, thousands of college kids descend on the town to drink beer and break windows, likely takers of the National Jerk Test. Earthquakes might be safer. This was certainly not Jayne's idea of progress.

She asked for directions at a gas station on Palm Canyon Drive, then took a series of back roads toward the mountains. Ten minutes later she arrived at Oasis Village, "AN ADULT GOLF COMMUNITY," according to the sign out front. There was a guard at the gate with a gun on his hip, presumably to keep out children and nongolfers. Jayne batted her eyelashes and explained that she wished to speak with the manager about the possibility of purchasing her own small piece of golf heaven. The guard directed her up the inclining Sand Trap Drive to the community center. The speed limit of five miles per hour was rigidly enforced by mountainous speed bumps every few yards. When she told me how old most of the residents looked, I wouldn't have been surprised to learn that they had speed bumps on the sidewalks as well.

Oasis Village consisted of semi-detached townhouses clustered around an 18-hole golf course. The landscaping and the course itself were lusciously green, in sharp contrast to the surrounding tan and brown of the desert. A sign informed her that golf carts had the right of way, and she saw quite a number of these little electric buggies, each with a brightly colored fringed top to keep out the sun. Apparently this was the favored mode of transportation in the community, from hole to hole and house to house. Elderly men and women, hidden beneath hats and dark glasses, glistening with creams designed to ward off skin cancer, guided their carts about with great solemnity. Jayne gave them the right of way and crept along at five miles per hour, all the while thinking that she *never* wanted to end up in a place like this, isolated from grandchildren and young people and totally removed from the hustle and bustle of the everyday working world. But then Jayne never plans to retire. Entertainers rarely do.

The director of Oasis Village turned out to be a manically pleasant young man by the name of Willy Marvin, whom Jayne found in his office at the community center, organizing the weekly Tea Dance. "We call it Tee for Two . . . T—E—E," he said, spelling it out in case she missed the point.

A mousy little man who sported a limp mustache and wore a green golf shirt and white shorts, Willy seemed to be working hard to appear California casual, but Jayne imagined him more accustomed to the Midwest and a suit and tie. "Well, what a great pleasure, Mrs. Allen. I assume that you and Mr. Allen are avid golfers?"

"Well, I used to play tennis and golf when I was much younger."

"You're in the right place to take it up again, then," he told her with a chuckle. "You can play golf here morning till night, seven days a week. And it never rains to spoil the fun."

"Isn't that lovely? It sounds like paradise."

"It is."

"It must be a pity, in this fabulous paradise, when someone occasionally dies."

Willy's smile froze in uncertainty.

"I'm referring to my old friend, Abe Brautigan," Jayne said.

"Ah, yes, Mr. Brautigan," Willy said, the smile transforming into a frown. "Most unfortunate. Most unfortunate indeed."

"You understand, of course, that as much as Mr. Allen and I might wish to enter our sunset years swinging a golf club, we'd have to be certain that this is the sort of place where such a careless accident wouldn't happen to us."

"Yes, naturally," agreed the manager hastily. "The community leases the golf carts to the individual members, of course, but each member is responsible for the maintenance of his or her own machine. We do everything possible to ensure safe operation. You've seen our speed bumps. We even offer a course in golf cart safety and etiquette. Still, it's rather unfortunate that—"

Willy cleared his throat and seemed reluctant to finish his thought. "What's unfortunate?" Jayne prodded.

"Well, some of our members race about at excessive speeds. Sort of a second childhood, I suppose. In fact, Mr. Brautigan had been cited twice for driving fifteen miles per hour. We're *very* strict about this sort of thing, you understand. A third violation would have resulted in his losing his golf cart privileges for six weeks."

"Yet speeding was not the cause of the accident," Jayne said. "I understand the brakes failed."

"Yes, that's right," Willy agreed unhappily. "We had one of our mechanics look the machine over after the accident, and he concluded the problem was with the master brake cylinder. For some reason, it simply went out."

"You know, Mr. Marvin, I can visualize what a terrible thing it would be to have one's brakes fail on the freeway, but in a residential community such as this, I don't quite grasp how . . . well, how the accident turned fatal."

Willy Marvin clearly hated the direction the conversation was taking; Jayne was forced to drag the words out of him. Apparently, Abe's semi-detached townhouse stood at the top of a small though steep hill— quite a *marvelous* hill, Willy assured her, from which one had a perfect view of the seventh hole.

On the afternoon of his death, Abe had backed his golf cart out of the garage to head down the hill for a bingo tournament at the community center, only to discover his brakes were completely gone. Unfortunately, it was the speed bumps themselves that proved so fatal; on a smooth surface Abe might have been able to have the ride of his life and coast to a safe stop where the road became flat. As it was, the bumps sent the cart out of control and flying into the side of a house near the bottom. "Abe pitched headfirst into a patio door. He never had a chance," Willy mourned.

"All due to a faulty master cylinder," Jayne mused. "Do you think it would be possible for my chauffeur to come here and inspect the golf cart? I'm curious to know if this master cylinder was tampered with in any way."

Blood drained from Willy's face. "Tampered with? . . . I can't imagine . . . Look, are you sure you're here to purchase a retirement home? I can't quite understand—"

"I assure you, Mr. Allen and I are *very* interested," Jayne said in her most regal manner. "We simply must make sure this community meets our standards of safety, that's all."

"We have an armed guard at the gate," Willy pointed out meekly.

"A good beginning," Jayne admitted. "But suppose someone managed to sneak in and tamper with a cart's brakes. That doesn't sound very safe to me."

"I assure you . . ."

"Did Mr. Brautigan have any outside visitors before his so-called accident?"

"Well, I suppose you could ask our activities director, Penny Tarrington. She has more daily contact with our members. But I . . . well, frankly I don't see how you can doubt that this was an accident. After all . . ."

Jayne stood up.

"You've been very helpful, Mr. Marvin. Perhaps you can tell me the number of Mr. Brautigan's house. I'd like to have a look at the hill for my report."

"Your report?"

"To Mr. Allen, of course. The *number,* please."

"Sure. It's 122 Five-Iron Lane."

"And Ms. Tarrington? Where can I find her?"

"I think she's giving an aerobics class at the moment. Next building over, as you go out the front door."

Jayne shook hands briskly and left a bewildered Willy Marvin slumped at his desk. The poor man probably didn't know what had hit him.

Before going in search of the activities director, Jayne climbed the hill to Five-Iron Lane. Number 122 was like all the other townhouses, beige and vaguely modern, with a small patio and a big picture window looking out upon the green of the golf course. From the garage, the road inclined steeply and passed over a tortuous series of speed bumps placed every thirty feet or so. A hundred yards farther along, the road took a sharp turn to the right. Apparently, this was where Abe had continued straight—and into the side of the house.

Jayne shook her head sadly. "Poor Abe," she murmured. "He really didn't have a chance at all."

Chapter 18

Jayne found Penny Tarrington, the activities director of Oasis Village, dressed in a tiger-striped spandex leotard, leading an aerobics class in a large, airy room with mirrors covering two walls. Penny was a young woman—less than thirty, Jayne judged—with dark blond hair tied back in a ponytail and a pleasant though somewhat horsey face.

There was music blaring, atrociously repetitive health-spa disco with a heavy bass beat. "Step to the left, two, three, four . . . now to the right, two, three, four!" Penny cried with military gusto into a cordless microphone strapped to her head. And twenty elderly men and women, dressed in various shades of gaudy exercise-wear, struggled to keep up.

Jayne observed the class, impressed with Penny's patience and expertise. From our own experience at the Pritikin Longevity Center in Santa Monica, she knew that classes like this for senior citizens were a very good thing. One could live a longer, happier, and more energetic life by exercising—as long as no one tampered with your master brake cylinder.

"Why, you're Jayne Meadows," Penny said, coming

over after the class. "Mr. Brautigan used to talk about you all the time."

"Did he? How sweet of him. Actually, Abe is the reason I'm here. I was hoping you could tell me a bit about his final weeks."

Penny invited Jayne into her office, a cubicle with a sliding glass door that looked out onto the omnipresent golf course. Jayne sat in a comfortable swivel chair and faced Penny across a cluttered desk.

"Did you know Abe well?" Jayne asked.

"Not very, but I liked him. He used to tell funny stories about his years in television. I always felt that he had retired too early. It simply doesn't suit some people to have endless leisure time, and Abe was one of those."

"He seemed restless?"

"Quite. I think he was lonely, too. I understand his wife died some years ago, and his children rarely visited. They came perhaps once a year, during Hanukkah."

"Didn't Abe have friends here in the Village?"

"Not really. To tell you the truth, the other members found him a little abrasive. He was always going on about how boring it was to be retired and what an important producer he'd been in his prime. It put people off a bit, particularly after you'd already heard the whole spiel a few times. So I was glad he had a few visitors shortly before his death. Contact with the outside world seemed to cheer him up."

"He had visitors? Do you know who?"

"Oh, yes. It was that pretty woman from TV—Amaretta. I recognized her right away. You can't believe the stir she caused. Old men drooling. Everyone asking for her autograph. She came with her new young husband . . . I don't recall his name."

"Christo," replied Jayne, who was surprised that a selfish creature like Amaretta would take the time to visit an old boss who could no longer advance her career. "Do you remember when this visit was, exactly?"

"Let me think. . . . Abe had his accident toward the end of February. . . ." Penny consulted her desk calendar a moment to determine that Abe had died on Thursday the twenty-seventh of February and that Amaretta and Christo had made their visit on Tuesday the eighteenth, just eight days before the fatal event.

"They met here at the community center? You didn't by chance overhear their conversation?"

Penny smiled. "No, they went outside—to that patio table you can see from my window, the one by the date palm tree. I have to admit I was curious about the visit myself, so I glanced out my window from time to time. They talked for perhaps twenty minutes, but the visit seemed to end in some sort of argument. I couldn't hear the words, but Amaretta and Abe started gesturing at each other in an angry way, and a moment later she stormed off, with her young husband trailing behind."

"And you have no idea what the fight was about?"

"Not a clue. Although when Abe passed through the community center a short time later, he winked at me and said, 'The old dog has a few tricks left in him after all.' "

"I wonder what he meant by that. . . ." Jayne was more and more curious about this strange visit. "So Abe seemed pleased with himself?"

"Very. He was cheerful for days afterwards."

"Were Amaretta and Christo his only visitors?"

"No, there was someone else. An elderly woman came to see him a couple of days later. I'm afraid I don't remember her name. I probably wouldn't have known about her visit at all, except that she stopped and asked me directions to Abe's house. I had the impression she had money—she was driving one of those Jaguar convertibles."

"Can you describe what she looked like?"

"Well, she was tall, with blondish hair that was beginning to turn white. Rather elegant, a bit . . . well, haughty in manner, if you know what I mean. She spoke in a very patrician New England tone, and I thought there was something a bit eccentric about her, though I can't quite put my finger on why I should have thought that."

"Sylvia Van Martinson!" Jayne exclaimed. "Good God, I wonder what *she* was doing here!"

"Sorry, I can't help you there. Abe never mentioned the meeting at all."

"Did he still seem cheerful after she left?"

"Oh, yes. I definitely had the impression something was going on—some kind of business deal or something—and Abe was awfully glad to be involved in something other than golf. What did you say the woman's name was?"

"Sylvia Van Martinson."

"Well, she came back to Oasis Village a few days after Abe's death. She was curious about the golf cart he'd been driving when he was killed. I was busy—I was about to teach a class—so I directed her to our mechanic, Ernie Solow. I understood that Ernie had given the cart a good going-over, and I thought he might be able to help the woman."

Jayne smiled grimly. Apparently, Sylvia had been following the same trail on which she now found herself.

"I'd very much like to speak with this Ernie myself. Where can I find him?"

"I have no idea. He quit soon after Sylvia's visit. I think it may even have been the next day."

"Quit? Did that seem unusual?"

"Not really. We have a fairly high turnover with our staff. Some young people find it depressing to work with the elderly, and they occasionally leave without much notice."

"How long did the mechanic work here?"

"It couldn't have been much more than two months."

"And his job precisely?"

"He did various mechanical odds and ends. He was very good at that. But mostly he worked on the member's golf carts when they broke down or required regular maintenance. It's a full-time job, since it's how everybody gets around in the community."

"So if someone had a problem with their brakes, for example, they'd have gone to Ernie?"

"Exactly. I remember him more than some of our other employees because he fixed my station wagon when I broke down one day. It turned out to be my water pump. Ernie got me on the road again fast. He was really good at his job."

"I'll bet he was," Jayne agreed. She said goodbye to the young woman and made her way to the employment office to ask for the mechanic's last known address. A bored, unpleasant woman gave Jayne a street number in the nearby town of Desert Hot Springs but told her she would not find the young mechanic there, explaining that when the man had left Oasis Village, he had taken some expensive tools from the shop. When the head of security had gone looking for the mechanic to reclaim the missing items, he had discovered that the young man had left town. No forwarding address.

"Somehow that doesn't surprise me," Jayne murmured as she left the office. She got into the Lazer and began the drive back to Los Angeles, trying to piece together everything she had learned.

It was all most curious. It certainly seemed out of character for a self-centered person like Amaretta to visit Abe in his retirement community. So why had she? And what had they fought about? And what had Sylvia Van Martinson discovered that drove the mechanic, Ernie Solow, to leave town in such a hurry?

Jayne was entering the metropolitan sprawl, passing the mammoth Forest Lawn Cemetery, California's supermarket of death, when inspiration struck.

She was remembering the strange note she had discovered in Sylvia Van Martinson's office: "VERDI. 10 AM UNDER THE PIER. MASTER C."

Jayne had always assumed Master C was a person, but now she realized that Master C could very well be an abbreviation for master cylinder!

There were mysteries still unsolved, including who or what "Verdi" might be, but one thing was clear: Shortly before her death, Sylvia had been greatly concerned with the small mechanical device that had robbed Abe Brautigan of his life.

Chapter 19

Jayne's head was spinning with questions and speculations. A few miles past Forest Lawn, it occurred to her that there was one person connected with *The Murder Game* who knew where all the bodies were buried, so to speak, and that person was Peter Grover. If anyone could shed light on the series of mysterious deaths, it might be our urbane host.

I have a phone in my car. Jayne does not. She therefore pulled off the freeway into a gas station to use the telephone there. A computerized voice suggested she deposit $1.25 for the first three minutes. Just as Jayne was searching through her handbag for the appropriate coins, a car with enormous tires pulled into the station, music blaring so loudly on its stereo that it caused her teeth to rattle as she listened to the phone ringing on the other end.

It took about thirty years of concentrated work by literally thousands of people, including the writing of books, the production of television specials, the recording of public service announcements, increasingly stern warnings from the American Medical Association, the American Cancer Society, and the American Lung Association, to finally awaken the American public to the dangers of tobacco smoke not just to smokers but to those around them. May I suggest that we now need a similar program of public education to deal with the offensiveness of noise pollution from car radios and boom boxes.

Jayne found Peter at his home in Bel Air but had to shout at him in order to be heard above the music. He shouted back that he had a dinner date but could always make time for his favorite panelist.

"If you can be here in an hour, we can have some tea," Peter bellowed.

"Tea will be lovely," Jayne yelled, and hung up the phone.

The car with the loud music belonged to a sullen young man who was checking the air pressure in his oversized tires. Jayne, not intimidated, marched over to him. "Young man, it is incredibly rude to play your radio at such a volume!" she told him. "And furthermore, it is people like you, as well as that screeching noise you mistake for music, that are contributing to the collapse of civilized . . . er . . . civilization."

The youth gaped at her in astonishment. For a quick moment, Jayne was afraid he might pull out a gun and shoot her—such things do happen in Los Angeles these days—but he was so surprised that he muttered a sullen "sorry" and turned down the radio.

"There may be hope for you yet," Jayne said, and stalked regally back to her car.

Bel Air was another world entirely. Jayne drifted through the main gate off Sunset Boulevard into a soft canopy of trees that marked the beginning of Stone Canyon Drive. The road wound its way upward into the hills, past huge homes with tennis courts only partially visible behind high walls and greens. There was the smell of flowers and newly mown grass in the air. Everything seemed sleepy with wealth—complacent, clean. Each home had a sign in the driveway announcing electronic surveillance and armed guard response. To be this rich in Los Angeles was to be both vulnerable and paranoid.

Jayne pulled into a driveway, spoke into the security telephone, and the gate across the entrance swung quietly open. Peter Grover lived in a mock-English estate, a Tudor mansion on a heavily shaded acre lot. The house was exquisitely tasteful, with lovely rosebushes in carefully tended flower beds lining the driveway. As a way of relaxing, Jayne tends to her own flower gardens meticulously, and Peter's grounds completely erased her lingering annoyance over the young man with the big tires and radio.

She rang a deeply sonorous doorbell and was admitted into a cavernous foyer by a uniformed butler. Peter himself appeared momentarily, stepping briskly out of a den. He wore trim-fitting jeans, a dark blue polo shirt, and leather sandals, but even in such casual attire he managed to seem an elegant figure with his neat, graying hair and cool blue eyes.

"Jayne, darling, welcome," he said, kissing her cheek. "You look slightly frazzled."

"It's a rude world out there," Jayne admitted. "But your roses are divine, Peter. And *look* at your lovely house! I always feel I've stepped back into the nineteenth century when I come here."

"A small reward for a life of hard work and inordinate good luck," Peter said modestly. "But, come, you have to see my new Renoir."

"My goodness, I didn't realize you'd become an art collector."

Peter's Renoir was a scene of the French countryside in the lazy heat of summer, painted in the soft, impressionistic pastels for which the artist is so justly famous. The painting hung on a wall in an oak-paneled dining room.

"You have to tell me, Peter—forgive my being so gauche—how much did you pay for it?"

"A million two," he replied with a shrug. "I got it from a producer desperate for funds to finish his first independent production. Now I must show you the Picasso . . . here, in my library. . . ."

Jayne got a tour of Peter's collection, and she was struck not only by his taste but also by the amount of money required to fill this Bel Air mansion with such treasures. Peter's fortune might have begun with dreaming up *The Murder Game,* but he certainly had added to it, cleverly turning his early success into a magnificent lifestyle.

"How wise you are, Peter!" Jayne said as she took his arm and they walked together out of the house onto a vine-covered patio for tea. Jules, the butler, served the tea along with finger sandwiches of smoked salmon, and then he quietly departed. After a day spent on the hot freeways, Jayne almost felt like purring in contentment. There was something well-ordered and restful about Peter Grover's self-created domain.

"Well, Jayne, I know you adore Renoir and Picasso, but you didn't come here to see my paintings."

"You're absolutely right. I spent the morning in Oasis Village, a retirement community outside of Palm Springs. It's where poor Abe Brautigan spent his final years. A depressing place, I must say."

"Depressing?"

"Oh, I didn't see anyone beating the old folks, and there were all the amenities of upper middle-class retirement, but the place lacked a certain dignity. I find it painful to see adults who have worked hard all their lives suddenly treated in a condescending manner, as if they were infants."

"Ours is not a society that respects old age," Peter agreed. "You know, I always meant to get down there to see Abe, but somehow it was something I kept putting off. Did you know he called me only a week before he died?"

"Really?"

"Yes. He'd heard rumors that *The Murder Game* was going back on the air, and he wanted to be part of it."

"He wanted his old job back?"

"Precisely. Abe was bored to death in the desert. He wanted to be back where the action was. He thought I might convince the network brass that he was the only person capable of producing the show."

"But he was seventy-eight years old," Jayne remarked. "What did you tell him?"

"What could I say? I told him I'd give it a shot but that he shouldn't expect too much. And, of course, I was right. I talked to a few executives, but they were in their thirties and early forties—aren't they all now?—and had never even heard of Abe. They certainly weren't going to entrust an expensive show in an important time slot to an old-timer just because he was bored playing golf."

Jayne sighed. "How terrible to be pushed aside. But Peter, did you really believe Abe was capable of handling his old job again?"

Peter shrugged. "Probably not, but who the hell cared? My thought was to give him the title of Executive Producer and then let some ambitious young creature deal with the day-to-day hassles. To be frank,

141

Jayne, I felt in the same predicament as Abe. I was bored. True, I wasn't retired in Palm Springs, but I might as well have been. I was fed up with the details of running a business. I wanted the excitement of being part of a hit TV show again."

Jayne laughed. "A lot of people would consider running a chain of hotels and a small communications empire excitement enough."

"Well, it comes easy to me—all that stuff. Making money," Peter said offhandedly. "It must be my horribly logical mind. But it's show business that I adore. All the glamour . . . I certainly wanted all my old friends along for the party. Even Abe."

"But the network wouldn't budge?"

"No. I had to call Abe back a few days later and admit I'd been unsuccessful. I was afraid he'd be shattered, but he took the news rather jauntily. I got the feeling he had a few tricks up his sleeve."

Jayne glanced at Peter sharply, remembering how Penny, the young activities director at Oasis Village, had described Abe after Amaretta's visit: *The old dog had a few tricks left in him after all.*

But what tricks?

"Abe didn't say what he had in mind?" Jayne quizzed.

"Nope. He said I shouldn't worry about him . . . that he'd find some way to be a part of our little television reunion after all."

"And that was it?"

"Yep. Well, except that as he rang off, he assured me he'd have the last laugh."

Peter and Jayne were momentarily silent, pondering this last laugh that had never sounded. "Peter, may I ask you a very personal question?"

"I have no secrets from you, Jayne."

"Oh, I hope you do. But there were rumors many years ago that you and Amaretta were having an affair. Is that by any chance true?"

Peter laughed charmingly. "I'm afraid it is. I know she's shallow, Jayne, but my God, that girl was pretty when she was young. I was head over heels in lust—not love—and only ended the relationship when I realized she was simply using me to advance her career. Why do you ask?"

"Because Amaretta showed up at Oasis Village to visit Abe shortly before he died. She came with that new husband of hers, Christo. Somehow it seems out of character for her to make a sentimental journey to an old friend."

"An old *boy*friend," Peter corrected, a twinkle in his eye.

"You must be kidding!"

"Not at all. Amaretta may not have been Einstein, but she was certainly the honey for us big bumblebees. As a matter of fact, she set her sights on Abe shortly after I departed the scene, romantically speaking. That was years ago. I suppose she thought Abe would help her career after I refused."

"But she already had the part on *The Murder Game.*"

"Yes. But the poor dear wished to be an actress—a rich and glamorous movie star."

"Wasn't she in a movie once?"

"A sci-fi thriller in 3-D. She portrayed the Amazon Queen of a distant planet—not exactly Shakespeare, but even with a role like that the critics panned her."

Jayne chuckled, picturing Amaretta as an Amazon Queen. "But why did she visit Abe now, so many years later? They even had a fight of some kind, I'm told.

There's some deep, dark mystery here, Peter, and you've got to help me figure out what it is."

Peter nibbled on a smoked salmon sandwich and grinned at Jayne in an altogether boyish manner.

"You *know,* don't you?" Jayne accused. "You know why Amaretta went to Oasis Village!"

"Well, I *suspect* why. But, Jayne, it's a rather delicate matter involving old friends. . . ."

Jayne studied Peter, and he smiled back in that boyish and well-bred way. She knew it would do no good to plead that this was a police matter and that people were dying and that he really should tell her what he knew. For Peter it was all an amusing game.

"Won't you at least give me a clue?" she purred.

"Mmmm . . . I *might.*" Peter's eyes got bright. "Are you ready, panel?" he said.

"I'm ready," Jayne said.

"Then here it is: What is the very deepest, darkest secret a woman like Amaretta might have?"

"That's the clue? Goodness, let me think. . . . She began her career on the streets?"

Peter laughed uproariously. "No!" he cried. "And you'd better not ever let her know you suggested that!"

"She had a child out of wedlock?"

"That sort of thing *used* to be scandal. Today it'll probably get you an extra million dollars for your next picture, so depraved is our society."

Jayne pressed for another clue, but Peter only smiled mysteriously.

"If I told you," he said, "it would take all the fun away."

Chapter 20

I can modestly claim indirect responsibility for helping Jayne solve the riddle posed by Peter Grover: What could be the deepest, darkest secret for a woman like Amaretta?

My part came in waking Jayne in the middle of the night—half past two in the morning, to be exact. I didn't mean to, naturally. I woke myself with a dream that I was playing an exceptionally gorgeous melody on a heavenly piano. The song emerged intact upon my waking consciousness, with a portion of a lyric. It was a fabulous song. A sure hit. I sat up in bed, reached for the small tape recorder I keep on my night table to capture such inspirations, and began to sing the song softly, so as not to wake Jayne.

"The ghost of the past haunts my dreams—a sudden laugh—and yet it seems . . ."

I was on the next line when Jayne stirred. "Mmmm, what time is it?" she asked groggily. "Why are you singing in the dark?"

"I'm sorry, dear, I didn't mean to wake you. I just dreamed up an idea for a tune and wanted to get it down on tape before I forgot it."

"That's it!" Jayne cried, sitting up fully in bed.

"It?" I questioned. "Well, the melody is—"

"Not your song, Steve. I've just figured out a riddle."

"What's the punch line?"

"It's not that kind of a riddle. This is more like what the Sphinx asked Oedipus on his way to Thebes sort of thing."

"Ah," I said meaninglessly. Jayne was not forthcoming with either the question or the answer to her mythological riddle, and when I had finished recording I saw that she had fallen asleep once again. I followed suit gratefully.

The next thing I knew it was morning, and Jayne was waking me with a mug of tea. "I have an interesting idea," she said. "Let's invite Amaretta and Christo to dinner."

"Good God, whatever for?" I asked in alarm.

"Don't be antisocial, darling. Amaretta's really amusing in her own way. Just because she's vain and shallow, it doesn't mean there aren't redeeming qualities somewhere inside her. And Christo . . . I'm certain if you only got to know him, you would find he's fascinating in his own sulky little way."

"I'll tell you what . . . you have them for dinner, and I'll pop in for a moment on my way out somewhere. I'll say it's my bowling night."

"You hate bowling."

"That's true."

Jayne consulted her address book and dialed Amaretta's unlisted number. Christo answered the phone with a sullen, "Who is this?"

"It's Jayne Meadows, dear. I was ringing to invite you two for dinner some night soon. Is Amaretta there?"

"No. She is-a out."

146

"I see. Well, do you know when she might be home?"

Christo sneezed into the phone so loudly that Jayne was forced to remove the receiver from her ear. "She's-a at the spa—what she called?—The Ponce de Leon Center, where she get rid of all her wrinkles. After that, she have-a *appuntamento* with a dressmaker in Beverly Hills, and after that, there is still more shopping. . . . So who the hell knows when she come home, eh, *cara?*"

Listening to him made Jayne slightly dizzy. It was a bit like trying to follow grand opera, but she did manage to get the general sense of things. The young Italian sneezed once again.

"You have a terrible cold, poor dear," Jayne observed.

"This-a place California—she do not agree with me. I think maybe I die from boredom. I must get out of this-a place, back to Roma."

"Meanwhile, you should drink plenty of orange juice and get lots of rest."

"Rest? My wife, she give me no damn money, so what the hell else I do but rest? All I do is sit around za pool and sit around za pool and sit around za pool some more."

Christo hung up, leaving a thoughtful Jayne with the receiver still at her ear.

"Well, how'd it go?" I asked, grinning broadly. Jayne had made the call from our breakfast room, and I was enjoying every moment. "Did you discuss New Wave Italian cinema? Or perhaps early Renaissance art?"

"Hush. You know what I think? I think our dear Christo needs a mother figure. Someone to confide in."

"And you're thinking of volunteering."

"Indeed I am. You don't mind sharing me, do you, darling?"

"Not at all. Go ahead and be the brat's mother," I offered generously. "But the kid's going to be one fatherless child."

Chapter 21

Jayne picked up an assortment of motherly goodies at a local health food store: freshly squeezed orange juice, vitamin C tablets, a vial of echinacea, and a package of herbal tea. Prepared to wage epic battle against the common cold, Jayne stopped at Jerry's Deli for a large take-out carton of homemade chicken soup, then drove with her bundles to Amaretta's house in Coldwater Canyon.

The house was white with gold trim and appeared a strange combination of neoclassic and postmodern—styles that more or less canceled each other out. There were Greek columns holding up a decorative portico, with an impressively thick front door and small windows of smoked glass. Instead of a front lawn, there was a stretch of decorative rocks, with a few tall cactus sticking up at various places and an oversized copy of the famous Venus de Milo. Blue and pink spotlights beneath the statue waited for the night to cast a gaudy glow on the stately figure.

Jayne stood for a moment, tying to decide if Amaretta's house reminded her more of a huge wedding cake or a mausoleum at Forest Lawn. Undecided, she rang the doorbell—which chimed the first four memorable notes of Beethoven's Fifth Symphony.

Christo opened the door, wearing nothing but a very brief European swimsuit and wraparound dark glasses. The young man was cinematically handsome, with a long black ponytail, smooth olive skin, and a true Roman nose. He stared at Jayne without comprehension.

"If you're selling something, I don-a want it," he said rudely.

Jayne put on her most motherly smile. "It's Jayne Meadows, dear. Don't you remember? We've met several times—and we talked on the phone this morning? I was in the neighborhood and thought I'd drop by with a few things for your nasty cold."

"Yeah?" Christo lounged in the doorway but did not invite Jayne inside.

"Why don't I just put these things in your kitchen," Jayne said firmly, walking past the young man and into the house. She had a vague impression of the living room full of feminine kitsch. She noticed a glass coffee table held up by four miniature naked Cupids with wings and a plush red velvet love seat that seemed out of a Paris bordello. There were huge paintings with elaborate gilt frames and Chinese vases full of artificial roses.

"What remarkable decor!" Jayne observed.

Christo only shrugged. "Come, I take you to the damn kitchen."

The kitchen was immense and modern and seemed to contain every known electrical gadget, including a computerized popcorn popper and an automatic sushi maker.

"Amaretta must do a great deal of cooking," Jayne ventured cautiously.

"No way, José. Usually we *telefonare* for the take-out Chinese. I tell her I wanna go out some-a-time to all the swell *ristorantes,* but Amaretta, she like to keep me prisoner."

"How sad," Jayne said, pouring a glass of the freshly squeezed orange juice and handing it to the boy with two tablets of vitamin C. Christo took the pills and juice without a struggle.

"She's afraid maybe I meet some-a young pussycat," Christo said with a sigh. "Pretty little girlies, you know. That is why she keep-a me locked up without no *denaro.* Why do you think she do this?"

"Probably she doesn't trust you out of her sight."

Christo raised his hands in operatic despair. "In Roma, she caught-a me with this-a juicy young *contessa.* One-a time! And now it is like I am some criminal she must always watch."

"It must be difficult to have such a great difference of age between you and Amaretta," Jayne consoled.

Christo sighed. "Tell me about it!" he said.

"Perhaps if you found a job, you would have a bit more freedom?"

He sighed even more deeply. "But what can I do? I am good for nothing except *amore.*"

"What did you do in Italy?"

"I was a hunk."

"I beg your pardon?"

"I was—how you say it?—a dancer in a male revue. The ladies, they-a come and take-a good look, you know."

"Ah," said Jayne, letting the subject drop. Christo was slouching against the kitchen counter, examining the muscles of his left arm. He had an aura of sensuality about him, but he seemed, alas, in love with him-

151

self. Jayne thought it time to guide the conversation toward the reason for her visit.

"Incidentally, I was down at Oasis Village in Palm Springs yesterday," she began, pouring the still-warm chicken soup into a bowl and motioning for Christo to pull a stool up to the counter. "I was surprised to hear that you and Amaretta were there just a few weeks before me."

Christo sneered. "A lot of old people," he said distastefully.

"Yes, human beings, if they're lucky, do grow old," Jayne said, but the irony was lost on the young narcissist. "I'm curious, Christo, why did Amaretta go to Palm Springs to see Mr. Brautigan?"

A sly smile crept over Christo's face. "You won't tell her you heard from me?"

"Of course not!"

Christo lowered his voice to a dramatic whisper. "It was blackmail, you see. This-a Abe guy, he do a big, dirty blackmail number on Amaretta."

"Blackmail! How awful!"

"Is-a a bit funny, actually," said Christo with a smirk. "You never guess what the guy use for blackmail."

As a matter of fact, Jayne *had* guessed: The answer to the riddle of Amaretta's deepest, darkest secret had come to her in the middle of the night. "It was her real age," she said now. "Perhaps he threatened to let the world know how old she was unless Amaretta did precisely as he asked."

Christo's smirk faded. "Hey, how do you know?"

"Just a lucky guess," Jayne said. "Was it money he wanted?"

"No, it was a job. Can you believe it?" Christo was obviously amazed that a person might choose employ-

152

ment over cash. "He wanted to be the producer of this-a show, *The Murder Game*. Amaretta, she was to go to the network, you see, and say she no gonna work 'less Abe is the producer."

"I see," Jayne said. And she did. For Abe, this was a clever though desperate card to play. Aging bimbo though she might be, *The Murder Game* would lose something without Amaretta hopping about in her revealing dresses. If she threatened to quit, the network might take her seriously—and give Abe Brautigan some meaningless executive title at the very least.

"He say unless she do what he say, he tell the world her real name, too."

"A double whammy," Jayne observed. "And what *is* Amaretta's real name?"

"Blech," Christo said with a snicker.

"I beg your pardon?"

"Evelyn Blech, from Staten Island. Whad'ya think about that?"

"Poor Evelyn Blech," Jayne said. The combination of Amaretta's real age and real name would certainly destroy the fragile aura of glamour that had made her a celebrity. And for Amaretta, of course, glamour was everything, since she did not possess talent.

"Did she go to the network as Abe wanted?"

"Who knows?" Christo said. "I don-a follow these-a things. But I'm not stupid. My wife, she pretend to be thirty-four, but that would mean she was fourteen when the TV show went off the air before. Does she think I'm a big-a idiot?"

"She's only trying to make herself attractive to you," Jayne said, suddenly feeling actual pity for the woman.

"Big deal . . . . She must-a be fifty, I think. But I *like* older women." Christo gave Jayne a smoldering look.

"My wife . . . I think she rather die than let the truth of her age come out."

Jayne smiled sadly, wondering if Christo hadn't gotten this slightly backward. A vain creature like Amaretta might not die—but she might kill in order to keep the truth from being known.

Chapter 22

"So you think Amaretta is the killer?" I asked Jayne, not convinced.

"Of course she is," she replied. "Why do you find it so hard to believe?"

It was Sunday evening after the third broadcast of *The Murder Game,* and Jayne and I were having a light supper at Spago on the Sunset Strip. Spago, of course, is one of those ultimate Hollywood places where you can hardly take two bites without some press agent or producer coming over to hobnob. Jayne and I were repairing our egos in this sumptuous setting. To put it bluntly, we had lost tonight's game—the celebrity panel had lost, that is. I would say it was that jerk Tommy Blue's fault, if I were the sort to assign blame. A more generous assessment would be that tonight's guest panel had been remarkably bright—brighter than we were, certainly—and they had correctly identified the murderer, a diabolic playboy who had arranged for his wealthy wife to fall off their yacht into shark-infested waters.

I was enjoying my salad of fresh baby greens, flower petals, and arugula—which I deliberately call Pete Rugulo (an arranger friend of mine)—when a woman writer from *Daily Variety* stopped by our table to ask about the "jinx" and if we were worried for our own safety.

"Do we look worried?" I replied, smiling and continuing to eat. Both Jayne and I brushed off the idea of a jinx and assured the woman that no one had died in over a week. Life was back to normal. Almost.

When the columnist had left, our smiles fell. The truth was, we *were* worried—and would have been fools not to be.

"Tell me more about Amaretta," I prompted.

"Well, I called a friend at the network—Jack Delancy, that nice young boy who used to be a page."

"That was twenty years ago."

"Right. Anyway, Jack's now vice president of daytime programming. He told me that Amaretta had indeed lobbied to get Abe rehired as producer of *The Murder Game*. In fact, she had worked hard at it, obviously taking Abe's blackmail threat seriously."

"But the network gave the job to our pushy friend, Phoebe North."

"Exactly," Jayne said. "The network wouldn't budge on this issue. They insisted someone young and with-it produce the show, and believe it or not, Phoebe is considered one of the network's *wunderkind*. Apparently, she took some sitcom that was at the bottom of the ratings last season, added an obnoxious uncle to the cast, a generous sprinkling of smut, and now the show's a hit."

"Did Amaretta threaten to pull out of the show unless Abe was the producer?"

"No."

"Then she *didn't* take the blackmail seriously."

"Yes, she did. But, darling, she was in a bind. When was the last time you saw her on television?"

"About two hours ago," I replied.

"Steve . . ."

"All right, before *The Murder Game* revival . . . let's see, wasn't she in a cat food commercial last year?"

"That was *three* years ago, Steve, and it wasn't the role of a lifetime to be upstaged by a cat. Amaretta's career has not been gangbusters lately. She knew the network wasn't going to give in to her demand regarding poor Abe, and she wasn't about to put her own position in jeopardy by threatening to quit. She needed the work. And besides, it was *The Murder Game* that made her a household name in the first place. This was her chance to get back into the public eye."

"And Abe?"

"Well, she couldn't exactly leave him around to tell the world she's fifty-something. Or that she is really the unglamorous Evelyn Blech from Staten Island."

"Why not? This is an American success story. She could be proud of working her way up from a nothing to becoming, through hard work, dedication, and large chydes, a *world-famous* nothing."

Jayne shook her head. "Steve, don't be naive."

"Not a bad song title," I said.

"A secret like this takes on its own life after hiding in the dark enough years. Amaretta is ashamed of her past. Her secret may not seem like a big deal to you, but it is to her. And the worst part of it, of course, is her fear that if her real age came out, it would not only hurt her career but her marriage as well. Remember, she told Christo she was thirty-four."

I laughed. "But you said even he was smart enough to do the arithmetic to figure out that's impossible."

"So you can see what a pathetic lie it is. But Amaretta is desperate. She believes she has nothing in life except the illusion of her youth, sex appeal, and glamour—and she might be willing to kill to keep the illusion intact."

I was intrigued by the tragic portrait Jayne was painting, but she had left out some practical details.

"So how did Amaretta get Abe's brakes to fail?" I asked.

"She seduced the young mechanic at Oasis Village, of course. The one who conveniently disappeared . . . that Ernie Solow character."

"Ah, I see. *He* did her dirty work. And what about Sylvia Van Martinson? Did Amaretta kill her, or was it Ernie again?"

"Steve, what if Sylvia somehow discovered the truth? Abe could have told her about the blackmail scheme when she visited him. Sylvia had always been outspoken about her dislike for Amaretta, calling her a disgrace to feminism and all. What if she was going to expose her in her magazine? Amaretta would have to silence her, too."

"And then she killed Susan and Dominic?"

Jayne tried heroically to keep her theory afloat, but the connections were weakening. "Dominic could have found out somehow, too. Maybe this was the big scoop he called Jeffrey about."

"Sorry," I said. "That was about Shadow's early career as a teenage runaway."

"But this is bigger, Steve. This is murder."

"And Susan?"

"Well, maybe that one was an accident," Jayne conceded. "An old woman, after one drink too many, might easily fall downstairs. . . . Steve, stop smiling! At least I *have* a theory!"

"However weak."

"I agree there are a few dangling ends, but I have a plan to tie them up."

Jayne, of course, wanted me to ask about the details of her plan, but I deliberately changed the subject. "Care for any more Pete Rugulo?"

"No, thanks," she said.

At that moment the talented film actress Susan Sarandon walked by, apparently in the company of a gentleman who the most impartial of judges would have rated very low on the attractiveness scale. I know I'm wrong to feel as I do on the point, but—perhaps from being conditioned by all those glamorous films of the 1930s—I still expect to see beautiful women in the company of at least reasonably handsome men, despite the massive daily evidence that they rarely are. I don't want to sound like the Reverend Moon, but I honestly feel I could do a better job of picking out husbands for most of Hollywood's young starinas than they seem to do for themselves.

At that point Ms. Sarandon moved within my wife's field of vision.

"Oh," Jayne said, "there goes Susan . . . er . . ."

"Saran Wrap," I said.

"Right," she said. Jayne does not always attend, with painstaking care, to what I say.

Because the suspense was killing me, I finally said, "You were saying you had a plan?"

"Certainly. I stopped by Amaretta's dressing room after the show and repeated my invitation for her and Christo to come for dinner. Tomorrow night, if all goes well, we'll have a confession for the main course."

Chapter 23

We had hors d'oeuvres in the living room, a plate of miniature crepes filled with crab and smothered, though very lightly, in melted cheese, along with a healthy lazy Susan of crudités—raw vegetables cut up around a bowl of low-fat dip—to which Jayne and I gravitated. I have no problem using the word *crudités* in print, but the word will never pass my lips, except in ironic jest.

Amaretta sat on our sofa, her long legs crossed daintily. She wore a dazzling red cocktail dress that was straining at the seams. Christo sat on a high-backed orange bishop's chair near me. He was dressed in a white linen suit with a lavender silk shirt. He seemed languid, bored. Out of earshot of the women, who were talking fashion, I made a noble effort to start a conversation.

"Jayne tells me you grew up in Rome? What a wonderful city . . . I haven't been there in years."

"Roma, she okay-a by me."

"What part of the city did you live in?"

"All over," he replied airily.

"Trastevere? Vecchia Roma?"

"Everywhere-a," he said, gesturing like a Sicilian rather than a Roman.

I'm not exactly sure what it was that suddenly made me suspicious of Christo's Italian accent, but there was something strange about it: It was too broad in some places, nonexistent in others, and reminded me of the marvelous Guido Panzini characterization comedian Pat Harrington used to do on my NBC comedy show.

"There was a fabulous restaurant I used to go to in Piazza del Popolo," I said. "It was called Ziggy's. Right next to the Hotel Excelsior."

"Yeah, Ziggy's," he agreed. "By-a the Excelsior. She's still-a there."

"Isn't it wonderful when things don't change?" Actually, I had just made up Ziggy's, and the Hotel Excelsior, of course, is in Florence, nowhere near the Piazza del Popolo, which is in Rome.

"How long have you been in America now, Christo?"

"A-two-a-year-a."

I smiled. *A-two-a-year-a* was Italian straight out of a Marx Brothers comedy. I leaned closer. "Look, man, why don't you drop the Panzini accent and tell me where you're really from?"

I had his attention. Christo stared at me with his big brown eyes, which had narrowed. For a moment I thought he was going to give me a hard time, but then he smiled, speaking softly so as not to be overheard. "Okay, so I'm not Italian. Big deal. I grew up in the San Fernando Valley—about two miles from here actually. But in Hollywood a guy's gotta have an angle. Know what I mean?"

"Sure. But does Amaretta know about this?"

"You kidding? She thinks I'm a real wop. So what

are you going to do? Expose me? Go ahead, man. It would be a relief. I'm beginning to feel like some goddamn French poodle."

"I'll be happy to let you decide when to tell your wife the truth."

"The truth," he said gloomily, sipping on his white wine. "Who the hell knows what *that* is in this town!"

Amaretta apparently thought she had ignored her young husband long enough. She came over, carrying a sofa pillow, and knelt at his feet. "Hi-ya, honeykins. What'cha boys talking about?"

"Ah, gimme a break-a," Christo said sulkily.

Amaretta giggled. "Isn't he cute?"

I was saved from commenting on the degree of Christo's cuteness by Jayne's summons to dinner. We made our way to the dining room. It was the beginning of the strangest dinner party I have ever experienced.

Amaretta, *née* Evelyn Blech, was a self-invented character and so was Christo, whoever the hell he really was. I had a crazy desire to introduce them to each other: "Miss Blech from Staten Island, I'd like you to meet your husband, Joe Krelman from Van Nuys, California." Would they like each other? Probably not. But they certainly would find something in common: two ordinary people desperately trying to be what they were not.

I had encountered a roughly similar instance back in the 1950s, while working on television in New York. There was at the time—and perhaps still is—a department store in Allentown, Pennsylvania called Hess Brothers. From time to time its management would import New York celebrities to add glamour to their parties. Nothing wrong with that, of course, but the odd fact was that the apparently invited guests were actually hired for the evening, though all they had to do was mingle with the party crowd.

I happened to be performing in Allentown at the time one of the parties took place. On the train back to New York, later that night, I found myself sitting next to a young actress whose first name, I believe, was Eva. She was pretty enough and had a Hungarian accent that made her seem even more interesting. After an hour or so of small talk, she confided in me that she had been paid to attend one of the department store parties and that during the evening she had met a fellow she described as "the most charming young man." Eva herself was single, and had I not been married to Jayne at the time, I might have developed a further interest in her myself. The man she had met at the party, she said, was clearly the most interesting person there, and she could tell he was quite attracted to her. Since most of those who attended such events were the area's social and financial elite, she immediately entertained romantic daydreams about her newly found beau. Since she was finding it tough going as a young actress in the New York jungle, she had permitted herself to dwell on what it might be like to live a wealthy suburban life as the eventual wife of the charming stranger.

Apparently, for the next few hours the two had eyes only for each other and thoroughly enjoyed their romantic evening together before the witching hour. The time finally came that if they were to see each other again, they would have to exchange phone numbers, addresses, and fuller details of their identities. After she had told the gentleman a good deal about herself, he said, "You're an actress? My God, I thought you were a society woman living here in Allentown. I'm an actor, and I'm here tonight because I couldn't think of an easier way to make five hundred dollars."

For the dinner party, Jayne had prepared a yellow-fin tuna, grilled with capers, lemon, and a hint of cilantro. Well, maybe more a rumor than a hint. It was moist and delicious. Accompanying the tuna were new potatoes, steamed carrots, a tossed spinach salad, and a bottle of Pouilly Fume. Jayne's style, as always, was simple but elegant. Amaretta missed the point; she began talking enthusiastically about some restaurant in Beverly Hills where her fish had come smothered in what sounded like an overly rich orange cognac sauce.

"When you're the genuine article, my dear, you don't need to put on a rich disguise," Jayne said, moving subtly from tuna to life.

"So true," Amaretta said. "Isn't that true, honey-kins?" she asked her sulking husband, leaning over to run a red-nailed finger along his cheekbone.

Christo poured himself another glass of wine and didn't answer. Amaretta giggled nervously and mumbled an excuse for his behavior.

I could tell from the way Jayne's brow furrowed slightly as she looked at them that the moment of *denouement* had arrived. Amaretta and Christo lived so blindly in their separate fantasy worlds I felt a strange urge to protect them from the harsh truths about to emerge. But there was no stopping Jayne; she was on the trail of a murderer.

"I'd like to propose a toast," she said, raising her wineglass.

"A toast!" Amaretta responded merrily, lifting a glass. "A toast to . . . to what?" Christo muttered something in Italian, and I held my breath. We clinked our goblets together.

"To blackmail," Jayne whispered.

Amaretta nearly dropped her glass. Her voice was hoarse. "Blackmail?"

"I've been to Oasis Village, dear," Jayne said, touching Amaretta's hand to soften the accusation. "I've put all the pieces together, haven't I, Steve?" She didn't give me time to answer but sped on, "I found out how Abe was threatening to tell your real age unless you helped him get his old job back."

"Darling, I've never tried to hide that I'm thirty-four."

Christo chuckled.

"As an actress," Jayne said, "I sympathize entirely. We all tend to subtract a year or two. But if people found out you were really fifty-four . . ."

"I am *not* fifty-anything! I—I'm—" Amaretta was almost shrieking.

Jayne smiled. "Amaretta, your secret is safe with me. But to have an old lover threaten blackmail like that . . . I quite understand why you had to kill him."

Amaretta's mouth dropped open. She was momentarily speechless.

"You don't have to pretend any longer, dear. I know how you seduced that young mechanic to tamper with the brakes of Abe's cart."

Amaretta's eyes narrowed to slits, and she almost spit the words past her clenched teeth. "I'll sue you!"

"If you do, the truth will come out."

"Ha! Try to prove it."

"Oh, I can. I've managed to locate the mechanic— Ernie Solow. Remember him? He's willing to testify against you."

This was Jayne's big bluff, of course, on which the success of the evening precariously hung. It didn't seem to be working.

Amaretta rose, her face red and blotchy with rage. She let forth a string of four-letter words. Buried in the expletives was the message that she had never heard of Ernie Solow, nor any other mechanic at Oasis Village, and that Jayne could go to Hades on a river raft. Then she turned to Christo. "Come on, we're outta here!" she said.

The handsome pseudo-Italian polished off his glass of wine with one gulp, winked at me, shrugged in Jayne's direction, flicked his ponytail off his shoulder, and followed his wife out the front door—which closed with a slam that could have triggered an earthquake.

"Great dinner party so far, dear," I said calmly. "What's for dessert?"

"She didn't confess!" Jayne seemed stunned. She made a mournful face at me, and I made one back. We were just trying to think of a reason to laugh when I heard two loud cracking sounds outside the window. They sounded like rifle shots. A moment later, there was a loud crash.

We ran outside, leaving our front door open behind us. Seeing nothing, we ran to the end of the driveway and peered down the street to the right. Amaretta's Lexus was wrapped around the street lamp at the corner, with two distinctive bullet holes creating a milky-looking web across the rear window. It was one of those scenes in which it takes a moment for the brain to believe the message the eyes are sending.

Jayne and I raced down the block to the car.

"Amaretta! Christo!" she cried, pulling open the door on the driver's side. Amaretta's head was slumped against the steering wheel. Christo was doubled over beside her, blood running from his forehead. I was sure the jinx had claimed two more lives, but as

I flung open the passenger door, Christo moaned and slowly straightened. Jayne had leaned Amaretta back against the seat by this time and was patting her cheeks, encouraging her to come to—which she did with a loud groan.

I helped the dazed San Fernando Valley Italian from the car and Jayne tried to do the same for Amaretta, but the woman jerked away, half falling to the ground with the movement. Regaining her balance, she stared wildly at Jayne. *"You* did this!" she shrieked. "If there's a murderer around here, it's *you!"* Then she began to scream for help, apparently convinced that Jayne and I had indeed made an attempt on her life.

Chapter 24

Amaretta and Christo refused to wait inside our house while the police and an ambulance were summoned by our 911 call. Christo's head wound was superficial, but it was bleeding down over his white linen suit.

"My God," he moaned, "I paid twenty-five hundred bucks for this suit. Twenty-five hundred smack-olas. Will it come off? Will the goddamn blood come off?" He kept repeating these same thoughts over and over while Amaretta fluttered beside him, talking baby talk.

"There, there, honey, momma is gonna take her sweet boy on a big ole shopping sprec to Rodeo Drive." She cooed and caressed—until she caught sight of herself in the window's reflection. She was bloodless, but her hair was a mess, her suit wrinkled, and she flew into a panic, apparently at the thought that she would look less than glamorous if a photographer arrived with the police. A neighbor who had heard the commotion and also come to the rescue finally invited the bruised victims into her house to tidy up.

I decided to explore the area a bit. On the far side of the road from our home there was a long driveway leading to a recently sold and still uninhabited California-style ranch house. I looked at the large Encino Realty sign and then up the driveway. A sniper might easily have waited in his car, partly hidden here, and observed the comings and goings at our home. Perhaps Amaretta and Christo weren't even the targets; maybe it was Jayne and me.

I walked about the empty driveway for a few moments, trying to fathom why anyone would take shots at any of us. As I started to leave, my foot hit a shiny piece of metal and sent it skittering across the concrete. I bent over . . . and picked up a brass casing for a rifle shell. It took only seconds to locate the second shell. They were still warm. Holding them chilled my blood.

I went back to the house and waited with Jayne in the driveway for the emergency vehicles to arrive.

"I suppose I owe Amaretta an apology," Jayne admitted unhappily. "She can't very well be the killer if someone is trying to murder her."

"Maybe this shooting was only a charade."

"As in Cary Grant and Audrey Hepburn?"

"As in the fact that Amaretta and Christo are still alive. The sniper had an easy shot as the Lexus came out of our driveway, but he waited until the car drove past and then fired at the rear window."

"Isn't that like one of the questions they have about who shot Kennedy? If Oswald supposedly had a clear shot as the cavalcade came straight at him, why did he wait until the car was making the turn?"

"In this case it might have been to cause the least amount of harm possible."

Police cars began to arrive, racing up our street with their flashing lights and sirens blaring. As soon as Amaretta saw the brigade, she rushed from our neighbor's house, pointing at Jayne and me and shrieking, "There they are! They tried to kill us! Arrest them, for God's sake!"

Seeing nearby residents beginning to walk out to the ends of their driveways to watch what was going on, I smiled sheepishly. "I love your dinner parties," I whispered to Jayne.

The ambulance arrived, and Amaretta fainted rather dramatically into the waiting arms of a handsome young medic. Christo's head had stopped bleeding. He had a large wet towel and was pointlessly attacking the stains on his suit as Amaretta roused to say, "Tell them, honey. Tell them the Allens did this."

Lieutenant Washington stepped from an unmarked police car and came our way. He wore a brown suit, his tie was askew, and he looked weary.

"What's this about you taking parting shots at your dinner guests?" he asked.

I could tell Jayne was about to say something probably better left unsaid, so I squeezed her arm and stepped into the conversation.

"The shots came from across the street, Lieutenant. I found two shell casings on the driveway over there. Since Jayne and I were in our house at the time, it would have been impossible for us to have done the shooting."

Lieutenant Washington looked back and forth from Jayne to me. "So where are these casings?" he asked grumpily. "I hope you didn't touch them."

"Well, I . . . er . . . as a matter of fact . . ." I reached into my pocket and pulled out the shells.

The lieutenant scowled as he took them.

"I guess I wasn't thinking," I offered lamely.

"You were in shock, dear," Jayne comforted.

"Mr. Allen, Mrs. Allen . . . attempted murder is a

171

serious offense. I want you two to wait inside your house. I'll be up shortly to get your statements."

Jayne and I gladly returned to the comfort of our living room. She sunk into the sofa, deep in thought, and I sat down at the piano and noodled a few melancholy notes. It was a long half hour before the lieutenant reappeared, walking through the front door that I had deliberately left open. He stared grimly from Jayne to me and back again for what seemed like another long time.

"Offhand, it seems that you're correct, Mr. Allen," he said at last. "The shots were apparently fired from the driveway across the street. The injured parties agree that you were inside your house at the time, so you're not suspects."

"Thank you," I said.

"I do have a question, though," the lieutenant continued. "Why did you invite Amaretta and Christo to dinner?"

"To eat, of course," Jayne replied.

"They don't seem quite your . . . type."

"Lieutenant Washington, may I ask you a question?" I said.

"What?"

"Don't you think this has all gone far enough? Too many people connected with *The Murder Game* have died or almost died: Abe Brautigan, our old producer, and then Sylvia, Susan, and Dominic. And now Amaretta and Christo have been attacked, which I might add could have been hit in error. Mrs. Allen and I might have been the intended victims."

"What do you want us to do?"

"Simple. Go to the network and insist they take *The Murder Game* off the air. It's become too dangerous."

The lieutenant chuckled without mirth. "Do you

think the sheriff's department can tell a television network what to do? I think you've got it backward. *They* control public opinion. They tell *us* what to do."

"But in this case surely—"

"In this case there's been a series of unfortunate accidents, but there is no indication of foul play—before tonight. Tonight a few shots were taken, but if a sniper had really wanted to kill your guests, he or she would have fired the shots as the car was leaving your driveway, *not* after it had made the turn and was driving away."

"That's what Steve said," Jayne said proudly.

"Do you think someone was just trying to frighten Amaretta and Christo?" I asked.

"Oh, I think there's even a better reason than that," the lieutenant said, and led us to the window. We peered out at a television news van that had just pulled into our street. The van disgorged a camera crew and an earnest young woman with a microphone. "It's interesting, don't you agree, that your damned game show has been front-page news for the past three weeks?" the lieutenant said. He stared at the van with a look of distaste.

"Are you saying someone shot at Amaretta's car as a publicity stunt? Something to up the ratings for the show?" In the hyped-up world of Hollywood even bad press is often considered better than none, so the suggestion didn't seem that farfetched.

"That's what I'm suggesting," Lieutenant Washington said coldly. "Now who the hell do you think is desperate enough to do a thing like that?"

Jayne and I looked at each other knowingly as the question echoed in our minds.

Chapter 25

Phoebe North was bustling about her office in the best of moods. It was a dreary afternoon, the day after our disastrous dinner with Amaretta and Christo, with intermittent rain pattering against the asphalt outside the window. Jayne and I had come to have a chat with our ambitious young producer but so far had hardly managed to get a word in.

"We beat Angela Lansbury last Sunday!" Phoebe cried the minute we entered the room. "And that was *before* someone took a shot at Amaretta and Christo! Can you imagine what the ratings will be *next* Sunday?"

"Let's just hope a few of us are still alive to enjoy them," I said.

But Phoebe could not be brought down by the prospect of mere death, not when her career was enjoying such a surge. "Look at *Variety*!" she cried. "Look at the *Hollywood Reporter*! We're on the front page again, second time in a week. Jayne, didn't I tell you at the very beginning—back when we met at that airport in Dallas—didn't I say this show was going to be a hit!?"

"What you *didn't* say, dear, was that people would be dead," Jayne remarked.

"Well, people do die. Particularly old people," Phoebe said airily.

She stopped for a breath, and I jumped in with the reason for our visit. "Phoebe, we'd like you to take *The Murder Game* off the air."

Phoebe froze, choking on air. "For heaven's sake, why? Just because there have been a few . . . accidents?"

"Phoebe, if you count Abe Brautigan—which we do—four people connected with this show have died. Last night the number almost went up to six." I was tying to be reasonable, but I didn't seem to be getting through the woman's cloud of joy.

"I know the show means a great deal to you, dear," Jayne said. "But no television show is worth people dying."

"*You* could even be the next victim," I added.

Phoebe laughed. It was a short laugh with a ring of falseness to it. "This is a Steve Allen put-on, right? A joke."

"No, Phoebe, the show has got to go off the air."

Her manner changed. The smiles were gone. "You know what? I don't need this. We've got a hit on our hands. Maybe some people can't handle success, but *I* can. If there was any vaguely *factual* evidence to suggest that we were in danger, I'd be the *first* to suggest we cancel."

"Phoebe, someone shot at Amaretta and Christo last night. That was no accident."

She laughed again. "Steve, you know as well as I do that in Los Angeles people take shots at other people all the time. You can't take it personally. Some guy could have been target-practicing last night and not

176

even realized he hit their car. You can't pull a hit TV show off the air over a thing like that."

There was no reaching her. "Phoebe, if you don't stop the show, then Jayne and I quit."

"Quit? Aren't you forgetting your contract?"

"Easily broken," Jayne said breezily, trying to lighten up the moment, which was becoming ugly.

I was amazed by the tremendous change in Phoebe's manner. She stood up, leaning forward across the desk, her face contorted into an angry snarl. "Try to quit," she hissed, "and you two are dead meat!"

"What?"

"In the business, I mean. You'll never work in this town again."

"Phoebe," I said, "you've been reading too much *Spy* magazine. The never-work-again thing is a comedy line now."

"I'll see you in court," she said.

Chapter 26

"What an unpleasant woman!" Jayne said as we left Phoebe's office and stood momentarily in the hallway of the huge network administration building. "So *are* we going to quit?"

"I'd love to, but we'd lose our inside track on the murders."

"So you finally agree they *are* murders?"

A loud ruckus coming from the outer office we had just left suddenly interrupted our conversation. Jayne and I stared at the door behind which Phoebe North was yelling at her receptionist. "You stupid bitch! You pathetic, depressing . . . loser! I want you out of this office. Now! Forever! DO . . . YOU . . . UNDER-STAND?"

"An unpleasant woman indeed," Jayne mused as we quickly moved down the hall. "I'm beginning to wonder if our Ms. North is capable of killing a few people in order to have a hit TV show."

"Only if she thought she could get away with it," I answered. I suddenly had an idea. "Let's split up for the afternoon," I suggested.

"You've grown tired of me?"

"Sure." I pecked her on the cheek. "But seriously,

we might cover more ground if we're apart for a few hours."

I told her what I had in mind. I would take Cass and pay a visit to Peter Grover. I had a few questions for him, and I thought I might enlist his help in taking the show off the air, at least temporarily. Jayne, meanwhile, would wait to intercept and befriend the recently fired receptionist as she emerged from Phoebe's office. Quite a few secretary/assistants know more about their employer's businesses than the bosses themselves. As soon as her mission was accomplished, Jayne was to call the car phone, and we would pick her up and plan our next move.

As I left the building, there was a sudden downpour, and despite holding a magazine over my head, I got drenched making the dash from the network building to where Cass was waiting for me in the parking lot.

I found Peter at his office in the heart of the glitz and glass of Beverly Hills. Grover Enterprises occupied a huge suite on the top floor of one of these massive buildings, towering high above the others to afford a view of both Rodeo Drive and the hills to the north. Peter squeezed in some time for me after a meeting with a half-dozen Japanese businessmen, who departed as I arrived, each wearing an identical dark blue suit.

"I'm a participant in a shopping mall in Toyko," he explained, ushering me into his inner office. "I don't know why I do it, except that it will be hugely profitable, I suppose."

"That's reason enough."

Peter shrugged. "Actually, I find myself looking forward only to Sunday night these days. The rest of my life is marking time."

I glanced at a series of photographs propped up on

180

his desk. In the pictures, a tanned and smiling Peter was standing at the helm of his sleek yacht, *Life is a Game*.

"You and Jayne will have to come for a cruise one weekend. We could zip over to Catalina and still make it back for the Sunday night broadcast."

"Sounds like fun. Actually, I wanted to speak to you about the show. You've heard about someone taking shots at Amaretta and Christo last night? I'm beginning to think *The Murder Game* is too dangerous for everyone involved. Jayne and I were just over at Phoebe's office, and we threatened to quit unless she took the show off the air."

Peter laughed. "Good luck."

"But honestly, this has gone on long enough. We can't continue until we *all* have unfortunate accidents."

"Yes, but are you certain these mysterious deaths will stop if the show goes off the air?"

"Well, there's no guarantee . . ."

"And you and Jayne are *not* going to quit the show anyway." Peter's eyes sparkled with good humor.

"Why do you say that?" I knew what he would say, but I let him say it . . . he enjoyed it so.

"Because you're much too curious to walk away in the middle of a spectacular mystery investigation."

We laughed together.

"You've called our number," I said. "Jayne and I are hooked. But, Peter, maybe you should at least suggest that the network put on reruns for a couple of weeks until we get a handle on what's going on. They'd listen to you."

"Perhaps. Unfortunately, I *need* our Sunday nights. We are putting extra security around the studio, but you'd have to convince me there is a definite danger of someone else losing his or her life because the show is on the air."

"What more do you want?"

"Proof."

I had a feeling he was being deliberately obstinate. I stared at him a moment as he sat behind his great desk in his handsome, well-organized office. I had to remind myself that Peter Grover was the ultimate game player—a person who hid his real thoughts and feelings behind an urbane and pleasant exterior. In his own friendly way, the man was hard as nails, which is to say a successful businessman.

"May I ask you a question?"

"Certainly."

"You gave Jayne an interesting clue about Amaretta's deepest secret. Did you know for a fact that Abe was threatening to reveal her true age if she didn't help him get his old job back?"

Peter's smile broadened. "Actually, yes. Abe was hardly a master criminal. As I told Jayne, I had tried myself to put in a word for him at the network, and when I gave him a ring back to report my lack of success, he said I shouldn't worry. And that's when he told me all about his little fiddle with Amaretta. He really thought it was harmless, not blackmail at all, and that if Amaretta was so foolish about her age, it served her right. He seemed certain she'd be able to do the trick for him with the network."

"Peter, why didn't you simply tell Jayne about this blackmail business when she came to your house?"

"Well, two reasons, really. The first was a reluctance to label Abe Brautigan as a blackmailer. He was a friend of mine and what he was doing wasn't *quite* blackmail."

"And the second reason?"

"I didn't want to deny Jayne the opportunity to use her reasoning powers to find out for herself. I did give her a marvelously helpful clue."

"Peter," I objected, "this isn't a game. It's real life!"

"And isn't that the biggest game of all?" he asked.

"But when people are being murdered, you have to at least *pretend* to take it seriously."

He laughed gleefully. "Steve, first of all, to get back to the beginning of this conversation, I am not entirely convinced there's been even one murder committed. No, before you object, listen to me. I know it seems overwhelming, all these so-called accidents, but poor Abe was almost senile and shouldn't have been driving at all, not even a golf cart. Sylvia shouldn't have gone swimming in the ocean on a rough day. Dear old Susan was in a fragile condition, mind and body, and could easily have fallen down those stairs. And Dominic was upset, it was late at night, the phone was ringing; it would have been perfectly in character for him to walk headfirst into his closing garage door."

"I agree that each of these individual events *might* be an accident. But all of them together?"

"You've done your time in Las Vegas, Steve. Think about the question of odds. When you sit down in front of a slot machine, each pull of the handle carries the same slim odds of hitting the jackpot. In other words, luck has no memory. You could hit the jackpot four times in a row, or you could sit there for a hundred years and win nothing at all."

"Someone fired a rifle at Amaretta and her young husband last night."

Peter shook his head. "I'm not convinced that's part of the same package. Maybe it's a one-shot crime, done by a totally different person. Imagine some very clever character who has managed to pull off four spectacular murders and made each appear accidental so that the police do not so much as launch a serious investigation. It seems inconceivable to me that this same individual would suddenly change his *modus operandi* and commit the grossly unsubtle act of blasting away with a rifle. And if this clever person *had* decided to change his style, he wouldn't have bungled the shooting. Amaretta and Christo would be dead."

"You seem to have a lot of respect for the killer, Peter."

"If there is a killer, yes I do. I admire intellect. But in this case, the crime is just too good, and that's why I suspect there is no crime at all."

"And the rifle shots?"

"Probably a crackpot. Los Angeles is full of them. Or maybe someone with a grudge against either Amaretta or Christo is taking advantage of the publicized jinx. Something like a copycat killer."

Only a day earlier, I might have agreed with Peter. Today I had crossed over to Jayne's side of the fence. Perhaps it was actually having been close to the rifle shots the previous night and holding the warm shells in the palm of my hand.

"But anyway, Steve . . . good luck. If there is a killer out there, I hope you find him."

"But you won't ask the network to take the show off the air?"

Peter pursed his lips thoughtfully. "Not yet. But keep me informed of your investigation, okay? If you come across something new . . . if you can convince me there's murder afoot, I'll refuse to do the show until the matter is cleared up. Fair enough?"

"It will have to do." I stood up and was about to leave Peter's office when an idea hit me. I knew it was crazy . . . that this was real life, not television. But it was difficult to disassociate Peter Grover from his role as host of a game show, the man with the sealed envelope who dispensed the final answer.

"You can't give me a clue, can you?"

He laughed. "Steve, I'm flattered . . ."

Looking at Peter, I somehow knew I was right. He might not have an envelope in his pocket, but he knew things he was not telling.

"Well, this isn't quite a *clue*," he said with a chuckle. "Let's just call it an idea worth mulling over: Let's pretend for a moment that you're someone like Bobo Van Martinson and you want to murder your rich mother Sylvia to speed up your inheritance. Now how exactly do you think you might go about this and not get caught?"

It took me less than three minutes. I was in the elevator, gliding down from the top floor, when the answer hit me like a baseball bat.

Chapter 27

Jayne waited in the hallway outside Phoebe's office until a frumpy young woman with thick glasses and fuzzy brown hair came stumbling out, carrying in her arms a loose stack of papers, a couple of framed photographs, an opened box of Ritz crackers, and odd bits of clothing—obviously all personal items she had cleared out of her desk.

Jayne came up beside her. "Excuse me," she began, but unfortunately the ex-receptionist was so startled that her sad collection of personal belongings flew out of her hands and scattered across the floor. Perhaps she had thought that Jayne was Ms. North, come to browbeat her some more.

"Oh, this is my fault," Jayne said, quickly kneeling to help the young woman, who had started to cry. "You poor dear. I heard that horrible woman screaming at you. Why don't you let me help you carry your things to your car?"

"O'm'God! You're Jayne Meadows! I wouldn't *dare* impose. . . . Honestly, I can get these—"

But Jayne wouldn't hear of it. She hastily helped the young woman scoop up her belongings, then led her to the elevator. "Let me buy you a cup of tea," she said firmly.

The girl was overweight. Now that she had stopped crying, Jayne noticed her eyes were a luminous green behind the lenses of her glasses. Her name was Agatha Welch.

"This is the second job I've lost in a year," she sniffed. "I was so excited to be working in television. . . ."

The elevator arrived, and as they got in, Jayne began to pry. "What exactly was your problem with Phoebe?"

"The computer. Again. Some people are computer literate; some aren't."

"But what did you do?" Jayne asked.

"Well, you see, there are two buttons close to one another—one is for saving and one is for deleting. Unfortunately, I occasionally get them sorta confused."

"That does sound serious," Jayne said.

"So I ended up losing this very important file. We didn't even have a hard copy. The whole thing is gone. I really can't blame Miss North for firing me."

"There, there," Jayne said. "Perhaps I can find you a job with my husband. He has an office with lots of computers in it."

"But I must be the worst secretary in all Los Angeles."

"Nonsense," Jayne said, patting Agatha's hand.

The two had reached the main lobby. Jayne was supposed to call Cass to pick her up or take a taxi, but when she saw it was raining again, she had an idea. "Look, dear, my husband's left me stranded here without a car. Instead of going to the coffee shop, perhaps I could talk you into giving me a ride home in exchange for some nice Chinese herb tea I have at the house."

"I'd be honored to drive you, Mrs. Allen. I'll get the car."

After a few minutes Jayne saw a fire-engine red vintage two-seater MG sports car, with Agatha behind the wheel, squeal up to the front door and stop. Jayne dashed out and settled into the passenger seat. The car smelled mustily of leather and motor oil—the way old British sports cars smell. The only working windshield wiper—thankfully, on the driver's side—was beating time erratically against the rain.

"This isn't the sort of automobile I would have expected you to drive."

Agatha chuckled. "You don't like my rocket ship?"

"I beg your pardon?"

"My rocket ship. When I want to escape from planet earth—you know, when people are giving me a hard time—I just get into my MG and drive faster than gravity."

"I see," Jayne said, searching about for a seat belt.

Agatha squealed out of the network parking lot onto the road leading toward the freeway. Jayne hoped for the best and tried to relax.

"Agatha, I was hoping you could help me with something. For a number of reasons, I'm trying to find out what kind of person Phoebe North is. Does she have a boyfriend? What is she like to work for? Does she have expensive taste? Things like that."

Agatha sped around a delivery truck, cutting sharply back over in front of him seconds later. "She was a terror to work for! I don't think she saw the rest of us as human beings at all, just machines to help further her career."

"Can you give me an example? Something specific?"

"Sure. Here's something strange. Phoebe wouldn't allow anyone in the office to wear the color blue. She reserved that for herself. She thought it was her most flattering color."

"Insecure . . ." Jayne mused. "Do you think she has many friends?"

Agatha snorted and swerved around a corner. "As far as I know, that lady has never had a personal life. Everything was business. All the lunches, dinners, even entertainment-type things she did were all work-related."

"What about boyfriends? No romance?"

Agatha shook her head, downshifting for a red light. "When I first got the job six months ago, someone in the office told me that Phoebe had been dating a young writer. But apparently he was just trying to get her to produce one of his scripts. The story I heard was that the guy eventually got a script picked up by another producer, and he dropped her cold. Who else'd want to go out with Amazon Woman?"

"How sad."

"Yeah, I guess so. Everybody should have *some* love in their life. Old Phoebe would be really lonely if it weren't for her brother."

"She has a brother? Where is he?"

"I thought I told you. Her younger brother lives with her. He's really a creep. He'd call the office all the time asking her for money. I get the impression that all he does is sit around the house drinking beer and watching television."

"I wonder why Phoebe puts up with him?" Jayne asked.

"Well, the way I figure it, he's the only person in her life who doesn't have anything to do with business. She needs some family around her, I guess."

"And he doesn't work?"

"No. Well, except for a few mechanic jobs he gets every now and then. He—"

"Wait a minute. You said *mechanic* jobs?"

"Yeah. You know, cars and stuff. He's great. Put new brakes on the rocket ship a few months ago. I wouldn't want to know the guy socially, though."

Agatha accelerated sharply and merged onto the freeway, expertly avoiding a city bus that had refused to let her in.

"Agatha, what is Phoebe's brother's name?"

"Ernie."

"Ernie North?"

"No. Phoebe's like practically everyone else in this town. She uses a made-up Hollywood name. She's really Sharon Solow."

"Ernie Solow," Jayne whispered and sank back in her seat, smiling broadly. She had found the missing golf-cart mechanic from Oasis Village. He was the brother of her new chief suspect.

Chapter 28

Agatha agreed to make a detour to Phoebe's home in Beverly Hills, with the hopes that Ernie would be there.

"We'll nail the bastard!" she said with a chuckle. She peered intently over the wheel of the red MG, reminding Jayne of Toad in *Wind in the Willows* going for his wild ride. Fortunately, she was an excellent driver, even if she occasionally went twenty miles over the speed limit.

"Wimp!" she muttered, leaving behind in her exhaust a Hell's Angel on a Harley. Jayne was struck by the amazing transformation from Agatha, Klutzy Receptionist to Agatha, Road Warrior.

"You know, Agatha, perhaps you're wasting your talents doing office work," Jayne suggested. "You could be a race car driver."

"Oh, Carl wouldn't like that."

"Carl?"

"He's my boyfriend. Runs a pharmacy in Pasadena. We've been engaged for ten years. He's not exactly a woman's libber. Says he likes his gals nice and feminine."

"But what do you like, dear?"

Agatha shrugged. "Who knows? I'm getting tired of being engaged, I know that. Carl keeps saying he has to save more money before we can get married, but at this rate . . ."

"Perhaps you should take matters into your own hands."

"You mean tell him to put up or shut up?"

"Loudly and clearly."

"Boy, he sure wouldn't like that."

"Maybe it's time Carl entered the twentieth century."

Agatha smiled. "Ms. Meadows, you're right!"

"That's the spirit . . . ah, but perhaps you should slow down a bit." In her excitement, Agatha had pressed the accelerator pedal to the floor. She looked at Jayne's nervous face and immediately slowed to 65 mph.

"Sorry," she said. "It's always scarier for the passenger when you go fast."

Even with closer attention to her speed, Agatha made record time crossing over curvaceous Coldwater Canyon to Phoebe's house in Beverly Hills. From the outside, the place showed no sign of life. Leaving the MG, Jayne and Agatha dashed through a new rainshower to the overhang of the front door and rang the bell. After a moment, a voice came through the intercom. "Yeah? What is it?"

"We've come from your sister's office," Jayne improvised. "She asked us to pick up a script."

"Yeah? Well, wait a minute."

Ernie Solow opened the door with a can of beer in his hand. He was wearing jeans and a T-shirt and looked generally disheveled, as if he had just awakened from a nap. He had a pale face shaped like a full moon, with a dark stubble of whiskers on his chin. His two-toned hair was sticking out in even more directions than usual. Jayne realized she had seen him before—at Phoebe's press party, where Susan Fitzgerald had fallen down the stairs.

"Hey, I remember you," Ernie was saying to Agatha. "I worked on your brakes once." He turned to Jayne. "And you're . . . don't tell me . . ."

"Excuse me, can we come in out of the rain?" Without waiting for an answer, Jayne swept into the house.

"Jayne Meadows! That's it! My sister didn't say anything about a script for you."

"Oh, I'm just along for the ride. Agatha, why don't you see if you can find the script Phoebe sent you for, and I'll have a short chat with Ernie about my brakes."

Agatha went up the stairs and around a corner to Phoebe's office. Ernie stood in the living room looking after her, bewildered.

"Mr. Solow, I've heard you're the best automobile mechanic in West Los Angeles, and reasonable as well."

Ernie turned toward Jayne, eyeing her warily. "Who says so?"

"Agatha, for one. And I have a dear friend down at Oasis Village in Palm Springs. He recommended you highly."

"Oasis Village?" Erie's eyes were coldly nonchalant. He slouched against the wall and slugged back some beer. "I just worked down there for a short time. I'm studying acting, and it got to be a major drag living so far away from town. So these days I only do mechanic stuff for friends . . . to pick up a little extra bread, you know."

"Marvelous. If you're available, my Lazer needs a brake job."

195

"They're going out?"

"Actually, someone suggested it might be my master cylinder." Jayne smiled but watched Ernie closely.

He betrayed nothing, shrugging and taking another gulp of beer. "Thirty bucks an hour plus parts," he said. "Your dealer would cost you seventy-five, eighty."

"That's quite a savings," Jayne said. "But more than the money, of course, there's the matter of safety. I live on a hill, you see, and I have the most dreadful fear of my master cylinder totally going out someday and taking my car and me careening into the side of some house."

"Yeah, that sort of thing can happen," Ernie said. "Okay, I guess I can do the work for you. Let me get another beer, and we'll set up a date."

"Splendid," Jayne said. Ernie departed through a swinging door into the kitchen just as Agatha came down the stairs with a script in hand.

"Do you think it's okay to take this?" she whispered.

"We can mail it back anonymously," Jayne assured her.

Jayne and Agatha waited in the living room, until it began to dawn on them that Ernie was taking a rather long time to fetch his beer. "We'd better take a look," Jayne finally said.

She led the way through the swinging door into kitchen. There was no sign of Ernie.

"Look, there he is!" Agatha cried, pointing out the window to the far side of the yard. Ernie was beyond the swimming pool, leaving through a gate on the other side.

"And I thought I was being so clever," Jayne said.

"We haven't lost the bastard yet," Agatha said.

"I'm going after him. You take my car around the block and drive up the alley. We can overtake him!"

Jayne was so impressed with the way Agatha took charge that she did as she was told. Agatha tossed Jayne the car keys and then sprinted out the back door.

Jayne ran out the front and fired up the MG. She immediately realized there was a choice to be made. The alleys of Beverly Hills went in a north-south direction, parallel to the main streets. Jayne could either drive north up Foothill to Carmelita and hope to cut Ernie off there, or she could go south to Santa Monica Boulevard. She decided to go south, reasoning that Ernie would be more likely to flee toward the business district of Beverly Hills where he could lose himself in the crowds.

Jayne's adrenaline was pumping. The tires spun on the wet pavement as she backed out of the driveway and roared down Foothill Drive. Santa Monica was surprisingly clear of traffic as she slid around the right-hand turn toward the alley. That's when she realized she had made a serious miscalculation. The alley ended before it reached Santa Monica Boulevard, at the narrow strip of park and flower beds that bordered the street. There was an outlet to the west but it was a long way around, especially considering the traffic that had appeared out of nowhere. Jayne had only a moment to decide what to do. She thought of the brave Agatha who was counting on her, reminded herself she was chasing a murderer, and threw caution to the winds. Gunning the sports car, she drove over the curb, through a flower bed, across a bit of public lawn—narrowly missing a homeless old man asleep on the grass under a tarpaulin—down a gravel path, and finally up the alley behind Foothill Drive. She saw

Ernie almost immediately, trotting her way, with Agatha in hot pursuit about thirty feet behind him. Jayne slammed on the brakes and angled the car to box him in.

Ernie, however, had different ideas. He kept running. When he reached the MG, he clambered onto the low hood, slid across the ragtop, and vaulted off the trunk, hardly breaking stride as he ran off toward downtown Beverly Hills.

Jayne turned to watch him, her mouth hanging open, but Agatha jumped into the passenger's seat, panting wildly for breath and yelling, "Back up! There's no room to turn around! Go! Go!"

Jayne jammed the MG into reverse and accelerated backward down the alley, sending plastic garbage containers flying in every direction.

"Ride 'em, cowboy!" Agatha yelled gaily. "Uh-oh, he's getting away! Faster, Jayne!"

Ernie had managed to reach the end of the alley, where he turned right and disappeared from view. Jayne stomped down hard on the accelerator.

"Hurray!" Jayne cried, for she had noticed a black-and-white Beverly Hills cruiser at the end of the alley, its red and blue lights spinning madly. Her foot dived for the brakes, but she was going too fast and the pavement was slippery from the rain. There was a sickening crunch of metal and shattering glass as the rear of the MG hit the cruiser broadside.

Jayne had the breath knocked out of her. A man in a dark blue uniform pulled open her door, pistol in hand.

"All right, ladies, step out of the car, please," he said brusquely.

"Please lower that weapon," Jayne said, gathering her dignity. "It's bad enough we let a murderer escape.

We can *certainly* do without rude behavior, thank you."

The cop sighed. He probably believed he had already encountered every kind of lawbreaker there was—but he had never met one quite like Jayne Meadows Allen.

Chapter 29

While Jayne was chasing murderers and crashing into cop cars, Cass and I were doing nothing so exciting. After leaving Peter Grover's building, I used the limo as an office while I tracked down Susan Fitzgerald's last address in Hollywood. I got the information finally from a publicist I know, Arnold Plum, an Englishman who makes it his business to keep abreast of everything worth knowing in this town. He told me that the ex-grande dame of the New York stage had spent her last months living at the Chateau Marmont hotel. It's a nice place, popular with celebrities, but there seemed something depressing about ending one's life alone in rented rooms.

Tracking down this final address took nearly an hour, and it was now a dim late afternoon with the rain fading to a fine gray mist. I was surprised Jayne had not called to be picked up. I considered phoning Phoebe North to see if my missing wife was still at her office but decided to wait. After our last snarling exchange, I thought it wise to avoid the woman.

"Let's drive over to the Chateau Marmont, Cass," I suggested. "Maybe the management can fill us in a bit about Susan's life there."

"Sure. What for?"

"Cass, if you were Bobo Van Martinson and you wanted to kill your mother to get an early inheritance, what would be a good way to go about it?"

"But what has this got to do with Susan Fitzgerald?"

"Just think about it," I told him.

He thought out loud. "Let's see . . . what was Bobo's alibi? She said she was in her darkroom when her mother drowned . . . hey, I've got it! Maybe Bobo fixed up some kind of robot she left behind in the darkroom while she sneaked down to the beach to drown her old lady. Probably worked on some kind of remote control and the—"

"No, Cass. Science fiction hasn't gone that far. What I'm getting at is a lot simpler. You see, what often gives a murderer away is the discovery of some very obvious motive. With Bobo, for example, she stood to inherit millions, so normally she would be the first person the cops would suspect. In order to get away with murder, she'd have to find a way of disguising her motive."

"But that's impossible. Either she inherits the money or she doesn't. And if she doesn't, why kill?"

"Ah, but let's suppose there's a *series* of mysterious deaths, all of which occur amongst a specific group of people who know each other—in this case the veterans of *The Murder Game*. The whole complexion of the case changes. Now it looks like the work of a madman, or some crazy jinx. The real motive is conveniently disguised."

"You're saying that Bobo wants to get away with killing her mom, so she knocks off Susan Fitzgerald and Dominic Carrow, too?"

"No, I say only that it's *possible* the other deaths are

202

smoke screens. Of course, I'm only using Bobo as an example, and in her case she would have an accomplice because Bobo wasn't at the party where Susan was killed. However, the intended victim—the *real* victim could have been Sylvia, Dominic, or maybe even Abe. And the killer could be anyone . . . say a third cousin who wanted to inherit Dominic's Laurel Canyon home."

"So basically what you're saying is the real murder might not have had anything to do with *The Murder Game?*"

"Again, it's possible."

"Here's an idea, Steve: Maybe the real murder hasn't even happened yet. See what I mean? Someone's just setting up a big alibi so that when the real victim is knocked off, everybody'll assume it's part of the series."

"Cass, even if you're wrong, that's very creative thinking." It was true. The killer could be any family member, personal enemy, or business competitor of any of the victims—if indeed a murder had actually taken place rather than a string of accidents. In fact, if you looked at it this way, this was the most confusing murder case I had ever been involved with. That's why I was on my way to the Chateau Marmont. I was hoping to simplify things, to satisfy myself that Susan Fitzgerald, at least, had not been the primary victim. It was hard to imagine someone wishing to kill such a harmless old soul, but we couldn't afford to take anything for granted.

The Chateau Marmont is a place rich in Hollywood history, an ornate Norman castle overlooking Sunset Boulevard. Greta Garbo had once lived there, John Belushi had died there, my friend, parodist Allan Sherman, had spent time there, and passing celebrities of various epochs have chosen the hotel's offbeat atmosphere for their California sojourn. Cass pulled off Sunset into Marmont Lane and turned into the basement garage. I rode the elevator one floor up to the lobby, where a carefully coiffured young woman behind the reception desk was patiently explaining to a man with shoulder-length hair that Warner Brothers records had agreed to pay for his suite but not his room-service bill, which apparently amounted to some twenty-three hundred dollars.

"But this is bullshit," the long-haired man complained, using the jargon of his class, if one may use such a word. "I wouldn't have ordered Moet et Chandon for breakfast if I knew I had to pay for the bloody stuff myself, would I?"

The receptionist refused to be ruffled. I had a sense that if she ever got tired of dealing with spoiled show-business types, she would make a splendid social director at an insane asylum. No sooner had she dealt with the long-haired fellow about his room-service bill than she was approached by a short-haired young man with a bad complexion. He was semi-hysterical.

"This is hurtful, positively hurtful," I heard him say. "I live in this damned hotel for nearly three months, and now you're telling me I can't even go back to my old room for the teeniest peek around?"

"Mr. Grusky, as I've just explained to you, there is a new guest living in your suite. . . ."

"But I'll only take a minute. Maybe the maid can let me in when the guest is out. I'm certain the vase is still there. Pretty please? It's the only memento I have of Susan. . . . Don't you have a heart, Miss Brown?"

"Mr. Grusky, Miss Fitzgerald was a charming woman and valued guest. I'll ask the head housekeeper to have a look for your vase, but that's all I can promise. Why don't you telephone me in the morning?"

"I'll stop by." The young man turned suddenly and made a sprint for the elevator, apparently hoping to storm his old hotel suite for the vase he'd left behind. Like magic, a hefty security guard with the build of a football player appeared and discreetly restrained him.

"It's mine! It's mine!" he cried, "And you can't stop me from getting it!"

"Mr. Grusky, you don't want me to call the police, now, do you?" the security guard asked softly.

I decided to intervene, since I recognized the fellow from the publicity party at Phoebe's house. He was Lance, Susan's private secretary. I remembered that Dominic had made some unpleasant comment about Lance and Susan's relationship.

"Maybe I could have a talk with the gentleman," I said, stepping up to the security guard. "Lance is upset, that's all. I'm sure there's no need to call the police."

The guard gratefully permitted me to take over, and Lance meekly allowed me to guide him toward a sofa in the big old-fashioned lobby.

"My life is over," he moaned. "Absolutely finished."

"Nonsense," I assured him. "Susan was a marvelous woman, and I know she'd be very unhappy to see you carrying on like this."

He looked at me suspiciously. Lance Grusky had a weak, ill-defined face, misty gray eyes, and a tuft of unkempt hair that rose up at the back of his head and gave him somewhat the look of a woodpecker.

"You're Mr. Allen."

"That's right. My wife and I were friends of Susan's.

In fact, that's the reason I'm here. I wanted to get a clearer idea of what her final days were like."

Unfortunately, I had to listen to the entire saga of the art deco vase: how Susan had bought it for him—it was quite expensive—at an antique store on Melrose Avenue and how it had been left behind when he had been ejected from the hotel following Susan's death.

"You were living here with her?"

"Yes. Oh, I know what dirty minds might make of that, but it was an entirely innocent friendship, I can assure you. She was like my mother."

"And you were her private secretary."

"That was my title, but there wasn't a lot to do. Susan's career was over . . . just a few commercials here and there, and *The Murder Game,* of course. I wrote letters for her, balanced her checkbook . . . stuff like that."

"So you were privy to her finances."

He also appeared to know everything about her career and private life, including her relations with her grown children—a daughter who lived in New England and a son in Baltimore. On the surface, it seemed an unusual friendship between a timid twenty-six-year-old and an old woman in her late seventies. But her social power, even though now diminished, and his youth were perhaps just what the other needed.

As I probed for details, I was able to form a picture of Susan's last weeks. Money had been a problem; she was barely able to pay the rent at the hotel. That meant there wasn't much a potential murderer could hope to gain from inheritance. She had left behind a few thousand dollars in a bank account, a cooperative apartment in New York (rented out the past few years), and a small mountain of debts.

The Murder Game had lifted Susan's spirits and given her hope. As far as Lance knew, Susan had had no contact with Abe Brautigan, or indeed any of the other veterans of the original game show, except at the one fatal party. Susan and Lance lived a quiet life, enjoying simple pleasures such as a certain ice cream parlor on the Strip. Their life contained no unexpected surprises or dramas. She had been hoping to visit her daughter sometime in the summer, but other than that, there had been little contact with her children.

"Lance, do you have any reason to suspect that Susan's fall down those stairs might not have been entirely accidental?"

The young man's eyes widened in horror. "Good God! You're not suggesting Susan was pushed!"

"No, I'm just asking."

"But what could anyone gain by killing that dear old woman? She didn't have an enemy in the world."

It seemed I was wasting my time. Of course, a great deal of detective work is like this—fishing blind, hoping for a bite. After about twenty minutes, I was relieved to see Cass coming my way through the lobby.

"It's Jayne," he said, a strange grin on his face.

"She's ready to be picked up? Is she still at the network?"

"Would you believe jail?" Cass said, in quite a creditable imitation of comedian Don Adams. "She suggests you bring a lawyer—and a checkbook."

Chapter 30

Jayne may not be good casting for a first-class criminal, but she had certainly managed to get herself incarcerated in a first-class jail—in the brand-new Beverly Hills Civic Center, a building complex that looks rather like a very large wedding cake.

The old Beverly Hills City Hall, a baroque Spanish tower built in the ornate government style of the thirties, was a more user-friendly place, with the officers and jail of the BHPD housed in a quaint basement warren. In the 1980s, however, the city fathers decided to keep pace with that decade of excess, and they built what may very well be the glitziest civic center on the face of the planet.

It was a massive undertaking beset by strange problems—the most publicized being the auditorium-cultural center that had been originally intended to stand at the heart of the complex. Soon after construction had begun, however, some bright person decided that Beverly Hills had a greater need for additional parking spaces than additional culture, so the auditorium was scrapped and converted to an underground garage.

This was where the problems began. An auditorium, of course, does not require automobile access, whereas a parking lot does. City government being what it is, someone had overlooked this essential fact. The new civic center was delayed for years, and many millions of dollars were added to the budget, while tunnels were dug deep in the earth to allow the citizens of Beverly Hills to safely park their Jaguars, Porsches, Mercedeses, and Rolls Royces with the least amount of walking possible. Funding for less important services—such as education for children—was slashed to the bone to facilitate the construction of this lavish parking structure, which gives you an idea of the high esteem with which automobiles are held in the City of Beverly Hills.

And this was the city where Jayne had so unfortunately wrecked a police cruiser and a poor red MG that would probably never ride the roads again.

Cass and I parked and made our way upstairs to the police station. A sergeant sat behind the bulletproof glass surrounding the front desk and eyed me coldly. It was clear that at least this particular Beverly Hills cop was unimpressed by celebrity, even if I had been inclined to use what modest amount I had.

"I'm here to pay the bail for my wife, Jayne Meadows Allen," I said, smiling.

"Can't do it," he muttered.

"Why not?"

"Because the judge hasn't *set* bail yet."

"Well, when will that happen?"

"Probably tomorrow or the next day."

"Good God, you mean my wife is going to have to spend the night here? What is she charged with . . . exactly?"

The sergeant studied a sheet of paper and read in a monotone: "Reckless endangerment, assaulting a police office with a deadly weapon, resisting arrest, destroying city property, vandalism, and felony littering." He looked up. "The lady ran down a few garbage cans in the alley. Made quite a mess."

The sergeant wouldn't even allow me to see Jayne, so I was reduced to phoning my attorney, Seymour Bricker, for the name of a good legal specialist.

The lawyer who eventually came got no further than I had. It seemed that Jayne was indeed doomed to spend the night in jail.

None of this, of course, happened as quickly as I'm telling it. Hours went by in bureaucratic wrangling. Outside the station the dreary rainy afternoon became a soggy night. I sat huddled on a plastic bucket chair beside my counsel, whose meter was running even as he gave me consolation, and my ever-faithful friend, Cass.

"Mr. Allen," the attorney said at last, "why don't you go and get yourself a bite to eat? There's really nothing more you can do here."

But I was too disheartened to move. "You go ahead," I told him. "I'll call you when something happens."

I tried to get Cass to go home, too, but he wouldn't budge.

It was a long, grim night. Sitting on the hard seat beneath the bright glare of lights, listening to the sound of Cass's knuckles cracking over the din, I felt that I was at least sharing a portion of Jayne's discomfort. Gloomily, I watched various malefactors being hauled to jail. There was an old producer from a bygone era who had attempted to light a cigar at the Polo Lounge, then acted rudely when told to stop; a Yuppie couple who had tried to walk out on their dinner bill at La Scala; and a mad revolutionary who had been picked up on Rodeo Drive for marching up and down with a preposterously subversive placard to which he still clung. It said: "LET THE RICH PAY THEIR SHARE OF TAXES."

Since I always carry a pocket-sized dictation machine with me, I was able to get in a couple of hours of office work, knocking off two business letters, three personal notes, a couple of pages of dialogue for a play I was working on, about a dozen jokes that had occurred to me during the day, and some philosophical observations to be added to a manuscript for which I had already signed a contract with a New York publisher.

After emptying out my brain, I dozed fitfully until around ten o'clock, when Cass poked me and nodded toward the main door. Lieutenant Washington had just come in. He shook the rain from his trenchcoat and gray felt hat and glanced our way with a scowl.

I jumped stiffly from my uncomfortable perch and hurried over. "Lieutenant, you have to help me get my wife out of here. It's all some sort of an absurd misunderstanding."

"Yeah, yeah," he said, heavy on the cynicism. He looked me over in a way that made me think he was going to throw me in the slammer as well, then he sighed. "Cool your heels a bit longer, Mr. Allen. I'll look into it."

"My goddamned heels are freezing," I muttered as he walked away.

Lieutenant Washington was buzzed through a heavy door into the inner sanctum of the police station. I waited for nearly another hour and then, to my relief, saw the lieutenant emerge from the same locked door, this time with Jayne by his side—as well as a strange woman with fuzzy hair and thick glasses, who looked vaguely familiar but whom I was too tired to place.

I leaped from my seat and embraced my wife. "Are you all right, dear? Did they feed you?"

"Wonderfully. Right, Agatha? We ordered Chinese from Mr. Chow's."

"It was delicious. Best I ever had. My fortune cookie said I was going to travel to exotic places."

"Steve, dear, I want you to meet Agatha Welch—your new secretary."

"My new—?"

"Well, at least a member of your office staff. Agatha is an absolute whiz with computers . . . or maybe she could run the company errands."

Agatha energetically shook my hand, as if I were a water pump. "I can't tell you how excited I am to join your team. I promise to be very careful and not delete any important files this time."

I shot Jayne a look as Agatha continued to rattle on about the several unfortunate mistakes of her secretarial career.

"Mr. Allen, please pay attention!" Lieutenant Washington's voice ended the small talk. Thank goodness. "The BHPD are still pressing charges, but I've managed to convince them that your wife and Ms. Welch were attempting only to pursue the cause of justice."

"Then we can go home?"

"*After* we all have a chat. Why don't we step outside?" He motioned to Cass that he, too, was invited to the conference.

The lieutenant's chat was the worst dressing-down I had received since I went through infantry basic training at Camp Roberts, California in World War II. He told us that from now on we were not to meddle in

213

police matters, chase suspected murderers through alleys, or back our automobiles into municipal vehicles. If we had any bright ideas, we were to come directly to him. Otherwise, we were to mind our own business and let the police mind theirs.

"I can assure you, Lieutenant, that Steve and I have learned our lesson," Jayne said solemnly.

The lieutenant looked at Cass and Agatha. "I hope so," he said. "You appear to have two loyal employees here. I trust you'll set a better example for them in the future."

"Absolutely," Jayne promised.

"Then you can go."

Cass went to fetch the limousine, and a few minutes later Jayne, Agatha, and I slid into the back seat.

"To Foothill Drive, Cass," Jayne said breezily. "I believe we need to have a little conversation with Phoebe about her disappearing brother."

"Jayne, you *promised*."

"Of course, darling . . . but I had my fingers crossed."

Chapter 31

During the short hop from the Civic Center to North Foothill Drive, Jayne gave me the lowdown on Ernie Solow, the missing mechanic from Oasis Village, and how he had turned out to be Phoebe's brother. She described how he had fled when Jayne and Agatha had confronted him, and generally had been the inciting factor in their arrest. "It's obvious that Ernie took the job in Palm Springs hoping to find some way to create a fatal mishap for poor Abe," she concluded.

"Technically not obvious, but certainly a possibility to be pursued," I corrected.

"Steve! How can you be so dense? He did it for his sister, of course, so our ambitious producer could get the publicity to turn *The Murder Game*'s reunion into the season's biggest hit."

"Hmm . . ."

"Is that a 'hmm' of assent or disagreement?"

"I don't know. I know Phoebe is ambitious, but isn't a charge of murder rather extreme? And besides, when Abe was killed, there wasn't any publicity. *We* hadn't even heard of his death until she told us."

"Yes, but she could have been planting the *modus operandi*. The famous jinx."

"Hmm," I said again.

"Well, if Ernie is innocent, why did he run? He *must* be guilty. Isn't that right, Agatha?"

"It *sounds* logical."

Jayne leaned forward in the seat. "What do you think, Cass?"

Cass thought for a moment. I could almost hear the cogs of his old cowboy mind turning around. Finally, he tossed us back a riddle. "What if Ernie's guilty but not *really* guilty? See what I mean?"

Neither Jayne, Agatha, nor I saw even vaguely what he meant.

"Well, let's say it *was* an accident. Maybe Ernie worked on Abe's brakes and screwed up—an honest mistake. He might have forgotten to tighten the master cylinder properly, left out the brake fluid, something like that, and then the next day there's the terrible accident and the fella dies. Ernie knows he's responsible, so he runs. But was it murder? Or just the way life is sometimes? Anyway, when Jayne and Agatha show up asking questions, maybe he gets spooked. Thinks someone's going to sue him or something. So he runs again."

Jayne had to admit that Cass had a point. One problem with a murder investigation is that you are always looking for the extraordinary, whereas in most cases human beings are motivated along the path of least resistance, the mundane. So it could easily have happened that Ernie simply did sloppy work and didn't want to stick around to face the consequences. Once again, damn it, we had come back to the possibility of there being no murder, no crime, nothing but a string of unfortunate accidents. A jinx, in fact, just as the headlines said, though as a rationalist and subscriber to the *Skeptical Inquirer,* I don't believe in such things.

"Yes, but what was Ernie *doing* at Oasis Village in the first place?" Jayne asked with a barbed smile. "Doesn't it seem too huge a coincidence that he should have a job there?"

This was a good point, too. We all agreed that we needed to have a serious talk with the aforementioned Ernie Solow, should we ever find him. I guess I'm as bad as Jayne. Within ten minutes of promising Lieutenant Washington that our days of amateur detecting were over, we were hot on the trail again, determined to unravel the puzzle of these deaths—or at least conclude, once and for all, that there was no puzzle to unravel.

Phoebe's gingerbread house on North Foothill showed lights behind the curtains on the lower floor, as well as the flickering blue-gray glow of a TV set in the living room. I was far from certain she would be glad to see us, but at least she hadn't gone to bed yet. Jayne and I decided it best to go in alone, so we left Cass and Agatha in the limo and made our way up the front walk.

The rain seemed to have run its course, and there was a clear star-lit sky. The night smelled wonderfully of wet greenery and flowers.

Jayne rang the doorbell, and in a moment I could see a suspicious eyeball in the peephole looking us over. Somewhat to my surprise, Phoebe opened the door. She wore a flannel dressing gown, and her hair was a bit wild. She was barefooted, and there was a glass of white wine in her hand.

"Well," she said, "come in." Strangely, she was more hospitable than I had anticipated. "That Lieutenant What's-his-name stopped by earlier and told me all about . . . I should never have let my brother come live with me. He's never done anything but cause trouble."

Jayne and I followed Phoebe into her living room. There was a sitcom on TV, which sent forth a roar of laughter following a very weak joke. Phoebe snapped it off with a weary twist.

"Listen, I'm sorry I was so rude earlier. I get so busy and stressed out. Would you like a drink?"

I was amazed. Was this really our producer-as-witch?

"A cup of tea might be nice," Jayne suggested.

We followed Phoebe into the kitchen, sitting around a formica-topped breakfast table while she boiled water and made three cups of Lemon Zinger, discarding her own glass of wine.

"The last time Ernie got into trouble I didn't see him for three years," she said.

"What kind of trouble was he in?" I asked.

"Stolen car. Back in Allentown, Pennsylvania—that's where we grew up. My real name isn't Phoebe, it's Sharon. Sharon Solow. I suppose you know that by now. Ernie and I didn't exactly have a swell childhood."

"What do you mean?" Jayne asked.

"My father was a drunk, my mother a frightened little schoolteacher who kept her mouth shut so she wouldn't get beat up—by my father or the system."

"I'm sorry to hear it," Jayne said.

Phoebe shrugged. "Well, there's nothing like a little misery to motivate a person. I dreamed my way out of Allentown, graduated Penn State, and went to New York City. Luck was on my side. I got a job as assistant publicist for a radio station. Worked night and day. But I managed to parlay my way into producing and finally into big-time TV."

"I can see why *The Murder Game* is so important to you," Jayne sympathized.

"It would be helpful if you'd tell us a bit more about your brother," I suggested.

Phoebe smiled sadly. "Ernie had big dreams of escape, too. Only he hated to work. So he dropped out of high school and came to New York. Borrowed money from me and then ended up living in my apartment for a while. Finally, I kicked him out, and I didn't see him for a few years."

"Any idea where he was?" I asked.

"Who knows. Last fall he just shows up on my doorstep. What could I do? Turn him away? He *is* my brother."

"But sometimes, no matter how much you love them, you have to let them go. They'll never be well if you continue to be their crutch," Jayne said.

Phoebe didn't seem to hear her. "I'm the success in the family," she said. "Or at least the lucky one. It seemed only right to try to do something for him."

"Did you try to find him work?" I asked.

"That was a disaster. I got him a job in the mailroom at the network, and he was fired after a week."

"How do you get fired from so simple a job?" I asked.

"Jerk started selling dope to some of the fast-lane, would-be young executives. Security found out. They didn't arrest him—as a favor to me—but they had to fire him."

"What about the job at Oasis Village?" Jayne asked. "How did that come about?"

"Ernie was always dynamite with machines. His one talent. I started getting him small jobs fixing cars

219

of people I knew. But I was ready to throw him out again. Then one day last December he announced that a friend had managed to find him a mechanic's job down in the desert, and he was going to give it a try, move down there for a while. I didn't question it; I was delighted."

"A *friend* found him this job?" I asked. "Did he say who the friend was?"

"No. Like I said, I didn't ask any questions."

"Do you have any idea who it could be? Did he hang out with anyone?"

Phoebe shook her head. "I told him never to bring any of his buddies here—and in that regard he respected my wishes. He was grateful for the free rent so he wasn't about to screw it up."

"But the job in Palm Springs didn't last long," I said. "When did he come back?"

"I guess . . . oh, around the end of February."

"Did he explain *why* he came back?"

"Nope. Just said he was laid off. Blamed it on the recession."

"I'm afraid that wasn't the truth," Jayne told her. "Ernie ran away the day after Abe Brautigan was killed in the golf cart. He took some expensive tools with him. Phoebe, did you know your brother was working at Abe's retirement community?"

"No. Well, not until a month or so later. All these accidents started happening, and Ernie . . . well, perhaps I shouldn't mention this . . ."

"Please do," Jayne and I said together.

"Well, after Susan fell down the stairs at my party— you were here—Ernie finally told me where he'd been working in Palm Springs and how it wouldn't look good for either of us if word got around that he was connected to these accidents."

"But *was* he connected?" I asked.

"He swore he wasn't, and I believed him. Ernie just has a way of being at the wrong place at the wrong time. He said he didn't have anything to do with Abe's brakes going out but that people would blame him anyway because he was the mechanic and was supposed to be in charge of these things. His friend told him he'd better just lay low."

"The same friend who got him the job?"

"I don't know."

"You didn't ask him about the friend at all?" Jayne found this hard to believe.

"Look, you have to understand; I didn't *want* to know. After the incident with the drugs in the mailroom, I realized Ernie had some bad connections. It was more than I could deal with. And I was busy, as you know. With my own work."

We were silent for a moment. I would have given anything to know who Ernie's mysterious friend was—if indeed there really was such a person and Ernie was not lying to his sister, or his sister lying to us.

"Besides working on cars, what other interests does your brother have?" I asked, fishing broadly.

Phoebe laughed harshly. "Nothing that's exactly going to help him get ahead in the world. He likes to watch football, drink beer, and surf."

"Do you know which beach he goes to?"

"Sure. Santa Monica. By the pier. He made me tag along one Sunday."

Jayne glanced sharply my way, her eyes blazing with I-told-you-so triumph. As for myself, I kept my voice deliberately neutral. "I see," I said thoughtfully. "Phoebe, by any chance do you have a recent photograph of Ernie you might lend us?"

Chapter 32

Mid-morning on Wednesday, Jayne, Cass, Agatha, and I went to the beach. I'm a little vague as to exactly how it was that ungainly, bespeckled Agatha—my new staff-member whether I liked it or not—had become one of our intimate group. Of course, Agatha and Jayne *had* shared a jail cell; I suppose this had created a bond as sisters-in-crime. Whatever the reason, Jayne does occasionally adopt stray creatures, human and animal, and Agatha had become a fact of life.

The rain of the day before had swept the city clean, washed the air, and left us with a sparkling, breezy morning of bright sunshine. On the way to Santa Monica, Cass and Agatha sat in the front seat of the limo; Jayne and I were in the back. Cass was describing his childhood in Wyoming, and summer storms over the Grand Teton mountains in which the sky turned almost pitch-black and full of sudden rain. I don't believe I had ever heard Cass, normally a laconic fellow, wax so poetic. Sitting by his side, Agatha listened with grave rapture. "You mean there really *is* life outside Los Angeles?" she asked, putting him on ever so slightly.

"You bet. There are people who've never even been on a freeway."

"Wow."

When Cass parked in the public lot at the foot of the Santa Monica pier, Jayne suggested we split up into two teams. We had spent the early morning making a dozen color Xeroxes of the snapshot Phoebe had given us of her brother. Cass and Agatha would canvass the beach to the south of the pier, and Jayne and I to the north. Our hope was to show the photo to the locals, those loose and generally suntanned souls who, for various reasons, had opted out of the harsher life inland. Perhaps someone would recognize Ernie; if we were lucky, someone might have seen him with a friend, maybe even know that person's name. This was legwork of the most basic kind, and of course, at the back of my mind was the slim hope we might even spot Solow himself on the Santa Monica sands.

Jayne and I began our search on the boardwalk, the small food concessions and beach stores clustered around the entrance to the pier. This is a strange area, part cityscape, part amusement park. The pier and beach are a kind of never-never land, attracting an assortment of drifters and seekers, bodybuilders and bums, tourists and hustlers. The beach, of course, is an elemental ingredient of the California dream. Here at the edge of Santa Monica, the dream had reached a scruffy end. We passed a group of young men sharing a bottle in a paper bag. Occasionally, the musty smell of marijuana drifted on the ocean breeze, along with the stench of urine and body odor from the poor unfortunates whose only home was a stretch of grass and park benches on the cliff above.

The photo we had of Ernie Solow had been taken by his sister on the afternoon they had come to this very shore. In the snapshot, Ernie, with his English-school-boy haircut, was bare-chested, unshaven, and carried a surfboard beneath one arm. We showed the picture to a woman who sold slightly smelly shrimp cocktails from a small stand, then worked our way down past a place that rented umbrellas, bicycles, and roller blades; a liquor store; a pizzeria; a T-shirt concession; a metaphysical bookstore that specialized in crystals and tarot cards; and yet another liquor store. No one seemed surprised that we were looking for a lost soul. The beach at Santa Monica was full of them.

After our home had been partly destroyed by fire some years back, Jayne and I had rented a house on the Santa Monica beach. Most of its nearby inhabitants had seemed physically and mentally healthy enough, but there had obviously been a terrible deterioration over the decades, a fact—sad to say—consistent with the increasing depravity and sickness of our society in general. Jayne used to like to go out in the early morning and exercise, chiefly by walking in the sand on the beach side of the house we were temporarily occupying.

At first she would leave her beach slippers or sandals at the water's edge, but after losing three pairs that way, she figured out that the same degenerate, who was in the area constantly, was stealing them, not despite but *because* of the fact that they were woman's slippers.

After an hour, Jayne and I had unearthed only one person who thought he recognized Ernie—a young white man with pink cornrow hair who worked in the place that rented roller blades. He thought he might have rented skates to Ernie and a young woman a few weeks before but wasn't certain.

"Can you describe the young woman?" I asked.

"She was a chick. You know."

"Tall? Short? Young? Old? Good-looking?"

"I didn't really notice."

I spotted a sign above the cash register requesting that a driver's license be left as collateral when renting skates. This gave me a short spurt of optimism. "Could you look in your records? Perhaps you have a name written down."

"We don't keep no records like that," the youth said sullenly.

"That's a double negative," Jayne mentioned. "What you mean to say is that you don't keep *any* records like that."

The kid's lips pursed sarcastically. Jayne and I wandered on.

After a time, when it was clear we were batting zero, we took off our shoes and socks, rolled up our pants, and wandered together down onto the warm sand. Two sea gulls soared overhead, making their lonely cries. Far out on the ocean a big sailboat moved gracefully among the whitecaps toward the horizon. It had been a while since Jayne and I had walked together barefoot on a beach. She momentarily took my hand and gave a deep, contented sigh.

We moved slowly toward the hard sand closer to the ocean. A wave broke and slithered up around our toes with a soft hiss. We stood for a moment beneath the shade of the pier, amongst the ancient, pitch-soaked timbers, suddenly realizing that this was the spot where Sylvia Van Martinson's body had been found. It was cool and quiet beneath the pier but somewhat sinister. It certainly was a curious coincidence that this was also the beach where Ernie Solow reportedly liked to surf. I guided Jayne away from the pier and out once more into the bright sunlight.

"Let's show the photograph to that fisherman," Jayne suggested, noticing a tiny Oriental man in huge rubber boots who was standing with his pole and line in the water a few yards down the beach. The little man was so old and wrinkled he seemed somehow eternal. There was a bucket by his side half full of shimmering kingfish. He didn't look up as Jayne and I approached. The man appeared to be Vietnamese; he couldn't have been much over four and a half feet tall.

"Excuse me, do you speak English?" I asked. I held up the photograph for him to inspect. "I wonder if you've seen this person?"

The old man glanced briefly at the picture, then reeled in his line and cast out once again. I held up the picture a second time and repeated my request.

"Why are you looking for him?" he asked finally with surprisingly little accent.

"We believe he's involved in a crime," I said.

"Murder?" The old fisherman grinned a toothless grin. "Maybe the murder of Sylvia Van Martinson? Is that what you think, Mr. Allen?"

I was shocked that the stranger knew my name as well as Sylvia's. "You know who I am?"

"Naturally. I watch television."

"Oh, you must be the fisherman who discovered Sylvia's body," Jayne said.

"I'm sorry to say I am. Mrs. Van Martinson and I have had several delightful conversations over the years."

"You knew her?"

"We were old friends from Vietnam. In 1965 she had come to do a story on the effects of the war on the civilian population. I was the Minister of Education, and I was able to supply some observations. Here in California we sometimes spoke on the beach. We were both here almost every day."

I examined the fisherman more closely. The wizened old man reeled in another kingfish, deftly took the fish off the hook, and dropped it into his bucket.

"As an educated person, you must be in the habit of observing things closely," I said. "Tell me . . . you just used the word *murder* in connection with Mrs. Van Martinson. That means you don't believe her death was accidental?"

"Of course not. Mrs. Van Martinson was too good a swimmer to drown accidentally so close to shore."

"And you were on the beach that morning. Did you see anything at all suspicious?"

"Nothing but fog and water, I'm afraid." He cast out his line again. "I support myself with my fishing, Mr. Allen, so I pay attention to my business, not to what's going on around me." He looked away uncomfortably, presumably reluctant to become involved in a police matter.

"But Mrs. Van Martinson was your friend. Surely you must have some interest in how she died."

He glanced at me quickly. "I've seen many people die. The whys and wherefores are not so important to an old man. It's the fact of death that's important."

I held up the photograph again. "Could you perhaps have seen this young fellow on the beach that morning?"

"No. I did not see him that morning. I saw no one that morning. As I told you, only fog and water. Until the body washed up almost at my feet."

"But you saw him some other time, then?" Jayne asked gently.

"Several times," the old man admitted.

"When, for instance?" I asked.

"He came here often, to surf." The old man's eyes twinkled and the almost toothless smile returned to his face. "He was not a particularly good surfer."

"Was he with other people?"

"Of course. People like that do not know how to be alone."

"Do you know who his friends were?"

"The sort you would expect. Young people without much direction in life. They laugh loudly and pretend to have fun, but they're bored and empty. They do not use their minds."

"Have you seen any of those young people here today?"

"No, not today. Not for some weeks, actually."

"Did you ever notice the young man with a woman?" Jayne asked.

The old man nodded. "A girl . . . yes."

"Could you describe her?"

The old man didn't answer at first. Instead, he looked half a mile up the sand toward Sylvia's large, old-fashioned beach house.

"It was the daughter," he said at last.

This seemed such a jump that my mind at first refused to make the connection. But Jayne's whispered "Bobo" finally penetrated my brain. Ernie's mysterious female friend was none other than the heir to the Van Martinson fortune.

Chapter 33

Bobo answered the door, staring at Jayne and me without apparent recognition.

"Hi, Bobo," Jayne said. "We just happened to be in the neighborhood. May we come in? You remember my husband Steve, don't you?"

"Oh, yes," Bobo said vaguely. "But the house is a mess; I'm redecorating."

"I'm always interested in interior design. I'd love to hear your plans." Jayne smiled kindly and moved closer to the door.

Bobo shrugged and backed into the cavernous old house. She had changed in appearance since Jayne had last seen her on the afternoon of her mother's drowning. She now had jet-black hair, cut in a short New Wave punk style with rainbow traces of iridescent green and red on the sides. A small gold ring pierced her left nostril. She was dressed completely in black. She wore jeans and a T-shirt, along with a silver-studded leather cuff on her right wrist, several chain-stitched friendship bracelets on her left, and rings on every finger.

"I've gotten rid of the clutter," the girl explained.

"You certainly have!" Jayne exclaimed. Bobo had

231

emptied the house of all her mother's sofas, chairs, tables, and bric-a-brac. She had emptied the house of everything, in fact, except for a few cushions on the living room floor. The old furniture had not gone far, however; it stood in a big pile outside the house, covered with canvas and sheets of green plastic, to one side of the swimming pool.

"I'm considering a bonfire," Bobo told us. "Let the past go up in flames, I say."

"Why don't you consider the Salvation Army instead, dear? There are many people who would appreciate these things."

"You think so?" As the girl smiled, she seemed rather sweet and vulnerable, in a slightly baffled way. Perhaps entering the Twilight Zone ran in the family.

"Bobo, we wanted to ask you a few questions about your friend Ernie Solow," Jayne said gently.

Bobo sucked in her breath. "You've seen him?"

"Yes. Yesterday in Beverly Hills . . . but only briefly."

"Well, if you see him again, tell him I think I'm pregnant. I don't want anything from him, but I thought he might like to know he's going to be a father."

Bobo said it all quite matter-of-factly, but Jayne's mothering instinct immediately shifted into gear, even while a desire to get to the truth took over. "Why don't we sit down on these cushions and have a little chat," she suggested.

"Why not?" Bobo plopped down in the middle of the empty living room. Jayne and I joined her, with much less agility. I didn't even want to think about getting up again. Since pregnancy seemed to be woman-talk, I kept mostly to the role of spectator, confining myself to studying Bobo's reactions to Jayne's questions and comments.

"When exactly did you meet Ernie?" my wife probed.

"A couple of months ago. I was taking photographs of people on the public beach, up by the pier. Ernie saw me and offered me a beer from his cooler. I told him I didn't drink, and he said he admired that. That most people drink too much beer."

"I see. So you had a nice chat?"

"Oh, yeah. He was sweet. I loved how disheveled he looked, like he had just woken from a long nap."

"I see. Eventually he asked you for a date?"

"A date? Kids don't go on dates anymore. I asked him to drive me up to Malibu one afternoon. We saw a movie. Some horror thing. And then we made plans to meet beneath the pier the following Thursday."

"Beneath the pier? Why didn't you ask him to come to your house?"

"Oh, sure. And have Mother freak out major league and scare him away?"

"Oh, because his appearance was a bit . . . scruffy?"

"No, because he was a *guy*. Mother was terrified that I would fall in love and move away. She wanted to be the center of my life, you know. Didn't want to share me with anybody. I don't know why . . . I was never exactly great company for her."

"So you saw Ernie secretly. Did you meet often?"

"Once a week or so, in the afternoons. We always met beneath the pier and sometimes he'd take me somewhere in his car. We went to a motel one afternoon. That's where I got pregnant."

"Bobo, did you realize Ernie's sister was Phoebe North, the producer of *The Murder Game?*"

"I think he mentioned that once, but I wasn't inter-

233

ested. Why should I care what his sister did for a living?"

"Were you in love with him?"

The girl shrugged. "Yes and no. He was kind of disgusting, actually, and he wasn't too bright. But there was something fascinating about him, too. Anyway, I was feeling kinda bored and lonely at the time, and I guess it was kinda fun to sneak around behind Mother's back."

I decided to jump into the conversation. "Bobo, did you ever meet any of Ernie's other friends?"

"Only the first afternoon. After that we were always alone."

"Who was he with on that first day?" I questioned.

"Well, there were a bunch of people, I guess. He didn't exactly introduce me to them or anything. I had the impression that everyone came separately and stayed kinda loose. Did their own thing."

"Were there guys? Girls?"

"Both."

"Can you describe them?"

"They were surfer types. You know, mostly kids in their twenties. Everybody had a super suntan. I remember there was a blond girl in a bikini and a good-lookin' guy who seemed kinda stuck on himself. But I didn't pay much attention to anyone but Ernie."

Bobo's description—or lack of description—was frustrating. Part of the problem, of course, is that young California surfers work hard to look and talk like everyone else in their group, to blend into a generic mode. We may have been close to the murderer, but he—or she—was enveloped in a sort of impenetrable mist.

"Did you hear any names?" I pressed.

234

Bobo screwed up her face thoughtfully. "Dude, I think . . . that was the name of one of the guys."

"Great. Think hard, Bobo. Do you remember if Dude had a last name?"

"No. I just remember that Ernie at one point said, 'Pass me a beer, Dude.'"

I sighed, my hopes deflated. Bobo had led a remarkably sheltered life. Meanwhile, my feet were falling asleep sitting cross-legged on the floor.

"Did you go on seeing Ernie after your mother died?" Jayne asked.

"No. As a matter of fact, I haven't seen him since he took me to the motel—that was a week or so before Mother drowned. I guess I disappointed him. The sex wasn't too great."

"Have you looked for him on the beach?"

"Not really. Maybe he was a disappointment to me as well. I'm not sure what I expected, but it was all sort of boring, really."

Indeed, the two did not exactly rival Abelard and Heloise. This was a minimalist modern romance between two lost and drifting souls. As for the alleged jinx, it still seemed Ernie Solow was connected with a number of the known facts: He had been employed as the mechanic at Oasis Village when Abe Brautigan had died; he had conducted secret meetings with Bobo beneath the Santa Monica Pier, where Sylvia's body had washed up; he had been helping his sister at the publicity party where Susan Fitzgerald had broken her neck. But how it all added up, and why, and who was behind it was more mysterious than ever.

And then Bobo dropped a new bombshell.

"Oh, yeah," she said vaguely. "I have something for you, Jayne. My mother left an envelope addressed to you in her safe."

I could see Jayne trying to conceal her excitement. "How interesting. May I have it, please?"

"Let me think where I put it. . . . I had a locksmith open the safe over a week ago, but I kinda spaced out calling you. Gee, I hope I can find the thing."

Under the circumstances, Jayne was remarkably patient. "Why don't you try to remember exactly what you were doing when you handled the envelope last. Think of it as a sort of mental exercise, Bobo."

"Okay . . . I took everything out of the safe, then I went to my darkroom. . . . No, wait! That's not right. I did yoga on the upstairs sun porch."

We dutifully followed the girl to a screened porch on the second floor. Sure enough, a small pile of papers had been left carelessly on the floor, along with an emerald brooch and what appeared to be a genuine diamond necklace. Bobo searched through some stock certificates, a copy of her mother's last will and testament, and what looked like a packet of old love letters. At last she handed Jayne a plain white envelope on which was written, in capital letters: "FOR JAYNE MEADOWS ALLEN, IN CASE OF MY DEATH."

The contents turned out to be six pages of lined yellow legal paper scrawled with notes. "Good God!" Jayne exclaimed, scanning the material quickly.

"What is it?" I asked.

"I don't believe it."

"Believe *what?*" I pleaded.

"Steve, this is incredible!"

"Jayne," I said, "this is earth calling. Do you read me? What did Sylvia write to you?"

Jayne seemed stunned. "They're notes Sylvia made about Peter Grover. She was investigating him right up to the time of her death."

"Peter? Why?"

"Because . . . well, it says here that Peter didn't invent *The Murder Game* after all. He *stole* the idea from a waiter he met at the Brown Derby. And you'll never guess the name of this waiter."

"Why don't you tell us."

"Verdi. The name on that mysterious crumpled note, remember? Carlo Verdi."

Chapter 34

I felt my world turn upside down. Jayne and I had always had a deep respect for Peter Grover, for his wit, charm, modesty, and erudition. Peter, in fact, was something more than a friend; we believed in him. He was one of those people you all too rarely meet who appear to have made the best possible deal with life, creating a small island of intelligence and gentility in a tumultuous sea of social chaos. Now it looked as if he was a cheat, a thief—and perhaps worse.

The pages Sylvia Van Martinson had left for Jayne were obviously preparatory notes for a magazine article. There were dates, names, and events, as well as some speculation as to how all the pieces added up. The notes were scrawled in pencil and not entirely legible or coherent, but I could get the gist of them. I sat in the back of the limo reading Sylvia's investigative report while we sped up the 405, homeward bound.

Carlo Verdi was described as a first-generation immigrant from Italy, a fast learner who had been able to land a well-paying job as a waiter at the old Brown Derby in Beverly Hills—a restaurant now closed for years but which had once been a central meeting place for show-biz executives and celebrities. The young man had been ambitious and smart, and he had had daily contact with some of the most important people in America—albeit in a less-than-equal capacity, serving the steaks, chops, and rich desserts of a bygone era that had never heard the word cholesterol. The Brown Derby was the sort of place certain patrons frequented several times a week, year after year. It was more than a restaurant. It was a place to pitch movie projects and television shows and to conduct interviews with the press, and your waiter was someone to befriend, an important ally in creating the right ambiance.

According to Sylvia's notes, Peter Grover had frequented the Beverly Brown Derby in the early 1960s, at a time when he was host of a TV game show that was a bit too intellectual to appeal to a wide audience.

The game was called *Quotations,* and the point of it was to successfully identify the originators of famous quotations from history. I remember wondering, at the time, if Peter had become aware of a board game created by the educator Robert Allen (no relation) and myself, which was based on the simple idea of linking up famous personages from history with things they had said or written.

Come to think of it, to this day there are people who suggest to me that the popular game show *Jeopardy* was based on the same question-before-the-answer gimmick as my old television comedy routine "The Question Man."

Carlo Verdi was a big fan both of game shows and detective novels; both genres require a certain type of mind that enjoys solving puzzles, and apparently Carlo had this knack. He came up with a radical idea that combined his two interests and created a TV game show based on the solving of a crime.

240

It must have been difficult to remain quiet with such a fabulous idea, when he was serving lunches and dinners to Peter Grover, week after week—a man who could help him bring this idea to fruition. The Brown Derby was a first-class establishment, however, and Verdi had to be careful how he approached a customer about anything personal. Peter might be friendly enough on the receiving end of a veal scaloppine but might easily resent a pitch from his waiter. And there were strict house rules. If a young waiter didn't go about this in the right way, he could lose his job.

But, according to Sylvia, Carlo was desperate, so one day, between dessert and paying the check, he made his move. He apologized in advance for taking such a liberty and then pressed an envelope into Peter's hand, which detailed information on how *The Murder Game* was to be played. Peter was quite pleasant about the whole thing. In Hollywood, of course, if you have any position of power, people hit you up all the time—waiters, cab drivers, gas station attendants—everyone hoping he can be the next Robert De Niro, or at least write the movie in which De Niro himself appears. Everyone is convinced that all he needs is a little break, and you—as a Hollywood insider—are the window of opportunity to that break.

So Peter smiled, left a nice tip, went home, and read the envelope he had been given. He saw the potential of *The Murder Game* right away. It was a brilliant idea, and it could make his career. But he was cagey. He phoned Carlo Verdi and said he might possibly manage to work up some interest for such a game show, though it would certainly take time. Meanwhile, Verdi was to mention his idea to absolutely no one else, lest it be stolen by some unscrupulous packager.

Unfortunately, the unscrupulous packager was already at work. Peter presented the idea to the network, claiming it as his own, the network loved it, and the rest, as they say, is history. Apparently, Peter managed to string Verdi along for a number of months, pretending the network had not yet made a decision, reminding the young man that for the time being it was best to maintain a low profile and not breathe a word to anyone.

Sylvia wrote: "By August 1963, Verdi had become suspicious. A month before the show went on the air, he was serving lunch to two network executives and overheard them enthusiastically discussing the new game show that was about to air for the fall season. The waiter quickly recognized his idea. He had been betrayed. Furious, he caused a scene that resulted in his losing his job.

"That night, after a few drinks, he drove to Grover's house on Mulholland Drive. There is no way to reconstruct the conversation the two men had. Verdi was killed later that evening in a single car accident, driving down from the hills. The police report indicates the victim was legally drunk and that the brakes of his car had failed. There was no further investigation."

"The brakes failed!" I looked up from the pages of notes. "This is getting too familiar."

"Another accident," Jayne said solemnly.

"I wonder how Sylvia found out so much about this Verdi character."

"Read the next page, Steve."

"Abe Brautigan," I said, focusing on the name.

"Right. Abe was one of the network executives Verdi overheard talking about the show at the Derby. The poor waiter was so upset he burst out with the truth right in the middle of their conversation, telling them *he* was the inventor of *The Murder Game* and that Peter Grover had stolen the idea. The executives didn't believe him, of course, and Verdi caused such a scene that the head waiter came over and fired him on the spot. So now he was not only robbed of his creation, he was also out of a job."

"Not to mention his life," I said, scanning the page for more details. "The other executive at the table was Willie Logan. Sylvia remarks that he died of lung cancer in 1973. I think I remember him."

"Of course you do. He was the one with that nice wife and the house at Trancas. He smoked like a chimney."

"For an eccentric old soul, Sylvia was still a sharp investigative reporter," I remarked. "This scene is fairly vivid, don't you think? I can just picture that poor waiter storming out of the Brown Derby after losing his job, tanking up on some booze, and going to see Grover. God knows a lot of drunk drivers have been killed trying to negotiate those curves coming down from Mulholland."

"Yes, but how many of those drunk drivers have had their brakes fail? Peter might have found a way to tamper with them. Maybe Carlo used the restroom or something."

"Jayne, do you *really* think Peter is capable of such a thing?"

"It's hard to believe—he's such a charm merchant— but he *is* the ultimate game player. I'm not certain he realizes the players sharing the board with him are living, breathing human beings "

Jayne had a point. Still, I found it profoundly depressing to think of my old friend in such a light. So once again the entire case had been thrown topsy-turvy. This was a lot to digest. During our ride home from the beach and well into the night, we discussed how all the pieces of the puzzle might fit together.

As it happened, Jayne and I had accepted an invitation for that evening to attend the premiere of a new movie that the son of a friend of ours had produced. We had accepted weeks before, but neither of us was great company. We sat in the dark, me in my tux and Jayne in a splendid jade-colored evening gown. The movie itself was a mindless thriller in which a lot of cars bashed into one another and the highly paid stars walked through their sometimes inane lines. It was an easy film to ignore, and although I am normally firm about not talking during movies out of consideration for those nearby, Jayne and I could not help but whisper back and forth.

"So Abe knew Peter was a fraud from the very beginning," I hissed. "Why the hell didn't he blow the whistle?"

"Darling, Abe was a dear man, but he was also very practical. He was the producer, after all, and if this came out, the negative publicity would destroy the show, even if a legal maneuver didn't stop production. Maybe Abe never quite believed the rantings of the young waiter. Grover probably provided him with a very persuasive counterstory. When the young man died, it seemed better just forgotten."

"Yes, but Peter was possibly a murderer."

"It's likely that Abe convinced himself the car crash was accidental. Why not? This Carlo guy was upset, and if Abe had investigated the matter at all, he would have found out that the police report said the man was drunk."

Personally, I supposed Abe was aware of the theft and the cover-up, if not the murder. He certainly remembered Verdi well enough to tell the whole story to

Sylvia more than a quarter-century later. Perhaps Abe had tried the same stunt on Peter that he had tried on Amaretta, saying, in effect, "Get me my old job back, or I'm going to start rocking the boat."

The big question was this: Had Peter responded to Abe's pathetic attempt at blackmail by hiring Ernie Solow to "fix" Abe's brakes? Had he learned from Sylvia that Abe had already blabbed—to her? If he thought Sylvia would use her magazine to broadcast the allegations, then Sylvia had to be killed as well. And after that, to make it look like some crazy jinx or the work of a madman, Susan and Dominic had to go. Or maybe he thought—or knew—that Sylvia had confided in Susan Fitzgerald. Maybe *this,* and not a betrayal of Shadow's confidences, was Dominic's big story! Peter was certainly clever enough to make the "accidents" happen. It would be the intellectual challenge of a lifetime, in fact, for the consummate game player to murder four, possibly five people without the police so much as launching a homicide investigation.

"It would have been the ultimate game for Peter," Jayne whispered in my ear, as if she had read my thoughts. "And Peter certainly had a lot to lose if even a hint of his theft was ever made public."

"The whole thing revolves around a waiter who's been dead for decades," I whispered morosely.

Mercifully, the movie ended at that point. As we sat and waited for the departing crowd to thin, I played out the murder scenarios in my head. Something didn't fit. "Jayne," I said after a moment, "can you visualize Ernie Solow as Peter's sidekick?"

Jayne knotted her brow and tried to see the two men plotting together. She shook her head.

"Neither can I. So where does he fit in? We must be missing something somewhere."

At Hollywood premieres, people generally mill around the lobby afterwards, convincing themselves and others they have just witnessed the birth of a new *Gone With the Wind*. This premiere was no exception. Jayne and I followed the crowd into the lobby, where the stars of the movie fielded compliments with technicolor smiles. "Better than *Lethal Weapon III.*" "Sort of a cross between *Dirty Harry* and *Married With Children.*" "Guess I'll have to wait till next year for my Oscar; you've got it sewed up this time."

Our friend, the father of the producer, came up and asked us what we thought of the movie. I assured him that, given the current cultural state of America, the film would make tons of money. Then Jayne and I left the theater and walked toward the lines of waiting limousines. Cass was easy to spot, his being the only burgundy-colored stretch Cadillac with rocket-ship fins among the dozens of more conservative vehicles. We settled into the back seat as the paparazzi snapped our photos.

"Well," said Jayne, "whatever the reason for all this, I think we should warn the others that we're in serious danger. Somehow I don't think this jinx is going to stop until we're all dead."

"And that's almost accomplished," I said glumly. "There's just you and me—and Amaretta makes three."

Chapter 35

The next morning Jayne phoned Amaretta's house but managed to get only Christo.

"Listen, *mia cara,* she don' wanna speak-a to you," Christo said.

"Young man, you already told Steve you grew up in the San Fernando Valley, so you can drop that ridiculous accent," Jayne told him curtly.

"Sorry. It's a bad habit. But no matter what accent I tell this to you in, it's the same story. Amaretta says she'll smile and be nice on Sunday nights, but every other day of the week you can drop dead for all she cares. She thinks you're crazy."

"Amaretta thinks we're crazy, Steve," Jayne whispered to me in a stagey aside.

"I'm not surprised," I said.

"Anyway, I gotta drive the old lady for her daily beauty treatment, so I'm gonna to hang up now. *Ciao, bambina.*" Christo hung up the phone.

Jayne pursed her lips thoughtfully. "Steve, I think I really need to talk with her. She doesn't understand the danger she's in."

"You'd think those two rifle shots through her rear window would give her a hint."

"But she thinks *we're* somehow responsible for that. If I can only make her understand that Peter is behind the whole thing, maybe she'll take it more seriously."

"Wait a minute," I said. "All we know for sure, assuming that Sylvia's story is reliable, is that Peter is a plagiarist and thoroughly dishonest. We're certainly not in a position to charge him with murder."

"Well, of course, I know that," she said. Whether she actually did at the moment or not, I don't know.

"But I'd never forgive myself if something happened to Amaretta and I'd never said anything. I think I'll run over to the Ponce de Leon. That's where she goes for her beauty treatment."

"I'll come with you. If Amaretta's at risk, you are, too. I'm staying close."

"Thank you, darling," she said.

We drove to North Bedford Drive in Beverly Hills, where the Ponce de Leon administered remedies, to those who could afford to pay the steep prices, to ward off the debilitations of age. From the outside, the building gave no hint of the miracles going on inside. One saw only an indistinct two-story building, a gray door, and a small gold plaque that proclaimed:

LE PONCE DE LEON
The Rejuvenation Center

We made our way inside. Once past the gray door, the wonders of the place began to make themselves apparent. The waiting room was splendid and modern, with long, plush black leather sofas, thick white carpet, strange chrome light fixtures, exotic plants, and a huge sprinkle-splattered Jackson Pollock painting on the wall. At the far end of the reception area there was a desk, manned—or womanned, as it happened to be—by a lovely young creature with smooth skin and long blond hair. She looked hardly eighteen, but knowing where we were, the thought crossed my mind that she might really be eighty-seven.

Christo was stretched out on one of the sofas, his legs resting on a spongy hassock. He was wearing jeans and a white T-shirt, and there was a copy of *Playboy* opened sideways to the centerfold. His hair, as always, was pulled back tightly from his forehead and clasped at the back of his neck in a long, dark ponytail.

"Hey, *paisano,*" he said. He looked over at the receptionist but did not sit up. "You don't have a cigarette on-a you by any chance?"

"Mr. Christo, you *know* you can't smoke here. It'll make you old before your time."

Christo growled and went back to his magazine, flipping through the pages so rapidly it was obvious that he was not reading the magazine for the literary experience.

Jayne approached the receptionist. "Why, hello, Miss Meadows," the girl said, smiling but looking puzzled. "I don't believe I have you down for an appointment." Jayne had never frequented the salon, preferring the Pritikin philosophy of healthful living to the minimally tested "miracles" affected here, but receptionists in Beverly Hills are sometimes aspiring starlets, and bright ones familiarize themselves with celebrities so as not to miss an opportunity of "discovery."

"That's because I don't have one," Jayne admitted. "My good friend Amaretta has been trying to get me here for ages. She suggested I come by this morning so she could show me around a bit. Is it all right if we go on through and say hello?"

"Normally, we don't allow visitors," the girl said, smiling hesitantly.

"And you shouldn't, but could you make an exception this time? After all, Amaretta and I have been doing a television show together off and on for nearly a quarter of a century."

"Oh, surely not *that* long," the girl said. She knew how to flatter, a necessary ability in our industry.

"Why don't you let them through," Christo offered unexpectedly. "Maybe *mia cara bambina* is-a bored and wants some-a company."

Christo rose indolently from the leather couch and sauntered over. He leaned over the desk and gave the receptionist a seductive smile.

The girl blushed. "Well, if you think it's all right, Mr. Christo, why don't you take them in?"

Christo winked at the girl and turned to us. "C'mon. It'll be entertaining to watch-a my wife scratch-a your eyes out." The accent was now a total put-on.

As Christo led us through the swinging door into the interior of the rejuvenation center, I was surprised to see a familiar face coming out—the young and pretty one of Shadow Bennington. We more or less collided.

"Goodness, I wouldn't have expected to find you here," I said.

She laughed. She was wearing jeans and a bejeweled T-shirt, but somehow managed to look elegant and lovely. "I had to stay up all night writing a paper on Dante's *Inferno,* and now I've got a long, hard shoot. There are times when going to college and being an actress clash. You should have seen me an hour ago; I felt about a hundred years old. Now I'm—"

"Rejuvenated?" Jayne interrupted.

250

"Totally. Look, I've got to dash. See you Sunday."

We wished Shadow luck and continued through the swinging door. The spa was a beehive of activity. Christo led us down a long corridor where lab technicians bustled to and fro, muttering over charts, treatments, details, and paraphernalia. This rejuvenation was a serious business.

We passed a line of discreetly closed doors. Christo rapped softly on one. "Hello, my little pussycat, I've brought you some-a visitors." He gestured for us to follow him inside—to the strangest-looking chamber I have ever seen. The entire ceiling was a dome onto which tranquil images of a meadow on a perfect summer's day were projected by a hidden light source. There were wildflowers, tall grass, and a sleepy weeping willow tree moving in a hypnotic breeze. The effect was more enveloping than Cinerama; one felt instantly transported into the beautiful outdoor setting. Lovely sounds pervaded the room: trickling water, soft birdsongs, and unearthly music that sounded like a gentle breeze rustling through crystal chimes.

Amaretta sat in the center of this serene capsule, submerged in a huge vat of some rich, milky substance. She had her eyes closed, and there was a look of serene ecstasy on her face. At the sound of Christo's voice, she opened her eyes. At the sight of us behind him, she screamed.

"Ssshh," Jayne said in a friendly tone. "We only want a few words with you."

"Christo, get them out of here!"

"Relax, honeykins, you will get-a wrinkles if you get-a upset. If you'll just-a listen to what they have to say, they will-a go away."

Christo cooed at her for a moment and then Ama-

251

retta turned our way. "Well?" she said coolly, her pouty lips pursed.

"We are truly sorry to disturb you," Jayne said quickly, "but I felt that I had to warn you. I believe our lives are in danger—yours and mine, and maybe Steve's—because we are the last survivors of the original *Murder Game.*"

"Aren't you forgetting Peter Grover?"

"He's the one who's trying to kill us," Jayne blurted out, to my dismay. She and I alternately went on to explain our latest theory—about the theft of the concept from the unfortunate waiter at the Brown Derby, Abe's possible blackmail scheme, Sylvia's investigation, and the ultimate game of murder-by-accident. Amaretta listened in shocked disbelief.

"But how could Peter do all this?" she asked.

"He has a helper," Jayne assured her. "We think it's Ernie Solow."

Christo laughed. It was the first sound out of him since we had begun our story. "Oh, come-a on now, Ernie's a harmless-a jerk."

"You *know* him?" I quizzed.

"Sure. We belong-a to the same health club on Santa Monica Boulevard. I work-a out several times a week. It's the only time Amaretta lets me outta on my own, isn't it, baby-doll?"

Christo kissed his wife's forehead, and she giggled.

"Have you seen Ernie recently?" I asked.

"Not-a for a week or so. But that's not unusual. He disappears every now and then—like last-a winter, for instance, when he had that job down in-a Palm Springs."

"Did he talk about that?"

"Sure, a little. He was afraid it was getting kinda tense living with-a his sister and thought it might-a be nice to be out on his own for a while. Palm Springs seemed like a good place to sit out the winter, and he liked working on-a machines. I think a friend turned him on to the gig."

As always, we were back to Ernie's mysterious friend. I was nearly bursting with curiosity. "Christo, did Ernie ever tell you who this friend was?"

Christo shrugged. "Nah. He was kinda cagey about that, really. I had a feeling maybe the guy had-a big bucks, some kinda position of power, and that Ernie wanted to keep-a him all to himself."

"Why do you say the friend had big bucks?"

"I don't know. Just the way Ernie kinda lit up when he spoke about him. And I remember one afternoon Ernie and I had-a side-by-side lockers at the club, and while we were getting dressed after a racquetball game, a big wad of hundred-dollar bills fell outta his pocket. I thought Ernie and his friend might've been selling drugs or something—who knows?—so I don't ask-a any questions."

Phoebe had mentioned that Ernie had been selling drugs during his brief stint in the network mailroom. Could this tie in somehow? I hoped not; things were complicated enough already without adding drugs to the picture.

"My Christo is very firmly against drugs, aren't you, sweetie?" Amaretta offered.

"You're all-a I need to get high," he told her, smiling down at her.

Jayne and I glanced at each other in dismay. Just then the door opened, and a young man in a white lab coat appeared with a large pitcher of a strawberry-colored liquid.

"Time for your elixir," he announced cheerfully.

"This is the magic formula," Amaretta confided. I

think she had forgotten she was angry at us. "It absolutely rolls back the years. You really should try it, Jayne; it will make you feel like a teenager."

"The prospect of feeling like a teenager again holds more terrors for me than old age!"

The young man in the lab coat poured out two large glasses, and Christo took his with a grimace of distaste. Apparently, he was required to drink the youth potion along with his wife. "Horrible stuff, but I guess it works," he said. "Sure you don't wanna try some?"

Jayne and I shook our heads.

Amaretta emptied her glass in one long series of swallows. Christo closed his eyes and took only a sip. The attendant smiled and left. I was eager to get back to the subject of Solow.

"Christo, when Ernie came back from Palm Springs, did he ever tell you why he had left his job?"

"He just-a said it was boring. Everyone there was old. And I got the feeling he had-a something better on tap in L.A."

"Like what?"

"I donna know. He didn't tell-a me much. But he was flush with money—took-a me out to lunch at some jazzy joint in Beverly Hills and told-a me he was going to leave L.A. for good come summer. Sail around the world on a fifty-foot yacht."

"He had enough money to buy a yacht?"

"No, I think it belonged to his rich friend. Ernie was excited about sailing off to the South Seas and meeting all kinds of rich, sexy babes. He said it was an old-a boyhood dream."

"Hmmm . . ."

"He even showed me a picture of the boat. It had a funny name. . . ."

"Do you remember the name?" I asked, having a hard time containing my excitement.

He was about to answer, when Amaretta began to cough. It was a strange cough that got progressively worse.

"Hey, are you okay, honeykins?" Christo peered at Amaretta, seeming genuinely concerned.

Amaretta shook her head, unable to speak, then began making horrible choking sounds.

"Oh, my God!" Christo looked in horror at his own half-finished glass of elixir. His chest began to heave with the same strangled cough. Jayne didn't waste time. She grabbed up the phone on a side table and dialed 911.

"What was the name of the yacht?" I asked hoarsely as I put my arm around Christo's shoulder and held him up.

"Life . . . Is . . . a . . . Game," he sputtered.

This was no philosophical statement. It was the name of Peter Grover's fifty-foot yacht. I told Christo to save his breath, that help was on the way. Amaretta looked in worse shape, so I waded into the vat of youth-restoring liquid and began giving her mouth-to-mouth resuscitation.

Christo collapsed to the floor, gasping and gurgling. Jayne began to scream. The once-calm rejuvenation chamber had become a madhouse.

Two paramedics burst into the chamber, followed by a gaggle of white coats and one blue coat—a uniformed BHPD officer. One medic took Amaretta from my arms, covered her with a sheet, and pulled her from the vat. A second bent over Christo. I sloshed out of the milky liquid and stood dripping beside my wife.

"She's gone," the first paramedic said after a moment. His voice seemed to come from a great distance. My knees felt weak.

"The man is still alive," I heard the second paramedic say. "But barely."

A dozen people seemed to surge into the chamber. The nice music disappeared in the middle of a note, along with the idyllic summer scene. "We're losing him! Where's the goddamn stretcher?"

Everything had happened so fast, I was in a state of shock. The policeman handed me a towel. "Life is a game," I told him dazedly.

"That's for sure, buddy," the cop muttered. And then he snapped a pair of handcuffs on my wrists.

Chapter 36

I was taken to the Beverly Hills police station, where my wife had so recently been a guest. I had a cellmate, a sensitive young man with smoldering dark eyes and a finely chiseled face like that of the old 1930s film star, Leslie Howard. He looked a little like Elvis on Slim-Fast. The fellow seemed an unlikely person to find in jail, but then, until recently, I would have thought I was unlikely to be found there, too. I caught him staring at me.

"Hey, you're somebody," he said at last. "Oh, I know . . . you're Steve Allen."

"He's much older than I am," I said.

"My parents are bananas over you. In fact, I've been seeing some of your old shows on the comedy channel. Laugh my butt off! What are *you* doing in here?"

I didn't know where to begin, and before I could open my mouth, the young man continued, "I slugged a cop, that's why I'm here."

"Not too bright a thing to do."

"I'm hip, but actually it was an acting exercise. Next week I have an audition for a Martin Scorsese thing. The part is this tough young kid who's spent most of his life behind bars. I just wanted to see what it was like—to be in the can—so I'd have something to draw from."

"Oh," I said. I was not in a good mood and did not encourage conversation. Besides, I had a lot of thinking to do—about the recent events and how they tied into our theory.

"So what are you in here for?" the young man persisted.

"Murder," I said grumpily, hoping it would shut him up.

"Fantastic, but why would you kill someone, Mr. Allen?"

"For asking too many questions." I gave the kid my most scorching look. It shut him up.

I sat on the edge of the steel bunk with my thoughts spinning around. At least I now knew who Ernie's mysterious friend was. And with the link between Ernie and Peter, the pieces of the puzzle were beginning to fall into place. Unfortunately, I still didn't have an iota of proof: no proof that Peter had stolen the concept for *The Murder Game* from Carlo Verdi; no proof that Peter had arranged Ernie's job at Oasis Village; no proof that Peter had offered Ernie the use of his luxury yacht for any but the most innocent motives of friendship. It was frustrating being so close to solving the case and yet so far.

In jail, time stretches out in a formless way. I filled an hour or so dictating, after which a police officer came for me, just about the time I had begun to fear the outside world had forgotten my existence.

"Good luck, Mr. Allen," my cellmate said. "Personally, I think you're innocent, but even if you're not, I hope you beat the rap."

"If I'm guilty, I *shouldn't* beat the rap," I lectured.

I followed the officer out of the jail, down a long corridor, and into a windowless room that seemed designed for confessions. I was not particularly surprised to see Lieutenant Washington waiting for me, sitting behind a drab gray metal table. The lieutenant had his shirt sleeves rolled up; his sports jacket was neatly folded on the table. He was drinking coffee from a Styrofoam cup, gazing at me with a hard cop stare, for which I didn't blame him. I smiled gamely, but found it difficult to take my eyes off his shoulder holster and the grim-looking weapon inside it. He indicated that I should sit on the hard metal chair across the table from him.

"Well, well. You and Mrs. Allen are turning out to be a pretty dangerous pair."

"Where is my wife, by the way?"

"Out in the waiting area, with two lawyers. Perhaps if we can clear up a few things, I'll let you join her." The lieutenant leaned dangerously across the table. "Let me tell you something, sir. I don't like smart-aleck celebrities who think they can go around this town doing whatever the hell they like. *Capisce?*" Because Washington is black, the Italian word made me laugh.

"What the hell's so funny?" He glared at me so hard that for a moment I thought he was going to hit me. Then his face turned to stone. He sat back in his chair and folded his arms across his chest.

"How long have you been having an affair with Amaretta?"

"I beg your pardon?"

"It's quite all right. Your wife doesn't have to know about this; just don't insult my intelligence by lying to *me.*"

"I'm certain your intelligence is beyond insult," I

assured him. "Amaretta and I are—were colleagues on a television show and nothing more. There was definitely no affair. She was vain and shallow, two qualities I find unattractive."

"Then you're not sorry she's dead?"

The lieutenant had a fine way of twisting words. "Of *course* I'm sorry she's dead! Half the people in Hollywood are vain and shallow, but I don't wish them all dead. I simply keep my distance the best I can."

"And yet you and your wife had Amaretta and her young husband to dinner recently. A dinner that ended, if I remember, in a murder attempt."

"We discussed all that at the time, and I think you cleared us."

The lieutenant tried another tack. "Were you aware that Miss Blech was sixty-three-years old?"

"Who?"

"Evelyn Blech. That was Amaretta's real name. Didn't you know that?"

"Oh, yes, now that you mention it, I think Jayne did tell me that once. But her real age was a closely guarded secret. Goodness, sixty-three."

"Why were you blackmailing her?"

"What the hell are you talking about?"

"You didn't threaten to reveal her true name and age if she didn't give you one hundred thousand dollars?"

"Absolutely not. Abe Brautigan threatened to make such a revelation, but that was months ago. And he didn't want one hundred thousand dollars. He just wanted his old job back."

"Read this," the lieutenant ordered, passing me a folded sheet of paper from a file in front of him. The paper had words and individual letters cut out from a newspaper and pasted on it. The words spelled out a

260

dire patchwork warning: "eVeLYN bleCH, you WILL pay $100,000 or the WORLD will lEaRN your true age is 63. Get Cash rEAdy in used twenty DOLLAR BillS. DElivery instructions TO FOLLOW."

"We found it on Amaretta's desk an hour ago, in an envelope postmarked last week. Are you claiming you know nothing about it?"

"You're damned right I am."

"I think maybe *you* put the arsenic in her glass, Mr. Allen."

"Arsenic? Was that what killed her?"

"There was enough in her drink to kill a horse. You're lucky this isn't a double homicide. It looks like the kid is going to pull through. He's young and healthy and, fortunately, didn't drink the entire glass."

"Thank God for that. So you've analyzed the elixir?" I asked curiously.

The lieutenant smiled coldly. "Yeah. The miracle drink was nothing more than colored mineral water with carrot juice, honey, and a few herbs thrown in. It was actually a clever idea to use this particular method of murder, Mr. Allen. The bitterness of the herbs concealed the arsenic taste very well."

"I'm sorry to disappoint you, Lieutenant, but neither Jayne nor I had occasion to do the deed. Did you question the spa attendant who served the stuff?"

"I'm the one asking the questions. *You're* the suspect."

"For God's sake, man, even if I had a motive—which I don't—I'm not stupid enough to give a woman and her husband poisoned drinks in a public place and then wait around for the cops to arrive. The whole thing is ridiculous."

"Then suppose you tell me what you think happened."

"May I ask you some questions first?"

The lieutenant hesitated, his face void of expression. Then he smiled. "All right," he said.

"Where was the elixir kept?"

"In the kitchen. They made a big kettle of it every day. There aren't any special security precautions, so anyone with access to the rejuvenation center could have sneaked in and doctored the stuff."

"Did you find arsenic in the entire batch?"

"No, only in the pitcher that was served to the deceased's room."

"So what does the attendant have to say about it?"

Lieutenant Washington cleared his throat. "Well, unfortunately, he's said nothing. He left the center before the police arrived. But his name is Matthew Wilson. He has a small apartment in Westwood. Goes to UCLA. He hasn't shown up at home yet, but we've got the place staked out. And we're looking for him, of course."

"UCLA."

"Yeah. What's so special about that? A lot of these college kids have part-time jobs to support themselves."

I didn't tell Lieutenant Washington what was so special about UCLA. Somehow, in all the excitement, I had forgotten our chance meeting with another UCLA student—Shadow Bennington. I suddenly felt as though someone had slapped me on the face. Shadow had been leaving the inner sanctum of the rejuvenation center just as Christo, Jayne, and I were entering. Could there be some connection between the missing Matthew Wilson and the pretty young soap opera star? UCLA was a vast university, but the coincidence of both of them going to the same school seemed too striking to ignore.

"Is something bothering you?" the lieutenant asked.

"No . . . I was just thinking about how Jayne and I nearly sampled that fatal mixture." I suppose I should have told the lieutenant what I knew, but I didn't want to implicate Shadow when I had only the vaguest suspicions. Besides, she really seemed like a person incapable of murder.

"Normally, I would suspect the young husband," the lieutenant said. "But in this case he was nearly a victim himself—both times."

"You don't think he could arrange to *nearly* die? It would certainly be a clever alibi."

The lieutenant shook his head. "Would *you* knowingly drink half a glass of something laced with arsenic, Mr. Allen?"

"Of course not."

I was feeling confused and exhausted. Christo had given me the link I needed to establish a connection between Ernie and Peter Grover, but then this new murder had occurred and now everything was in a jumble again. My problem was one of predictable personality. If Peter wished to rid himself of Amaretta, I couldn't imagine him shooting at her car and, when that failed, somehow slipping arsenic into her drink. All the other murders—if, indeed, that's what they were—had been subtly and intellectually planned to appear as accidents. It would not be Peter's style to blow that perfect cover with attempts that were clearly murderous.

Could there be two killers involved in this rash of deaths, as Peter himself had suggested? An original killer, perhaps, and then a copycat killer who wished to take advantage of the general confusion and jinx-headlines to get rid of Amaretta and Christo, possibly for reasons totally unconnected with the show?

I didn't confide my suspicions to the lieutenant or even tell him what I knew about Grover's theft of *The Murder Game*. Everything still seemed too tentative, and despite Jayne's mood of intuitive certainty, I was not ready to actually point the finger at an old friend until I was convinced I knew the entire truth.

It was certainly the riddle of a lifetime—even without the new, unlikely element of Shadow Bennington.

Chapter 37

On Thursday, Jayne and I moved incognito into a tower suite on the twenty-ninth floor of the Century Plaza Hotel, telling neither our son Bill, who is president of MTM studios, nor any member of my office staff where we were going. Only Cass and Agatha were let in on the secret. It seemed a wise decision to drop out of sight for the time being, away from would-be murderers and the tabloid press who were hot on our trail, lusting for the intimate details of Amaretta's final moments on earth.

The Century Plaza Hotel soars dramatically into the futuristic high-rise landscape of Century City, a rich but vastly impersonal place. Wags sometimes call this the city that Elizabeth Taylor built, for all these many acres once comprised the back lot of 20th Century Fox studios but were sold to land developers in the early sixties to pay for the wild Roman extravagances incurred during the filming of *Cleopatra*. From the floor-to-ceiling windows of our suite I could see the palm trees of Beverly Hills shimmering in the distance and, beyond that, the Hollywood Hills rising into a brown mist. Farther to the south and east lay the smoldering poverty of Watts and South Central L.A.

This was a city of contrasts. I tried to imagine what it must have looked like from up here on the fateful nights of rioting, and my heart grew heavy contemplating the sad state of human affairs. Jayne called to me, and I gratefully turned away from my thoughts.

She and I organized our forces, first sending Cass and Agatha to Bel Air to keep an eye on Peter Grover. Cass had his limo and Agatha her little sports car, which a gifted artisan of repair had managed to save. They were to work in tandem, trailing Peter wherever he went. There was a slim chance that Peter would fail to spot a fire-engine red MG and a burgundy-colored stretch limousine (which he would probably recognize as ours) on his tail, but it seemed worth a try. Our admittedly long-shot hope was that Peter might lead us to Ernie Solow. It was difficult to imagine getting to the bottom of this quagmire without the producer's brother.

After Cass and Agatha set out on their assigned task, Jayne drove her Lazer to the beach at Santa Monica, where she had set up a lunch date with Bobo Van Martinson, feeling that an intimate one-on-one talk might reveal previously forgotten details about Phoebe's missing sibling. After our earlier conversation with the girl, this, too, seemed a long shot, but we reasoned that if Jayne fed Bobo some of the new information we had acquired, it might jog her memory or bring sense to some remark she had forgotten simply because it had seemed unimportant at the time.

This left me by myself in our hotel suite. My mission was to do some creative telephoning to learn whatever I could about Carlo Verdi, the obscure waiter who had been dead nearly twenty years. I was less than optimistic that I would get anywhere in this search, but it seemed important to try to confirm Sylvia's notes on

Abe's accusations, even though a blackmailer might not be considered too reliable a witness.

I sat with my feet up on the king-sized bed, address book and notepad in my lap, and began a journey into the past, phoning old friends who I thought might have frequented the Brown Derby in its heyday.

It was slow going.

My first call was to a movie producer I used to know, but my friend had died a year before, and his widow and I ended up talking for ten minutes about death and the good old days.

Depressed, I tried a second old friend, a press agent, only to find his number had been disconnected and reassigned to a dry cleaning business on Fairfax.

My next call was to an aging songwriter, but he said he had always gone to the Hollywood Brown Derby, never to the Beverly Hills branch, which he considered inferior. Somehow we ended up talking about other long-gone Hollywood landmarks—Ciro's and the Macambo and Trocadero—all torn down to make way for new glitzy buildings. My songwriter friend began to wax nostalgic.

"It sure was fun back then," he said mistily. "Tell me the truth, Stevie, wasn't Hollywood a more glamorous place in those days?"

I kept calling, working the memories of old, old friends, until at last I reached a screenwriter who remembered a young waiter named Carlo.

"Beverly Brown Derby? Early sixties?" I clarified.

"That's the one. Nice kid. Bright as a penny. I remember him because he died young, a car crash I heard. There had been some kind of scene or something at the restaurant, and then bam! the guy turns up dead. Something like that sort of sticks with you over the years."

"It certainly does. Do you remember anything about him? Did he have a wife, a family?"

The screenwriter didn't know a thing about Carlo personally, except for the fact that he could toss a great Caesar salad. He did, however, give me the name of someone who might help—Maxie Tannenbaum, former head bartender at the Derby. Maxie knew everything, I was assured.

"We used to spend long hours in conversation, Maxie pouring, me drinking," the screenwriter told me. "You know, it's funny. I hadn't seen him for twenty years, and then just a few weeks ago I was buying toothpaste at Gelson's and someone taps me on the shoulder . . . and damned if it wasn't Maxie. We shot the bull for a few minutes and exchanged numbers, promising to get together soon. But of course we never did."

"Could I have the number?"

"Yeah. Hold on, it's right here in my wallet . . . somewhere."

After two hours, I had a semi-definite lead. I hung up the phone and rewarded myself by calling room service for a turkey sandwich and fresh grapefruit juice. Then I dialed the retired bartender.

"Yeah?" came a gruff, smoky voice. There was a television set on high volume in the background. I could clearly hear the announcer calling the plays of a Dodgers game.

"Is this Maxie Tannenbaum?"

"Who wants to know?"

"My name is Steve Allen. I was hoping I could ask you a few questions about the Brown Derby."

"Who?"

"Steve Allen."

"No one here by that name."

"No, *I'm* Steve Allen," I explained patiently.

"No kidding? I used to know his first cousin, Morty Allen. Ran a bookie joint downtown."

"My only two cousins are women."

"Who'd you say you were again?"

This went on for a while, until I began to suspect that Maxie Tannenbaum was either drunk, approaching senility, or both. It was obvious that a phone call was an impossible way to gain any information from him. Somehow I managed to get his address—an apartment in Hollywood. I told him not to go anywhere; I'd grab a taxi and be right over.

"There used to be a guy on television named Steve Allen," he said finally. "Are you any relation?"

"In a sense, yes." I hung up the phone, then picked it up again to call the front desk to arrange for a cab. But the doorbell of my suite rang. I assumed it was my sandwich arriving, so I was startled to see Shadow Bennington behind the door.

"Hi. I hope you don't mind me coming up. I've been trying to call you for the last two hours, but your phone's been constantly busy." Shadow was wearing jeans, a simple white blouse, and Birkenstock sandals—the casual attire of the young, which Shadow wore so elegantly.

"How in the world did you find me here?" I asked.

"Cass told me. Goodness, are you supposed to be in hiding?"

"Something like that."

"Well, don't be mad at Cass. I finally got your car phone number from Phoebe North, and when I reached Cass I begged desperately for your room number. I hope you don't mind."

"No, it's okay. But I'm afraid I'm out the door. I need to grab a cab and meet someone in Hollywood."

"Why don't I drive you? I'm not taping today, and I'm actually caught up on my schoolwork for a change. It would give us a moment to talk."

I hesitated briefly. Shadow was as pretty as a ray of spring sunshine, but there was something cold in the way she was looking at me. Something dangerous. I had seen enough death recently to be cautious.

"It's important," she said. And then she smiled, and the coldness gave way to sincerity and the danger seemed to fade away. Perhaps I had only imagined it.

"Let's go then," I smiled back. "As a matter of fact, I want to talk with you, too."

Chapter 38

Shadow drove a sleek white BMW with tinted windows and a stick shift, guiding us through Los Angeles traffic with aggressive ease. The car was so new it still smelled of the factory. I sat back in the soft black leather seat, embraced by the seat belt, and found myself studying the girl's profile. She was definitely tense. Her mouth and chin were set with determination, and her eyes seemed to be constantly judging and calculating the risks of the road, seeking maximum advantage against the other cars. This was more than driving a car; it was waging a battle against the world. She drove with the same determination that had propelled her out of an abused childhood, into college and a tough profession as an actress, and would undoubtedly one day carry her onward to her distant ranch in Montana.

She glanced my way while waiting for a red light to change. "You're studying me pretty hard, Steve. What's your conclusion?" she asked.

"I'm thinking that you're a young woman who usually gets what she wants."

"I try," she admitted with a laugh. "Is that wrong?"

"Not at all. As long as you have concern for others and *their* wants."

"Of course, but most of them generally just want to take advantage of me—sexually, financially, or psychologically."

"That's a harsh judgment. Perhaps if you opened up a little. Allowed yourself to love and be loved in return . . ."

"Ha!" It came out like a harsh bark, but then her voice softened. "Actually, I *do* have a friend. It isn't exactly a great passion, but for some reason he seems to need me. As a matter of fact, he's the reason I wanted to talk with you."

"Let me guess his name," I suggested. "Matthew Wilson."

Shadow turned my way with obvious surprise. "Good God, do you know *everything?*"

"I saw your Mr. Wilson briefly at Le Ponce de Leon. He served a pitcher of their so-called elixir—which in this case brought eternal death instead of eternal youth."

"Goddamn it!" she said. "That means the police are looking for him."

"They wouldn't be doing their job if they weren't."

Shadow turned off Santa Monica Boulevard onto Maple and headed north toward Sunset. She guided her BMW down the beautiful tree-canopied residential street in silence.

"I think it would help if I told you a little about him," she said at last. "Matthew Wilson III, only son of a wealthy Sacramento family. Matt got the full rich-kid treatment—private schools, trips to Europe, a Porsche at seventeen. All the stuff *I* missed out on. But then two years ago Matt's father went bankrupt and committed suicide. It turned out the house was mortgaged to the hilt; the bank owned the cars, the furniture, everything. So in an instant the rich kid became a poor kid—and he doesn't know the first thing about surviving in this world. He's a gentle, dreamy guy who's never had to hustle. I guess that's why he needed me so much."

"So you're taking care of him?"

"To a degree. I met him in an anthropology class last fall, and I guess my heart just went out to him. Matt's really very imaginative and sweet, and I think maybe he's the only person I've ever met who didn't have a hard edge to him. He's never tried to con me or use me. That's what I like about him. He's just my friend."

"Do you live together?"

"No, I need my own space too much. But I've been helping out with his rent and we spend weekends together, usually at my place. When I met him he was working his way through school as a waiter, but he got fired because he wasn't aggressive enough to keep up with the pace. That's when I helped him get the job at Le Ponce de Leon."

"So you know the rejuvenation center fairly well?"

"I've been going there for a few years. When I decided to be an actress I wanted to look good, *really* good, and there are some people at de Leon who know how to work magic. Even more importantly, though, is how relaxing it is to go there. The owner has become a friend."

"Okay, so what happened yesterday? Have you talked to Matt? What's he say about the fatal elixir?"

"I have to warn you this isn't going to sound good."

"That's okay. Maybe I can help."

"About a week ago, Matt received a letter with ten one-hundred-dollar bills in it and a small package of powder. The letter instructed Matt to pour the powder into Amaretta's elixir on a certain date—yesterday. It was supposed to be a harmless practical joke. Matt was told the powder was an aphrodisiac that would cause Amaretta to make a fool of herself for about twenty-four hours, but that there would be no lasting harm. If Matt did as he was told, he would receive another thousand dollars in the mail. So he did it."

"And he believed such an outrageous story? He wasn't even the least bit suspicious?" I couldn't believe anyone could be so naive.

"I told you . . . the guy is without any practical experience in the world. And he was desperate for money. The fact that I've been helping him out so much financially had begun to bother him. His pride was hurting. It was just too tempting. . . . If only he had talked to me."

"But he didn't until afterwards?"

"Right."

"Did he have any idea who the letter was from or why he was singled out for the honor?"

"None at all. Both the letter and envelope were printed on a computer. It was only when Amaretta and Christo collapsed that he realized everything wasn't kosher. He panicked and ran. He called me last night and told me the story. He's really miserable."

"Shadow, if you care about this young man, you must advise him to turn himself in—immediately. If he tells the truth, shows the police the letter . . . If they can't find any motive for him to want Amaretta dead, he'll probably get a break."

Shadow looked sick.

"Has he refused to do that?"

Shadow shook her head. "Not refused. He just can't. He threw the letter away, so he has no proof that he believed he was only acting out some kind of a practical joke."

"Bad, bad, bad. But he should get himself to the nearest police station anyway. The letter wouldn't necessarily have been convincing proof; it could have been printed out after the crime as an alibi. If he doesn't turn himself in, he'll be on the run for the rest of his life. That can't be what he wants."

"That's why I've been trying to get in touch with you all morning."

"Me? What can *I* do about the matter?"

She looked at me, deliberately turning on the full power of her big, beautiful chocolate-colored eyes. "You can find the real murderer, Steve. Then Matt will be in the clear."

Shadow told an interesting story, but I wasn't entirely certain I believed a word of it.

"He may be naive, but he's a good person, Steve. And he isn't only running from the cops, you know. What if the person who sent that letter tries to kill him so he can't talk?"

There was something in Shadow's eyes that puzzled me, even as their plea reached out to my heart. I reminded myself that not only could Shadow herself have slipped the arsenic into Amaretta's drink, but she also had a motive to murder one of the other victims—Dominic Carrow. If she had found out he had been preparing a column to expose her not-so-distant profession of the streets . . .

I didn't know what to think. Shadow was an actress, after all. Maybe even a very, very convincing one.

Chapter 39

Shadow and I drove briefly along Hollywood Boulevard, a street where dreams end. Here prostitutes, drug addicts, rock 'n' rollers, bikers, social zombies, and the ragged homeless mix with tourists who have come to see the names of legendary stars set in the pavement. At night the neon signs and glowing movie marquees hide some of the dirt and desperation, but daylight shows all its shabbiness and sadness.

Shadow was familiar with the street name I gave her, so she didn't need my assistance as she guided the BMW eastward past the Pantages Theater and made a left turn toward the hills. Maxie Tannenbaum lived in a sleepy stucco apartment building on a quiet street. The building had a quasi-Spanish feeling, with a red tile roof and a courtyard out front. The place was run-down but clean. I found the bell for Tannenbaum, 3-C, and rang several times before an answering buzz opened the door. Shadow and I fitted ourselves into a tiny elevator and made our way slowly upward.

"This city is full of the poor and forgotten," Shadow said with a shudder. "I never want to end up like that."

"I'm sure you won't."

We got out on the third floor and made our way down a dark hallway to 3-C. The door was open a crack, and the sound of a television set drifted out into the hall.

I poked my head in the door. "Hello? Mr. Tannenbaum?"

An old man in shapeless trousers, hat, and undershirt waddled our way with some difficulty. He had a huge potbelly and would have made a great Santa Claus. Or maybe the famous reindeer. The blood vessels on Tannenbaum's red nose and his watery blue eyes spoke of years of alcohol abuse. Maxie had shocks of white hair on the sides of his head. Maybe a circus clown . . .

"Come in, come in," he said in a deep, raspy voice. He smiled and tried to make us feel welcome. "Don't get many visitors these days."

We entered a world of neglect and disarray. There were old newspapers and magazines piled up in the middle of the floor, and a sad old sofa covered with socks and underwear. Maxie stared at Shadow like a man seeing a beautiful mirage.

"Amanda Laslow," he whispered. *Nights of Passion* . . . I watch you every day."

"Shadow Bennington in real life," she said, holding out her hand. "But I'm just along for the ride. It's Mr.—"

"Steve Allen! Damn, in the flesh."

"Nice to meet you," I said. "We spoke on the phone."

"Hot damn! Two stars in one day. I feel like I'm back at the Derby. I used to serve everybody then—Bogart, John Wayne, Marilyn Monroe. Even old Ronnie Reagan. He was a good smiler, but he never left much of a tip. And Alan Ladd . . ."

"Mr. Tannenbaum . . ."

"Call me Maxie. I've been thinking about writing a book—*Cocktails of the Stars*. I have a great memory, ya see. That was the secret of my success. A regular customer would walk into the Derby, and I'd have their drink ready by the time they sat down. I knew who wanted their martini on the rocks, who wanted theirs up, who drank straight vodka—that was Joan Crawford—who wanted an extra cherry in their Manhattan. I'm a walkin' encyclopedia on celebrity booze."

"I'm glad you have such a good memory, Maxie. It's the old days I want to talk about."

"No kiddin'?" He beamed. I had the feeling no one had asked Maxie about the old days for a long, long time. "Hey, you want to sit down? Let me just get rid of these old socks and things."

Maxie brushed off the sagging sofa, and Shadow and I sat down. He mercifully flicked off the television and sat across from us in an armchair that tilted slightly to the left and was losing its stuffing out the back.

"Hey, where's my manners? Would you like a drink? I got bourbon or vodka but no mix, I'm afraid."

"No thanks, Maxie. What I would like, however, is your help. I'm trying to find out everything I can about a waiter who used to work at the Beverly Hills Derby in the early sixties. A young man named Carlo Verdi."

"Carlo? Good-lookin' kid, but he got himself killed in a car wreck about, oh"—he thought back—" '65. Yeah, it was '65."

"Exactly. Do you remember anything about him?"

"Yeah. He was a good worker, kinda quiet. You

meet some guys in restaurants you know are going to be waiters the rest of their lives, but Carlo was just passing through. He was a guy with a dream. I used to rib him, you know, about his big ambitions, but deep down inside I believed he would make it one day. The guy was smart."

"Tell me about his dreams, Maxie."

"Well, the kid was an inventor. He could just think things up, you see. He got this idea for an automatic pet-feeder that would feed your animals while you were away for the weekend. Pretty clever, I thought, but Carlo didn't have any way of marketing the thing. Still, I told him not to give up."

"He invented other things, too?"

"Sure. There was an electric duster, and a game—a cross between bingo and checkers; he called it "Chingo." He sent that off to some of the big toy manufacturers, but no one was interested. But Carlo wasn't discouraged. He started thinking games might be a good way to make his fortune. It didn't cost much money to build a prototype. All you really needed to do was to come up with a dynamite idea."

"So Carlo invented more games?"

"Dozens of 'em. It got to be a joke. He would come into work each day and tell me all these crazy ideas he'd had. I'm not much of a game player myself, so I didn't know if any of his ideas were good or not; but I got a kick out of hearing about them."

"Was there any one particular game he was more excited about than the others?" I didn't want to put words into Maxie's mouth, but I was trying to guide him along.

"One particular game? Yeah, there sure was. He called it "Detective." Carlo always read a lot of paperback mysteries, you see, and he came up with this idea that people would like a game where they could figure out a bunch of clues and solve a crime."

I heard Shadow catch her breath. I had not told her the reason for my visit to this old former bartender, but she immediately realized the significance of Maxie's revelation.

"This game . . . was it for television?" I asked.

"Well, that came later. First Carlo thought of it as a board game, but because of his lack of success with manufacturers, he decided to turn it into a TV game show. You know, he was meeting all the important TV executives and stars every day. Serving them lunch and dinner. I tried to warn him that those big shots who were friendly enough when he was serving food and keeping their glasses full would turn on him if he started pitchin' a show idea to them, even if it was good. It was against the rules of the Derby, you know. If these people thought they were gonna to be hassled by every crackpot in Hollywood when they were trying to have a relaxing evening or conduct an important business meeting, they'd find a new place to hang out."

"But he did it anyway?"

"Yup. Couldn't help himself. One day at lunch he laid out his idea to this TV emcee who had always been nice to him. Tipped top dollar."

There was a long silence. "Do you remember the name of the emcee?" I persisted.

"Sure. Grover. Peter Grover."

I smiled. At last I had more than speculation. Here was concrete proof of the validity of Sylvia's notes, and a live witness that could be produced in a court of law.

"So what happened after he pitched the idea to Mr. Grover?"

"Oh, nothin' for quite a while, but then Carlo got it

281

in his head that they had stolen his idea. One day he overheard two producers talking over lunch and his suspicions were confirmed. He went off his rocker at the height of the lunch rush. I couldn't hear what it was all about, but the manager fired Carlo right then and there. And then he went out and got drunk and crashed up his car. Terrible way for a nice young fellow to end."

"What do you think?"

"About what?"

"Maxie, you watch a lot of television. I'm sure you've seen Peter Grover's game show *The Murder Game.* Is it Carlo's "Detective" idea?"

"Close enough."

"You've known about this all these years. Why didn't you say anything to anybody?"

"Say what? To who? I wasn't about to mix it up with important people and get myself fired, too. Especially when Carlo died. How would it help him anyway for me to say something? Nope. Just get me in trouble. Better to keep my mouth shut."

I felt sure that Maxie's testimony, coupled with Sylvia's note to Jayne, gave us enough to nail Peter Grover and possibly build a murder case against him. It almost seemed too easy.

"Did Carlo have a family?" I asked.

"Sure. Married to a nice girl. Pretty. She picked him up once or twice from work. Last time I saw her was at the funeral. I remember it was a scorcher of a day, and she was pregnant. I felt bad for her. That baby was one of the reasons Carlo was so anxious to make more money."

"So the baby—"

"I don't know if there was a baby. That lady looked mighty sickly at the funeral. Stress and pregnant women are sometimes a dangerous combination. And like I said, I never saw her after that."

"Where did the Verdis live?"

"I don't know, I never saw him outside work."

"Do you remember his wife's name?"

"Maria? Nadia. Somethin' like that."

Maxie's memory was getting vague, but I was satisfied with what I had.

"Maxie, would you be willing to tell the police what you've told me?"

"The cops? Hey, I don't want to cause no trouble." He glanced around the room. "Ah, what the hell. I guess I don't have anything to lose anymore."

Shadow and I stood up to leave. Maxie made a valiant effort to rise from his overstuffed chair to see us out, but I told him he needn't bother. He told us if we ever needed a bartender for a party, he could still mix a mean cocktail. We said we'd keep it in mind. He had the television blaring before we reached the front door. A sitcom's laugh track echoed mockingly behind us.

Shadow and I rode the narrow elevator in silence down to the lobby and walked out into the brilliant southern California sunshine. I found myself wondering if Mrs. Verdi had given birth to her child and whether it was a boy or a girl. The child, I figured, would now be twenty-seven years old.

I looked sharply at Shadow as I had a crazy thought. She appeared to be barely twenty-one, but, I reminded myself that she had admitted to going to Le Ponce de Leon for several years. What if that rejuvenation business really worked? What if Shadow was older than she looked and her real last name was Verdi, not Bennington?

"You're giving me that look again." She smiled, and I smiled weakly back.

"I was just wondering how old you are."

She laughed softly and winked. "Steve, I never tell anyone the truth about that."

Chapter 40

On Friday morning, my new staff member Agatha answered the phone in the sitting room of our hotel hideout. "It's Christopher Fitzgerald," she announced, putting a hand over the receiver.

"Who?" I asked. The name didn't ring a bell. "Whoever he is, how'd he find us here?"

I glared momentarily at Cass, who was eating a room-service breakfast of eggs, bacon, and pancakes. "It wasn't me," he said. "Honest."

Agatha, meanwhile, was grilling the unknown caller. "Hmmm . . . uh-huh . . . I see," she said into the receiver. "Will you hold, please? . . . Steve, he got your number from Lieutenant Washington."

"Now the cops want to get me killed," I muttered. "They're afraid of the competition."

"Shall I tell this guy to take a hike?"

"It doesn't matter now," I grumbled. "I might as well take the call."

"Hello, Mr. Allen," said a male voice on the other end of the line. "I'm calling from Baltimore. Sorry to trouble you, but I was hoping you could help me sort out something in regards to my mother's estate."

"Ah," I said, the light dawning. "You're Susan Fitzgerald's son."

"I understand you were present at my mother's death."

"Along with quite a few others."

"My mother's attorney tells me she either fell down a flight of stairs at a party in Beverly Hills—or was pushed. By any chance was a man named Lance Grusky present at the party?"

"Yes. Lance was your mother's personal assistant."

"Right," he spat the word out, saying it in a tone that left little doubt things were definitely *not* right. "My private investigator tells me that two years ago Grusky called himself Blaize Trudeau and lived with an elderly woman from Pasadena, who conveniently died and left him all her money."

"Is that right?"

"Mr. Allen, three weeks before her death my mother changed her will and left nearly everything to that bastard. My sister and I were . . . shocked."

"Mr. Fitzgerald, I'm confused. From what I understand your mother was . . . well, there wasn't much of an estate to leave—to anyone."

"Wrong," he said angrily. He had an unpleasant way of speaking, and I imagined him as a schoolmaster in an old-fashioned boys' school—ruler in hand, roaming the aisles, seeking knuckles to rap.

"My mother's co-op apartment in Manhattan was appraised last year at a million, two hundred thousand. She had an additional million in stocks and bonds she bought back in the big years of her career. She never touched those assets because she wanted to leave something to Gladys and me. She didn't want to die without leaving us something."

"And yet she changed her will, which *is*—was—her prerogative."

"Unless she was under duress or not completely in her right mind. Exactly where *was* this Mr. Grusky at the moment my mother fell down those stairs?"

"I'm afraid I can't help you there. He was at the party, but I had turned off the lights—they were bringing a birthday cake in—and I had some trouble finding the switch again. The house was dark for a while."

"Was my mother bonkers?"

"I hadn't really seen her for some time. She did seem a little . . . confused at the party."

"She left my sister and me a thousand dollars each, with the stipulation that if either of us challenged the will, we would forfeit even that pittance. Does that sound like something a sane woman would do to her own flesh and blood?"

"Well, not knowing the background of—"

"It's not just the money, Mr. Allen. We've got to prove that Lance Grusky pushed my mother down those stairs. Lieutenant Washington said the police have found no reason to pursue the matter. But he told me you were carrying on an unofficial investigation of your own."

Was the lieutenant giving me some kind of green light? Was he hoping I would break this case he couldn't pursue because of lack of enough evidence to justify the manpower? "Do you really think your mother was murdered?"

"Don't you?"

"I have to admit I have some suspicions. But Lance is not my number one suspect."

"But it *has* to be that son of a bitch. She left him all her money. What better motive could someone have?"

"I'll look into the matter," I told him.

287

"Will you contact me if you find out *anything?* You can call me at the Oakwood Academy for Boys in Baltimore. I teach Latin and Greek there."

I smiled, took the man's phone number, and promised to keep him informed of developments. Jayne had listened to my side of the conversation and smiled sympathetically as I hung up the phone.

"So now we have another suspect. With a very strong motive," she said.

"As far as I can tell, nearly everyone connected to this case had reason to murder everyone else."

"We must find Ernie Solow. He's got the answers. I just know it."

"He could be anywhere in the city. Hell, he could be back in Pennsylvania by now."

"Life's a game!" Jayne said suddenly. I gave her a puzzled look, then realized what she was telling me.

"Of course! Peter's yacht."

"If you wanted to drop out of sight in comfort . . . if you had a rich friend who also had a stake in making sure you stayed lost, where would you hide?"

Chapter 41

It was a windy afternoon on the coast, with bright yellow sunshine. Whitecaps and foam stirred the deep blue waters of the Pacific. We left Agatha behind at the Century Plaza to make some calls for my office, and Cass took us on a course west on Sunset to the beach, then north on the Pacific Coast Highway to Paradise Cove. I wasn't sure where Peter harbored his yacht, so my plan was to start as far north as we thought he might be and work our way south, checking each marina for *Life Is a Game*.

Paradise Cove is an atmospheric spot, an upscale trailer park in a woodsy setting, with a sleepy wooden pier stretching out from a perfect white sandy beach. This is where James Garner kept his trailer on the old TV show *The Rockford Files*. Sam Peckinpah had also kept a trailer at the cove, along with many other movie people. Over the years so many TV shows and movies had been shot here that folks back in Iowa probably knew the place as well as Jayne and I did.

Cass and I bought ice cream from a vendor at the foot of the pier. Jayne reminded me of my cholesterol level, but there was something about the sun and the sound of the surf that took me back to my childhood, and I couldn't resist the cone. Unfortunately, that was the most exciting thing that happened to us at Paradise Cove. Scanning the boats riding at anchor we saw no sign of *Life Is a Game*.

"I've got an idea," Cass said as we walked back to the limo. "Why don't we call Peter up and *ask* him where he keeps the boat?"

"Even if he was innocent, Peter wouldn't tell us."

"Why not?"

"But he might give us a clue, Steve," Jayne offered.

"I don't want to play Peter's games today. Anyway, if we can't find a fifty-foot yacht, we should retire from the amateur detective business."

We headed south toward the great boat basin at Marina del Rey, the world's largest man-made harbor and waterfront community, built in the sixties on marshy land between Venice and the airport. I doubt if anyone can fully appreciate the place now unless he or she knew it in the old days, as I did. I'd arrived in L.A. in 1944, having come over from Phoenix, only to discover that the rumors about the housing shortage were all too true. I finally found a second-floor apartment in a none-too-sturdy building that overlooked . . . well, a puddle about a hundred feet wide and an ugly view of two abandoned oil wells. The area was so primitive that our street wasn't even paved.

Two decades later the transformation began, reminding me of George S. Kaufman's line: "It just goes to show what God could do if he had money." Now, thousands of boats created a forest of masts that lurched rhythmically against the sky. This was the good life, California style. Huge cabin cruisers glided at five miles per hour through the narrow channels toward open water. Girls with marvelous figures hoisted sails, while their husbands/boyfriends hoisted bottles of imported beer and manned the wheels. We passed yachts that were a hundred feet long, sleek little speedboats, even an occasional rubber dinghy.

"We could walk around here for days," Jayne complained.

"Let's go to the harbormaster. He could tell us if Peter's boat is here," I suggested.

We walked to the huge harbor headquarters, a building bristling with all sorts of electronic gear and antennae, and eventually found a busy, bright-eyed young man who deigned to talk with us. He said he wasn't allowed to give out that sort of information.

We wandered back along the dock, questioning everyone we saw, and finally got lucky at the marine gas station—a fueling stop for boats rather than automobiles. A hefty middle-aged salt with arms like Popeye told us that *Life Is a Game* had at one time been anchored at Marina del Rey, but a few years back Peter Grover had moved it to Newport Harbor.

We thanked the man and hurried excitedly back to the limo, glad to be able to bypass the huge harbor at Long Beach and all the other scores of marinas, large and small, between Santa Monica and San Diego. As Cass opened the door for us, we told him of our new destination.

"Real stroke of luck," he said without enthusiasm. Cass, who knows something about boats, reminded me that Newport Harbor is a huge waterfront playground with ten separate yacht clubs that have berths for more than ten thousand boats. And if this weren't enough, scattered throughout the bay were a number of small islands—Lido Isle, Linda Isle, Harbor Island, Bay Isle, and Balboa Island. All these islands are crowded with luxury homes, private docks, and rows of yachts. Finding *Life Is a Game* in all this aquatic

291

splendor was going to be a proverbial needle-in-a-haystack chore. And, come to think of it, what if we happened to pass Grover's private dock or mooring spot at a time when his craft was out to sea?

"If we don't find her tonight, we'll rent a hotel room and look tomorrow," I told Cass.

"Whatever you say, boss."

At Newport we parked in a municipal lot by the water, climbed out of the limo, stretched our legs, inhaled the salty air, and stared out in dismay at the crowded miles of waterways and expensive homes. This seemed a last bastion of white America, most of its residents somewhere to the right of Dan Quayle though vastly more relaxed and charming than Rush Limbaugh.

"What's the plan, darling?" Jayne asked.

"If you can't beat 'em, join 'em."

"Which means?"

"We're about to get our feet wet, dear."

Chapter 42

Cass steered us along a watery avenue, a channel perhaps a quarter mile long that was bordered on either side by waterfront houses. Luxury cars were everywhere in evidence, most of them foreign. Other than the soft putt-putt of our motor, the only sounds were the lapping of the water, the snapping of flags in the light breeze, and, I thought, behind-the-scenes whining about taxes, the payment of which did not seem to have deprived local residents of any actual luxuries. The community reminded me of the Grand Canal in Venice, Italy, except that the California version has modern two-story houses with sun decks and sliding glass doors rather than Renaissance *palazzi* with barber poles outside.

We had rented a simple twelve-foot boat with a 35-hp outboard engine. "Just like steering a Cadillac," Cass assured us. "I used to drive these babies all the time, fishing the lakes in Wyoming."

"How long ago was that, Cass?" Jayne asked, gripping the side of the boat nervously.

"Thirty-five, forty years. But it's like riding a bike. You never forget."

"Er, Cass, do you see the cabin cruis—Cass!" A

floating motel crossed our bow, making a left turn into a yacht club. Cass's quick reaction to my cry prevented a nasty collision, but the wake nearly swamped us, hitting from the side. Our small boat rocked and yawed wildly. The bow crashed down on the far side of the wave, sending up a plume of oily salt water that slapped me in the face. Then we leveled out.

"That was fun," Jayne said, tightening her bright orange life jacket.

"Give a guy a great big boat, and the son of a bitch thinks he knows how to navigate," Cass grumbled.

I coughed loudly. I didn't think I had swallowed any of the sadly polluted water but I wanted to be sure. "Let's just keep looking," I said.

"What does she look like?" Cass asked.

"Who?"

"The yacht. You call a boat a *she,* don't you?"

My clothes were damp, and a sharp breeze had come up from the ocean. The sun was sinking low in the western sky.

"It's white," I said. "With sails."

Jayne scanned the boats to our starboard side, and I those to port. Cass was instructed to keep his eyes straight ahead, in case we ran into any more cruisers. We passed scores of sailing yachts with interesting names—*Xanadu, Tahiti Wind, Latin Lover, Storm Rider*—but no *Life Is a Game.*

The sun was close to setting, lighting up the wispy clouds on the western horizon into lovely shades of orange and pink.

"We'd better turn around," I suggested. "We'll get a hotel, get dry, and have dinner somewhere." We had not had a thing to eat since our ice cream cones at Paradise Cove, and after inhaling deeply of the sharp sea air all afternoon, I was beginning to visualize sizzling swordfish steaks in some nice seafood grotto with a view.

"Okay," Cass agreed. "We can go around this island and get back to the rental place quicker."

"What island?"

"Don't you see all those houses on our left? That's an island."

"Oh," I said. The land Cass referred to seemed to stretch into the sunset as far as the eye could see.

"Trust me. I studied the map when we got the boat."

Cass was getting sulky, his common response to doubts about his ability to navigate the roadways and waterways of this world. Since our little craft had running lights, I thought we might go forward another ten minutes or so. If this *was* an island to our left, it seemed advantageous to return on the other side, where we would have new territory in which to look for Peter's elusive yacht. Maybe we'd get lucky and be able to return to the secure dry land of the Valley early in the morning.

Our engine whined like a mosquito at a summer barbecue. We buzzed forward into the setting sun, which turned into a mushroom cap of color, then slipped quickly and soundlessly beneath the far edge of the world. The channel was wider here, the ocean breeze stiff and cool. Coastal twilights are misty and unreal. Magical. Jayne began softly singing the old 1930s ballad "Harbor Lights." After the sun disappeared, the western horizon suddenly exploded with red, as though some ancient god had set a torch to the sky. It was spectacular but short-lived, and as darkness caused Cass to flick on our running lights, my uneasiness returned.

"Perhaps we should turn back," Jayne said, reading my thoughts. "I don't think this is an island."

"Yeah, it looks like we're heading out to sea all right," Cass agreed. He was starting to make the turn, when I saw her—*Life Is a Game*. Peter's yacht was like the man himself, elegant and charming. Her pristine bow bobbed on the waves, canvas furled along the mast, her whiteness accented by a chunky red buoy that floated nearby. If it had been light enough to see the blueness of the ocean, I would have been tempted to sing "The Star-Spangled Banner."

We glided over to the yacht. There was no sign of life above or below deck. Cass guided us around the craft in a gentle circle.

"My, she's big," Jayne commented.

"I'm surprised they can park a boat near the mouth of the harbor like this," I said.

"It doesn't look like very good mooring to me," Cass said.

"I think we should go on board," Jayne said.

This proved more difficult to do than to say. Cass cut the engine and let us drift right up to the steep sides of the boat. There were no ropes or ladders.

We floated around the stern, where a single rope dangled invitingly down to us. *Life Is a Game* undulated gently like a silent ghost in the deepening twilight.

"I can shimmy up that rope," Cass said.

"Shinny," I said.

"What?"

"Cass, although I've never actually seen you dance, I doubt very much that you could actually shimmy up that rope. You know, as in wish-I-could-shimmy-like-my-sister-Kate."

"Oh, okay," he said, somewhat grumpily. "Shinny,

shimmy. But there's got to be a ladder or something up there I can throw down for you two to use."

A chill ran down my spine that had nothing to do with the ocean breeze. "Maybe we should wait. Call the police."

"And tell them what?" Jayne asked.

She had a point. The harbor patrol might not respond to a call about a sinister-looking rope dangling from a yacht. Still, my heart was beating almost audibly in my ears, and I felt there was something strangely dreadful about this silent ship. Having written background music for films and television dramatic shows, I suddenly heard a low-key, ominous phrase, played by cellos and electronic keyboard, somewhere in a dim corner of my mind.

"Go ahead," I told Cass reluctantly. "But be careful."

He stood up in the bow of our motorboat, grabbed the rope, and launched himself upward. For a moment, he dangled in a crazy way above the water, his legs kicking empty air. Then he dipped his shoulders and pushed. He swayed a little, and his feet landed against the side of the boat. Putting hand over hand on the rope, he climbed slowly up the sleek white fiberglass mountain, banging against the side and cursing loudly from time to time. The hollow words seemed to echo through the twilight, then dissolve into the playful lapping of the waves. With a loud guttural gasp, Cass finally pulled himself over the rail and landed on the deck with a flop.

"Umpf!"

"Cass, are you okay?"

"Just peachy."

As he had expected, he found an aluminum ladder, which he quickly lowered over the side of the yacht. I

297

tied our boat to the end of the dangling rope and followed Jayne up. As I stepped on board *Life Is a Game,* a bell sounded, startling me. It took a second to realize it was merely the nearby buoy catching the wake of a brightly lit cabin cruiser that was gliding in from the sea.

"Let's look around," I said brightly, trying to ward off the spookiness that seemed to descend over the deserted yacht.

I led the way down into the cabin, half hoping the interior of the boat would be locked and we could go no farther. But, alas, the door was wide open, as sinister and inviting as the dangling rope.

We climbed down steps into what appeared to be the kitchen.

"Oh, good, the galley," Cass said at my back, causing me to jump. "Wonder if there's any grub around."

"Shhh," Jayne whispered.

Only the dim light of the fading day reached us through the portholes. I stumbled against a table, and my hands found a box of kitchen matches on top. As I picked them up I had the eerie sensation that they, like the rope and open hatch door, had been left deliberately for us to find.

I lit a match and in the incandescent flare saw we were in a sumptuous wood-paneled salon. There was a kerosene lamp on the table, and I quickly lifted the glass and lit the wick.

"Why don't you two stay here while I take the lantern and look around a bit," I suggested.

"Be careful, dear."

I was gone for no longer than three minutes. When I returned to the salon, the lantern was shaking noticeably in my hand.

"Steve, what is it?" Jayne asked before I was even in the door.

"We've found Ernie Solow," I said.

"Did he tell you the whole story? Is Peter the mastermind of this murder game?"

"I'm afraid Ernie told me nothing. He's hanging from a rope in the master stateroom."

Chapter 43

I had only seen Ernie once in life, and very briefly at that—at the press party at his sister's home. Still, I felt the pathos of his death as I stared at the man dangling from the rope that came down from a closed air hatch. His eyes were open and bulging; his tongue protruded from his mouth, ugly and swollen. His two-tone hair stuck out at crazy angles. Even his clothes evoked pity: blue deck shoes, white cotton slacks, and a gaudy Hawaiian shirt of green and orange. A suitable wardrobe for a journey to Tahiti but not to cross the River Styx.

"Holy God," Cass said, holding the lantern.

"This isn't suicide," Jayne said.

"I'm afraid not. Cass, give me the lantern for a minute."

I had just noticed a scrap of paper pinned to Ernie's sleeve. As I reached for it and brushed across the dead hand, I shuddered. A shiver scurried up my spine. What I read made it cascade down through my entire body. Written in pencil, in block letters, were the words "THE JINX IS ON YOU!"

Cass chuckled grimly. "Dumb move, man. I bet a handwriting expert can tell us who wrote it."

Jayne and I were silent, fearing a more ominous meaning.

"I think we'd better get out of here," I suggested in my calmest voice.

"I agree," Jayne said.

The master cabin was a pie-shaped room at the very front of the boat. I led the way, lantern in hand, back into the main salon. My heart did a little gallop when I saw that the hatch to the deck was now closed; we had certainly left it open. I climbed up the steps and pushed on the door. As I'd feared, it was locked tight. Fighting a dizzy surge of claustrophobia, I came back down the steps.

A strange grating sound came from the bow of the boat. "What's that?" Jayne asked.

"It's the anchor being raised," Cass whispered.

We stared at each other, trying to comprehend what was in store for us. Then we heard footsteps on deck.

"Peter," I shouted, "let us out of here!"

The only answer was a growl in the bowels of the boat as the engine sputtered to life. Cass peered out a side porthole. "We're moving," he said. And, indeed, the boat had come alive. The wood softly creaked and yawned, the engine changed pitch, and we began to roll on the swells.

I tried to remember the layout of the upper deck. The pilot wheel was in the back near the rudder. That's where our captor would be standing right now, steering through the darkness to God-knows-where, a place I had no desire to visit. I didn't want to live there. I certainly didn't want to die there. I came up with a desperate idea.

"Jayne, Cass, in a moment I want you both to start pounding on the hatch and shouting as loudly as you can to be let out. That air hatch in the master cabin must lead to the bow. I'll climb out there, sneak around—"

"Are you sure you can manage it, dear?"

"No problem." I was angry. Angry at Peter and his damned haunted ship. Angry at myself for letting us get trapped, especially at sea. I rifled through the galley drawers, looking for a weapon. There were kitchen utensils, can openers, and silverware. I chose a lethal-looking kitchen knife with a wooden handle.

"Steve, maybe you should let me be the one to climb out there. I'm a little more . . . spry."

"I'll tell you what, Cass, we'll both go. It may take both of us to overpower him. Jayne, can you make enough noise so he'll believe we're all still down here?"

Jayne smiled and began to pound on the closed hatch. Then she started shouting, first in a deep voice, then in a high one, really throwing herself into the role. I took the lantern and led Cass back to the master cabin at the front of the boat. I looked at Ernie's swaying body. "We'll have to cut him down."

I held the lifeless feet; Cass climbed up on a chair and sawed at the rope with the kitchen knife. Ernie lurched into my arms, then landed with a thud in the middle of the stateroom's elegant Oriental rug.

Cass and I were both panting for breath, more from horror than from actual exertion, but there was no time to stop. I gazed upward to where Ernie had been and examined the hatch, which was at the top of a kind of square airwell several feet deep, rising to the outside deck from the suite's ceiling. The killer had used this extra space to hang Solow more efficiently. I lifted the lantern as high as I could and was pleased to see that the hatch was not locked. Luckily, the rope from which Ernie had been hanging led out a small crack to the outside and was most likely tied on the far end to some solid part of the bow. All Cass and I had to do was climb up the rope.

"I'll go first," I said. "You can give me a foot up and then when I'm out, you can use the chair to give yourself a start."

"Let's do it the other way around," Cass suggested. "I can stand on your shoulders and not even have to use the rope."

Looking down from my six-foot-three perspective to Cass's five-foot-eight frame, I could see he had a point. Cass put the handle of the kitchen knife in his teeth pirate-style, stood up on the chair, and grabbed my shoulders. It took a few tries, but finally, using the sides of the airwell to support himself, he managed to dig his heels into my shoulders and stand up.

"Can you touch the hatch?" I whispered.

"You bet. Here I go."

Cass lurched upward and my shoulders contracted with pain. Rubbing them, I looked up to where he had disappeared through the hatch. But he suddenly reappeared, tumbling back down the airwell on top of me. We did a little dance together and then landed, hard, on the corpse of Ernie Solow.

"What happened?"

"He slammed the hatch down on my head! The son of a bitch guessed what we were up to and slammed the hatch down on me!"

I looked at Cass on top of me and Ernie below me. We did not make a pleasant sandwich. "Well, don't just lie there," I said.

As Cass found his feet and started to stand, the rope began slithering up the airwell. I stared glumly as our last chance of escape disappeared, the hatch slammed shut, and the latch of it slipped into place. Hope is a

304

fragile thing in a situation like this. I felt it draining away.

"Are you all right?" Jayne entered the stateroom, tripping on Ernie's body and almost landing on top of me as I attempted to stand. Cass caught her and pointed morosely up to the locked hatch.

"Well, we'll just have to find another way out," she said positively.

"Sure," Cass said. I was not optimistic enough to comment.

We filed back into the main salon and sat around a heavy mahogany dining table. None of us dared look the other in the eye. The feeling of uselessness was hard to bear.

"We're out on the open ocean now," Cass told us, cracking his knuckles nervously. "Feel it? Instead of trotting over short, choppy swells, we're cantering up and down over sloping plains of water."

"Why, Cass, that's very poetic," Jayne said.

Suddenly, the engine changed pitch, sputtered, then died. We held our breaths, listening to a winch turning on the deck above us.

"What is that?" I whispered.

"He's putting up the sail," Cass said.

We listened intently for other clues. After a few minutes, we heard a familiar whine. It was the outboard engine of our rented motorboat starting up. We hurried to the portholes to try to see what was going on.

Outside, night had fallen completely. We were perhaps a half mile off the coast, with the lights of Los Angeles blazing brightly in the distance, sending a static glow high into the sky. Closer at hand, I saw the red and green running lights of the rented speedboat.

It was about a dozen feet from the yacht, riding over a swell toward the twinkling lights of the city.

"The rat has jumped ship," I said.

"But how can we sail without someone at the wheel?" Jayne asked.

"He must have put us on some kind of autopilot."

At that moment, the yacht heaved slightly on its side, the sails caught a stiff offshore wind, and we began rushing over the waves—on a blind race out to sea.

Chapter 44

I stood at a porthole and watched the lights of Los Angeles twinkle, fade, and finally disappear. The bow of our boat rose and fell through the waves. The wind was steady, carrying us westward.

"At least we won't starve." Jayne usually looks at the practical side in disasters, and she had been opening and closing the galley cabinets. "There's caviar, tins of salmon *pâté,* Greek olives, tea biscuits from Fortnum and Mason's."

"Calories be damned," I said. "How's our water supply?"

Jayne tried the tap on the sink. A trickle of rusty water gurgled out and then ceased to flow. Greek olives, salty fish eggs, and tea biscuits were going to be rather dry fare without something to wash them down.

"Maybe there are some cans of soda somewhere," Cass offered. He and Jayne rummaged through more cupboards, while I sat wearily down at the table and tried desperately to think of some way out of our predicament.

"Well, lookee here," Cass said. "A case of French champagne."

"Tattinger '86," Jayne observed. "Expensive stuff."

"Great. Shall we toast to our deaths?"

"Darling, don't be so negative. Surely the Coast Guard or some nice cruise ship will see us sailing off to nowhere, and we'll be back on dry land in no time."

"Right," I said, mimicking Christopher Fitzgerald's reading of the word. I began to wish timid little Lance *was* the murderer. At least we probably wouldn't be stuck out here on the briny waiting to die a soggy death. I wasn't at all optimistic that this adventure was going to have a happy ending.

Jayne's mind works so fast that I wasn't at all surprised to hear her say next, "But if we don't survive this thing, I hope they don't run that *horrible* picture of me that was in the *New York Post* recently. Remember? I was wearing that dress that I'd given Audrey, and she gave it back to me because it was too tight in the waist."

"Jayne," I said, "the day is past when newspapers run those flattering eight-by-tens that make all of us look ten years younger than we are."

"Oh, I know that," she said snappishly. "But Roger Kornblatt takes lovely pictures of us every time we run into him at a premiere or a party."

"Fine," I said. "If we ever get out of this cabin, I'll inscribe some suitable graffiti on the deck to the effect that when we buy the farm, we want Roger Kornblatt photos of us run in all the major papers."

Cass and Jayne busied themselves opening tins of *pâté,* boxes of crackers, and a bottle of the Tattinger. Peter had thoughtfully left us with crystal champagne flutes and Waterford china. It seemed as if to our host not only was life a game but death as well. My fury exploded again.

"Damn him! He's been one step ahead of us all the way. Peter knew exactly what we'd do . . . that we'd go off looking for his yacht. The son of a bitch made it just hard enough for us so that we would feel the thrill of the chase but not so tough that we wouldn't find the damn boat. He must have been waiting for us. Waiting and laughing."

Jayne came up behind me and silently massaged the back of my neck. I was as angry about being outmaneuvered as I was about the prospect of impending death.

"You'll think of something," Jayne said.

"Yeah," Cass said. "Meanwhile, have a glass of the old plonk."

"I've never liked champagne."

"Well, eat a few crackers at least, darling. We have to keep up our strength." Jayne led me over to the table, and we passed olives, caviar, and biscuits. Picking up the butter knife gave me an idea.

"Cass, where's that big kitchen knife we had?"

"I put it on the sink," Jayne said.

I walked over and picked up the knife. I felt the sturdy blade, five or six inches long, and the solid wooden handle. I smiled—for the first time in several long hours.

"What're you going to do, Steve?" Cass asked, coming up beside me.

"I'm going to cut through the hatch door, get up on deck, and turn this boat around."

"That could take all night."

"Cass, we *have* all night. So unless you have a better idea, let's get started."

We worked in turns. I took the first shift, scratching the tip of the knife against the locked wooden hatch. The wood was hard and had been lacquered to a fine finish. I began by etching a line around the lock and then started to saw and stab at it, trying to work the line gradually into a deeper cut. After fifteen minutes the results were hardly visible. After an hour, however, there was at least the start of a groove around the lock.

When my hands and shoulders got tired, Cass took over, scratching away at the wood. The sound he made was like a gnawing mouse.

Jayne took a turn when Cass became tired, and then I struggled for another hour or so, until my hands cramped around the knife's wooden handle.

When Cass took over for the second time, I stretched out on a couch in the main salon and managed to sleep for a short while.

Hours passed, with each of us alternately sawing and sleeping. Desperation kept us going.

The pink dawn broke on the water and a gray morning light filtered through the portholes into our posh prison. We still had not managed to work our way through the wood around the lock. Our faces were haggard with worry and exhaustion.

Jayne opened a new box of crackers and found a can of smoked oysters. She poured me a glass of champagne and this time I took a few sips, though I've always felt that champagne was one of the big nothings of the world. When I finished my gourmet breakfast, I took the knife from a bleary-eyed Cass.

"It's coming," he said encouragingly.

"Sure, just a little longer and we'll be sailing home."

I studied the door in the morning light. It didn't look as if we had made any progress in hours. Perhaps there was harder wood on the outer side of the hatch, or even metal. For the first time I began to panic. I sawed feverishly at the wood. "AGHHHH!" The blade snapped in half, the tip flying across the room. I stared at the broken tool in horror.

"Maybe we can use the corkscrew," Jayne said.

"Cork is soft. Wood is hard."

"Well, we can't give up."

"Of course we can't. I'll get us out of here somehow!" Knowing it was foolish, I nonetheless pushed out with my hands, slamming them at the door with all my frustration and might. A bolt of pain shot up my arm and across my shoulder. The impact made me stumble on the stairs. I looked over at Jayne, feeling worse than foolish. But she was staring, wide-eyed, at the door. I followed her gaze . . . to the most beautiful dawn I had ever seen. The hatch door had broken open; only a jagged edge of wood around the lock remained in place. The early morning sun washed over me, infusing me with renewed vigor.

"You did it, man!" Cass hooted and scampered out on deck.

"I never doubted you for a moment, darling," Jayne said, helping me up and leading the way out into the glorious seascape.

I looked around. The eastern sky blazed red and orange with the start of the day, and the ocean mirrored the steel gray of the sky. Both went on forever, unbroken by even the tiniest portion of land. Above, the white sail stretched out against the wind, like a big, wonderful sea gull. The fresh, salty smell of the open sea hit my nostrils with heady ecstasy.

Then, remembering our predicament, I glanced at the position of the sun, hurried to the steering wheel, and began to turn the craft around.

Cass let out a big cowboy yell, which died in his throat as he peered over the side of the yacht. "Jeez," he said, "we're awfully low in the water."

I looked down at the side of the boat and could see he was right. The ocean was nearly at the deck.

"Is there a bilge pump we can fire up?"

"I'll go check." Cass climbed down into the engine area and began to putter. "Hmm," I heard him say several times. "Well, I'll be damned."

I was getting very nervous. *Life Is a Game* had taken on so much water that she was riding sluggishly over the gratefully calm sea. I noticed that every few moments the bow was actually submerged beneath the waves as we moved awkwardly through the swells. A school of dolphins broke into the air a few feet from the deck. I tried to take their appearance as a good omen.

Cass finally reappeared from the engine hold, his clothes wet and greasy with oil. "Grover must have sabotaged the damn thing," he said. "It's not about to start." He grabbed a rag and began to wipe the oil from his fingers, one at a time. "I did manage to find the intake valve that had been left open, though. I closed it, so at least we don't have to worry about any more water coming in."

"Do you think we'll be able to stay afloat?" Jayne asked.

"If we don't get any wind and the ocean stays flat."

Fortunately, the ocean did remain fairly level—for an hour or two. The wind, when it came, was from the southeast, bringing with it dark clouds. Then the ocean swells increased in size, until our crippled yacht was riding sluggishly up and down the sides of what seemed like small mountains.

I'm sure it's a tribute to the yacht's sleek design that we managed to say afloat as long as we did. But, sometime after noon, one swell too many seemed to seal our fate. In horrifying slow motion, *Life Is a Game* yawed to one side, and the bow refused to come up out of the water. With a kind of lazy grace, we began sinking into a glittering, gray ocean grave.

Chapter 45

Life Is a Game disappeared forever beneath the waves at a few minutes past nine on Saturday morning. By noon the Coast Guard had mounted a major search operation after receiving an urgent phone call from Peter Grover's insurance agency informing them that the expensive yacht had been stolen and was last reported heading on a course due west from Newport Harbor.

At 1:45 Saturday afternoon, the Coast Guard helicopter discovered an oil slick and floating debris miles off the California coast. A frigate, called in to search the waters, discovered, bobbing on the waves, a couple of stray paper plates; a sofa cushion; a mostly empty, corked bottle of champagne; a deck chair, open and upright; and a life preserver with the yacht's name written across it in black letters: *LIFE IS A GAME*. Ten minutes later a sailor spotted a woman's purse. It was retrieved from the waters, and its owner was identified as Jayne Meadows Allen.

There was no sign of Mrs. Allen.

Agatha Welch told police that Mrs. Allen, her husband Steve, and the chauffeur Jimmy Cassidy had all been missing since the previous afternoon.

313

Somehow Western civilization continued on its course.

At 3:57 Saturday afternoon, Phoebe North was standing in the Beverly Hills showroom of a luxury car dealership, gazing adoringly at a light blue Jaguar while a slender, middle-aged salesman with jet-black hair and an accent like David Niven's extolled its virtues. "It's perfect for you," he said. "Aristocratic—"

"I wouldn't want people to think I was flaunting my good fortune. . . ."

"Subtle authority."

Phoebe contemplated the machine for another moment, torn between the attainable luxury and her frugal Pennsylvania upbringing. "It's a lot of money for a car. I suppose I should think this over for a while."

"Your investment will pay for itself many times over with the increased prestige and respect it will give you."

"Yes, but—" The beeper went off in her handbag, interrupting the sale. The number that lit up told her to call her production assistant, a young man by the name of Marcus Sanders. The salesman let her use his phone.

"Have you heard?" Marcus said. "Steve and Jayne are dead!"

"Oh, no! My God, what happened?"

"They drowned . . . somewhere in the Pacific. It just came over the radio. And someone named Jimmy Cassidy."

"Cass," Phoebe whispered. "Are you sure, Marcus?"

"Well, they haven't found the bodies, but the Coast Guard said it's impossible to survive in those frigid waters for more than a short time. What are we going to do about the show tomorrow night?"

Phoebe didn't answer.

"Shall I tell the network to cancel?"

"Cancel? Are you crazy? Ratings are going to top the Super Bowl!"

"But without Steve and Jayne—"

"Relax. I've already arranged their replacements."

"Already *what?*"

"Well, not theirs exactly. But with everyone dying off, I had the foresight to have a few other panelists standing by. Marcus, call the other networks and the papers. I want to arrange a media conference for seven o'clock tonight. That way we'll hit the eleven o'clock news coast to coast." Phoebe's face was grim with determination as she hung up the phone. She marched back into the showroom.

"I'll take the car," she said. "You can draw up the papers, and I'll come in Monday morning to sign them. Will ten thousand be an adequate deposit?" She pulled out her checkbook.

"Certainly, Miss North. Shall I draw up our thirty-six-month plan for the balance?"

"No!" she said, marching toward the door. "I'm paying cash."

Chapter 46

"O'm'God!" Shadow Bennington managed to turn the phrase into a single word. It was twenty minutes to show time on Sunday evening, and Shadow had just seen Phoebe North walk into the Green Room wearing a tight silver dress, black stiletto heels, and a new but retro-style hairdo that looked like a honey-colored beehive perched high on her head.

"Phoebe, you look so . . . different," she said.

"I'm Amaretta tonight," Phoebe confided. "That is, I'm taking her part on the show until we can find a replacement."

"And what about Steve and Jayne?"

"Biff Cornell and Chelsea Martin have agreed to replace them. Isn't that fabulous? What we have here, Shadow, is a brand-new show for a brand-new generation."

"Fabulous," Shadow said faintly. Biff and Chelsea were a married couple in their late twenties, an actor and actress who had been box-office attractions in trendy teen movies a decade earlier but had not been doing much since.

"Do you really think they're capable of intelligent conversation?"

"Of course! It was time to get rid of all those tired old-timers anyway. I have so many exciting new ideas. Starting next week, we're going to have a hard-rock theme song and all sorts of changes. MTV, look out. *The Murder Game* is taking over."

"But the MTV audience is mostly teenagers. Thirteen- and fourteen-year-olds," Shadow said, but Phoebe had already sailed out of the room.

The Green Room where Shadow was sitting was, of course, not green at all but a light shade of gray. Shadow had arrived early at the studio, had gone through makeup, and was now sitting in this traditional actor's waiting room studying a book on religious art in the Middle Ages. She had difficulty concentrating, however. At first she couldn't put her finger on the reason for her unease. She walked to the door and looked out at the strange men wandering about backstage. They didn't seem to be the usual stagehands or network executives she had become familiar with in the few weeks the show had been on the air.

Shadow glanced at one man, who leaned forward against a pulley rope. There was an outline of a gun beneath his shirt. She looked around at the other strangers, suddenly realizing they, too, were cops or security people. The place was swarming with them.

She returned to the chair and opened her book again, but a new distraction presented itself. A pair of Gucci loafers stopped by her side, at the bottom of her field of vision.

"Hey, babe." Tommy Blue stood in the Gucci's. "I forgive you for the scene with the hairpiece. Wha'd'ya say we let bygones be bygones and grab some dinner after the show?"

Shadow used an uncharacteristic four-letter word to

let Tommy know what she thought of his suggestion.

"Whoa, I bet you're fantastic in the sack," he replied, ever the gentleman.

Shadow raised her book like a shield in front of her face and stared hard at the pages. Just then Phoebe came back, with Biff Cornell and Chelsea Martin in tow. Phoebe gently lowered Shadow's book and began introductions. Shadow groaned. She had met—and dated—Biff a few years earlier. He had been nice enough at first but had turned out to be very self-absorbed once she'd gotten to know him. When he tried to pursue their relationship, even after his marriage to the empty-headed Chelsea, Shadow realized what a dreadful mistake she had made.

"Well, we meet again," Biff said, giving her a little wink.

"I just *love* your part on *Nights of Passion,* Shadow," Chelsea gushed. "You play the most fabulous slut!"

Shadow smiled coldly. "And what have you been up to, Chelsea?"

"You all know each other? How nice," Phoebe said. Insincere smiles were exchanged.

"Five minutes, everybody," the stage manager said, poking his head momentarily into the Green Room.

"Excuse me, I think I'll use the ladies' room," Shadow murmured. She escaped and hurried toward the dressing rooms—where she ran into another surprise. Christo was walking down the hallway, his arms full of personalized props used by Amaretta. A framed photo of her in a slithery game-show costume began to slip from his grasp; Shadow stepped forward and caught it. As she placed it back on his pile, she saw one tear escape Christo's eye and trickle down his smoothly shaved cheek.

"Amaretta was a foolish old woman, but now that she's-a gone, I miss her. I never thought I'd-a miss her. The house in Coldwater is-a big . . . lonely. I thought I'd be glad to come and go and do what I liked, but all I do is sit around all day and cry. Security found these things laying around, and I hurried over to get them. I don't wanna lose one thing that reminds me of my . . . *amore.*"

Shadow resisted the temptation to blot the tear. "You poor thing. Why don't you stick around? I'll buy you dinner after the show."

"I don't think I'd be such hot company."

"I'm not such hot company myself right now. . . . What do you say?"

Despite his sorrow, Christo's dark, languid eyes could not resist a quick look up and down Shadow's exquisite female form. "Well, maybe dinner would be nice. But I'm not sure Phoebe will like me hanging around during the show."

"It'll be fine. You can wait in my dressing room."

Christo's puppy-dog look made Shadow grin. "I'm just talking about dinner," she told him sternly, even though her eyes twinkled.

"Absolutely."

Shadow returned to the Green Room, where she found Peter Grover holding court with the panelists, a glass of mineral water with a slice of lime in one hand. He smiled smugly at the group, nodded at Shadow, then glanced past her to the door. Suddenly, his smile froze. The glass crashed to the floor, mineral water splashing over Shadow's legs. She turned to see what had startled him.

It was Jayne and I. The Allens back from the dead—which, I can assure you, had not been an easy journey.

"Good evening, ladies and germs. Are we all ready to play a little murder game?" I said.

Phoebe gasped. "You're not supposed to be here! You've been replaced!"

"Try it, and we'll see you in court," I told her pleasantly. "We've got a contract."

"Places, Mr. Grover," the stage manager said.

The show was about to begin. Consummate showman that he was, Peter recovered from his shock and quickly took charge. "Biff and Chelsea, I'm sure Phoebe will pay you well for your trouble this evening. Perhaps we can use you on the panel another time."

Phoebe sputtered objections, but Peter's natural authority silenced her. Putting one arm around Jayne and the other around me, he smiled brightly. "Welcome back. I can't tell you how glad I am to see you. It would be a very dull *Murder Game* without my dear friends."

"Tonight, friend," I said, "the game is for keeps."

Chapter 47

This Sunday night's edition of *The Murder Game* promised to be a dilly.

Whatever Peter was thinking to himself on the inside, on the outside, at least, he was wrapped in his usual unflappable urbanity. In fact, he seemed to be positively enjoying this new twist to the game, smiling elfishly at one and all. He introduced those of us on the celebrity panel: first Jayne, then me, Shadow, and finally Tommy Blue. It felt peculiar to greet Phoebe North, rather than Amaretta, on the way to our seats. She wore a slinky silver dress in a valiant attempt to be glamorous, but her smile was desperately forced and I felt a moment of pity for her, especially knowing what was to come.

After we were seated, Peter introduced the guest panelists one by one. There was a professor of criminology from John Jay College in New York, an always-busy celebrity divorce lawyer from Hollywood, a woman who had just written a book on a serial killer, and an attractive black female police officer from the LAPD. The audience was a typical Sunday night group.

As Shadow had already noticed, the place was

crawling with cops—in the hallways backstage, in the auditorium, at the rear of every aisle—and Lieutenant Washington himself was sitting in the front row, looking large and forbidding.

Shadow had been sending me strange piercing glances ever since Jayne and I had come back from the dead. "What's happening, Steve?" she whispered while the guest panel was being introduced. I smiled innocently, shrugged, and said nothing.

After the introductions had been made, Phoebe began to read from a TelePrompTer the text that would narrate the night's crime. She began boldly enough but stumbled as strange words appeared on the screen, words she knew had not been written by the show's writers. In an uncertain voice, she continued to read: " 'Tonight . . . uh . . . for a very special edition of *The Murder Game,* Steve Allen will narrate a real-life crime' . . . Good God!"

"Indeed I will," I agreed, rising from my seat and walking over to where Phoebe stood centerstage. "Phoebe, why don't you take my chair next to Jayne? You can be on the panel tonight."

Phoebe blinked and looked as if she was about to faint—both from stage fright and confusion. She glanced toward Peter for help, but he just smiled back and said, "Yes, that's a lovely idea. Why *don't* you sit down, Phoebe?"

I faced the cameras and the studio audience. The moment of truth had come, and I didn't need the TelePrompTer. I knew the details of the case all too well.

The stage grew dark, and the game board transformed itself into a video screen, showing a greatly enlarged black-and-white photograph of a sternly handsome young man with jet-black hair, a trim mustache, and piercing dark eyes.

"Ladies and gentlemen, panelists . . . please meet Carlo Verdi, born in southern Italy in 1939. For those of you who have enjoyed *The Murder Game* over these many years, this is the man you must thank."

A murmur rippled through the theater.

"Carlo came to this country in 1958, at the age of nineteen, determined to make his fortune. He settled for a few years on the Lower East Side of New York City, where he met and married a pretty Italian girl, Maria Grazia Sacrepanti. The young couple, like many before them, moved west to California, hoping to find new opportunities. What Carlo Verdi found, however, was a food service position at the old Brown Derby restaurant in Beverly Hills, a position that brought him in daily contact with the most powerful members of the Hollywood community."

I paused and glanced briefly at Peter, who—imperturbable as ever—nodded once, his faint smile urging me to continue.

"Carlo Verdi had a knack for games and intricate puzzles. Perhaps it was in the boring moments of clearing tables and emptying ashtrays that he dreamed up one of the most successful games of all time—*The Murder Game* . . . the very show we're enjoying tonight. But what was a mere waiter to do with such an exciting concept?"

I paused, looking briefly at Peter.

"Carlo took a chance. He confided his idea to someone he thought might help him, an important customer at the Brown Derby—a man who, sad to say, turned out to be unscrupulous. The man stole the idea, pretended it was his own, and made a fortune. That man, ladies and gentlemen, is . . ."

The photograph on the video screen faded out and was replaced by an early clip of Peter Grover hosting the original *Murder Game*. The audience, as well as both sets of panelists, gasped.

"That's right. Our charming friend, Peter Grover, betrayed the young waiter's trust, plagiarized his creativity, and shared none of the resulting gold. There is no doubt that our host is a thief. But now we must ask ourselves: Is he a murderer as well?"

Every eye in the auditorium turned to Peter to see his reaction to the charge. He merely shrugged and, to my surprise, maintained his amused smile.

"Please continue," he said, in a very sporting manner considering the circumstances.

"I will," I assured him. The video screen returned to the earlier photo of Carlo Verdi, which Agatha had cleverly found on file at the restaurant union to which the young Italian had once belonged.

"One day, a few months after Mr. Verdi confided his idea to Peter Grover, the waiter happened to be serving two network executives who were discussing an upcoming show—which Carlo immediately recognized as based on his idea. The young man, understandably furious, caused a scene that resulted in his losing his job. He went to a nearby bar, had a few drinks to bolster his courage, and then made his way out to confront Mr. Grover at his hilltop home on Mulholland Drive. We can only imagine what words were exchanged at this meeting. Carlo left Peter's house distraught and not entirely sober. His brakes failed coming down the curving road from the hills, his car smashed into a tree, and the young man was killed. Police ruled the mishap an accident. It was, in fact, the very first of a series of mysterious accidents that the media would later ascribe to 'a jinx.' "

I paused, and again there was a commotion as the audience and two panels realized for the first time how far back the mystery reached. I noticed Lieutenant Washington in the front row, staring at me with steel-cold eyes and a tense frown.

I continued. "Now, of the two executives who had been chatting at lunch about the upcoming game show, there is only one whose identity need concern us here. That man was Abe Brautigan, who became the original producer of *The Murder Game.*"

The screen lit up with a film clip of Abe in a tuxedo attending an Emmy Awards show sometime in the mid-seventies. He had silver hair by this time and a sharp wolfish face.

"Those of us who were fortunate enough to have known Mr. Brautigan remember him as a hardworking, down-to-earth guy who amused us with his constant complaints that you couldn't find a good corned beef sandwich anywhere in California. Abe was a sweetheart in the rough but, unfortunately, he had a touch of larceny in his soul.

"After the scene at the Derby, he knew the secret of *The Murder Game*'s true origin. Abe thought he might use this knowledge to better himself. Mid-level executives at large television studios, after all, come and go with regularity. As the producer of a hit show, however, you can pretty much call your shots. So Abe blackmailed his way into becoming Peter's partner in *The Murder Game.* Peter went to the top brass and convinced them that he needed Abe at the helm. Abe became producer, and Peter's theft remained a secret.

"And so the years passed. Peter Grover grew very rich; Abe grew rich enough. Eventually, of course, *The Murder Game* went off the air. Abe produced another game show that didn't do as well, and in the mid-eighties he retired to a golfing community outside Palm Springs."

On a hand-signal from the floor manager, we broke for a commercial. I saw Lieutenant Washington move from his chair and onto the stage. Everyone was stunned to silence as he took Phoebe to one side, where the two held a whispered conference. Only Jayne and I knew, of course, that he was giving her the news of her brother's death. We had not wanted it sprung on her in the middle of a game show on national TV.

Peter was giving me a bemused smile, but I avoided his eye. He started my way, but the floor manager called for places, and he automatically obeyed.

Phoebe returned to her seat on the panel, her emotions held professionally in check. But there was a sad glint of determination in her eye, and I knew her interest in solving this mystery had just become very personal. I gave her a sympathetic look as I turned toward the video screen.

A recent picture of Abe beside his golf cart, club casually resting on his shoulder, appeared on the screen. Abe was smiling, but his eyes and stance revealed his apathy. Agatha had tracked down this picture from Penny Tarrington at Oasis Village.

"Many might be satisfied with having had such a long and successful television career, but after a few years of endless golf, Abe Brautigan found himself bored. Retirement did not suit this brash go-getter. He was longing for action, when he heard rumors that the network was planning to update *The Murder Game* and put it back on the air. Peter would be the host, Amaretta his female assistant, and Jayne, Sylvia, Susan, and Dominic would reprise their roles as the celebrity panel. Abe desperately wanted to come out of retirement, join his friends, and produce the show once again.

"Unfortunately, what seemed clear to Abe was not at all plain to the new generation of network decision-makers. Abe was too old. Unlike the other members of the original *Murder Game* team, he had done his labors off-camera, so America would not miss his face. The network wanted someone young and hip, someone who would gear the show to today's audience. They settled on the talented Phoebe North."

I nodded toward Phoebe. She gave me a subdued smile, and there was a sprinkling of applause. I went on.

"Abe, alas, did not take this rejection lying down. He resorted to his old tricks. He blackmailed Amaretta, threatening to reveal her true age if she didn't help him get his old job back. When this didn't work, he used his blackmail trick a second time with Peter Grover.

"But then, quite unexpectedly, Abe suffered a fatal accident when the brakes of his golf cart failed on a hill—just as the brakes of Carlo Verdi's car had failed so many years before. The press, in their selective wisdom, did not notice this unimportant death miles from Hollywood. But it was, nonetheless, Mysterious Accident Number Two."

I had my audience spellbound, and I continued into details of the more publicized deaths—those of Sylvia, Susan, Dominic, and Amaretta—repeating the facts that were mostly well known: a drowning, a fall, an electric garage door slamming down unexpectedly, and finally, arsenic poisoning. Lastly, I spoke of Ernie Solow, brother of Phoebe North, and how Jayne and I had discovered him hanging from a rope on Peter's yacht. Phoebe's eyes filled with tears, but she willed them away as I quickly went on.

"And so we have what appear to be five mysterious accidental deaths, as well as two deaths—Amaretta's and Ernie's—that cannot be construed as accidents at all. Your job, panelists, in order to win this final edition of *The Murder Game,* is to examine these seven cases, decide who was really murdered, who the killer is, and what is the motive for the crime. You will need clues, of course, and they will be supplied to you in the usual fashion. Answer a question correctly, win a clue. Due to the reality of this evening's crime, however, no money will be awarded. And the usual time limits will not apply. The network has agreed to preempt its customary Sunday-night lineup; the game will continue until the crime is solved. And now another word from our sponsor."

The minute the stage lights dimmed, I heard someone clapping. It was Peter.

"Bravo!" he said, coming forward. "This will be the ultimate *Murder Game,* Steve!"

"But aren't you afraid you might lose, Peter?"

"Lose, win—what does it matter? All I care about, my friend, is how we play the game."

Chapter 48

During the commercial break, there was a small disturbance at the rear of the auditorium as a handsome woman in her mid-fifties arrived late for the show and tried to get seated. The woman had a grave, dignified face and wore a small black hat with her long, graying hair pulled back tightly into a bun at the back of her head. She was dressed in an unstylish sacklike black dress that looked as if it belonged in another era; there was a single strand of cultured pearls around her neck. There was something European about her, something alien to the sunny styles of southern California.

"Sorry, but the auditorium is closed for the live broadcast," said a uniformed page, blocking her way.

"But I have a note from Mr. Allen requesting my presence. I flew all the way from Florida to get here, and there was unbelievable traffic from the airport. You won't keep me out after such a long journey, will you?"

The woman produced the note from an oversized black handbag and gave it to the page.

He frowned and examined the letter, which was typed neatly on the stationery of "Steve Allen Productions." The young man had no way of knowing there was no such company, that Jayne and I called our outfit Meadowlane Enterprises.

"Who let you up here?" inquired the page. "The doors are supposed to be closed downstairs."

"I showed the note to a nice security guard, and he put me in the elevator. I don't want to get anyone in trouble. I've never been in a television studio before."

"Would you wait here, please," the page said. He disappeared momentarily inside the auditorium, taking the note to his superior. He returned shortly. "You're in luck. They're on a commercial break right now, so if you'll follow me, I can seat you."

He led the woman to an empty seat at the extreme left-hand side of the auditorium, in the sixth row. She settled in just as the stage lights came up in preparation for going back on the air. Two rows ahead of her and closer to the center sat Lance Grusky, and in the very front row was Bobo Van Martinson. Both of them had also received special invitations to the show from Lieutenant Washington, who glanced around from time to time, curious as to their reactions to the various clues and questions.

The APPLAUSE sign flashed, the audience cheered, and we were once again on live coast-to-coast.

"Peter," I said, "you're the host." He took over his customary job and I stood a few feet away, at the spot where first Amaretta and then Phoebe had been.

"I'll remind you, panelists, that in this special edition of *The Murder Game* the rules may have to be modified slightly, but as always, the point of the game is to name the correct murderer," he announced cheerfully. "And now let's have the first question, please."

The game board did its customary song and dance and lit up with flashing lights, which formed the words I had earlier supplied to the director: WHERE WAS

THE BODY OF SYLVIA VAN MARTINSON DIS-COVERED? As usual, this first question was given to the guest panel.

"Beneath the Santa Monica pier," replied the female officer.

"That is . . . correct!" Peter said. The audience applauded. "And now . . . er . . . for your clue," he hesitated, looking my way for assistance.

"I'll give out the clues tonight," I told him. The guest panel chose Forensic Lab from the clue categories on the board, and I was able to oblige them. I printed a clue on a piece of paper and handed it to the guest panelists. I gave them a riddle that had long puzzled Jayne and me: "THE FOLLOWING NOTE WAS FOUND IN SYLVIA'S WASTEBASKET: 'VERDI. 10 AM UNDER THE PIER. MASTER C.' " They studied this briefly with interest and confusion, which I well understood.

The guest panel won the next four clues in a row. I was afraid Jayne, Shadow, Phoebe, and Tommy wouldn't get a chance to get into the game, but finally the guests failed to answer correctly who it was that had left a message on Dominic Carrow's answering machine, causing him to rush heedlessly into his garage door.

"It was Peter Grover," Phoebe said, looking at our host suspiciously when the question was thrown to our side.

I should mention that since Jayne had an unfair advantage, she kept fairly silent throughout the game, allowing Tommy, Shadow, and Phoebe to field the various questions and clues. I admired her restraint.

Actually, we had done much the same thing in the old days, when Jayne was on *I've Got a Secret* and I was a panelist on *What's My Line?*, and, for whatever reason, one of us had happened, accidentally and innocently, to discover the identity of a mystery guest. I can still hear publisher Bennett Cerf saying, "I'm going to disqualify myself here because, as it happens, I had dinner last evening with our guest and her secret slipped out."

The game went back and forth from panel to panel, and I handed out the bits of information Jayne and I had accumulated over the previous few weeks: how Ernie Solow had been employed at Oasis Village but had disappeared after the death of Abe Brautigan; how Ernie had mentioned a mysterious friend who owned a yacht; how Lance Grusky, assistant to Susan Fitzgerald, had stood to benefit from her estate; how Bobo Van Martinson, the quirky daughter of Sylvia, had dated Ernie after meeting him by the Santa Monica pier . . . and more.

The clues spared no one. I disclosed the fact that Shadow Bennington had been at Le Ponce de Leon shortly before Amaretta was poisoned and that it was her shy boyfriend from UCLA, Matthew Wilson, who had served the fatal elixir. I didn't give away Shadow's youthful secret, but when the guest panel won a clue, I told them that Dominic had learned something quite sensational about Shadow's life and had been planning to expose her when he died.

Christo, too, was a suspect. I had learned from Lieutenant Washington that he stood to gain 4.3 million dollars from Amaretta's estate. I passed this information on to the celebrity panel when it was their turn.

All this took some time. The special edition of the show was becoming a marathon.

We broke for another commercial, and then, ten minutes later, we broke again, giving local stations around the country a chance to identify themselves.

Gradually, after nearly an hour on the air, the entire case had been laid out in front of the two panels, with all its contradictory facts. I could tell that the panelists, with the exception of Jayne, were properly bewildered.

It was at the top of the second hour that the guest panel finally made an accusation. The policewoman from the LAPD acted as their spokesperson. "I think it's fairly obvious," she said, looking long and hard at our urbane host. "You masterminded the murders, Mr. Grover, and Ernie Solow was your accomplice. He actually carried out the killings. Your motive was to cover up your theft of *The Murder Game* and create what would appear to be a series of accidents that would divert suspicion away from yourself."

Peter smiled. "Well, let's see if you're right. Steve, do you have an envelope for me?"

"I do indeed," I told him. I took an envelope out of my jacket pocket and gave it to him, watching closely as he read the name inside. A game player to the end, Peter betrayed no expression at all.

"Your accusation," he announced dramatically, "is absolutely . . . *in*correct."

There was a collective sigh from the audience, who had been sitting on the edge of their seats.

"I have it!" shouted Tommy Blue. He was out of turn, but no one really minded. "It's Shadow Bennington! Don'cha see? She had the motive *and* the opportunity. . . ."

"You're crazy," Shadow interrupted. "It's *you!*"

"Me? Why the hell would *I* kill anyone?"

"For laughing at your hairpiece, probably."

Tommy and Shadow looked as if they were about to get into a fist fight, and several of the audience members were standing to get a better look.

"You're all wrong," Phoebe said. "It was Lance. He's a serial killer who has affairs with rich older women and then kills them off, just like Bluebeard."

"Please, let's have some order here," Peter said. "We can't have a proper game unless everyone plays by the rules!"

But the rules had gone by the wayside, and this wasn't a game anymore. Peter looked at me helplessly. I decided to end the game and simply name the killer. But before I could speak, I noticed the late-arriving elderly woman in black stand up and walk closer to the stage. Normally, a page might have stopped the woman and asked her to return to her seat, but like everyone else, the young ushers were watching the stage, mouths agape.

A loud crack of a pistol shot echoed through the theater. Several people screamed. We all ducked for cover. At first I wasn't certain what had happened or if anyone had been hit. Then I saw the woman in black standing at the foot of the stage, pistol in her outstretched right hand. She was about to shoot again, but Lieutenant Washington rushed her, tackling her to the floor. The gun exploded a second time, hitting an overhead light bulb, before the lieutenant wrenched it from her hands.

There was more screaming, and some of the audience at the rear of the auditorium charged the exit. I glanced at Jayne to make sure she hadn't been hit. She was all right, on her feet, mouth open. I looked frantically about the stage.

Peter was standing by himself, a look of shock on his face, clutching a bleeding shoulder. He sank slowly to his knees. "Holy hell," he whispered, collapsing face forward onto the stage floor. Undercover policemen swarmed the stage and surrounded him.

Shadow Bennington was by my side. "It's Verdi's widow, isn't it?" she asked, staring at the front of the stage where Lieutenant Washington was struggling to get handcuffs on the lady in black. She was putting up a good fight, and a second officer stepped in to help subdue her.

"This has all been about revenge, hasn't it?" Shadow continued. "Mrs. Verdi's been killing off everyone who benefited from her husband's stolen idea."

"You're almost right," Jayne said, coming over to us. "Revenge was the motive. But that person in black is *not* Carlo's widow."

"Then who the hell is she?" Phoebe asked, joining us.

I stepped down beside Lieutenant Washington and his prisoner. "First of all, this isn't a she. It's a he. May I, Lieutenant?"

The lieutenant nodded.

I yanked off the hat and the gray wig. A long black ponytail flopped down the young man's back. He glared at me from behind woman's lipstick and mascara.

"Christo!" Phoebe and Shadow said it together, their eyes wide in disbelief.

"Meet Lorenzo Verdi, only son of the late Carlo. Raised on venomous stories by his mother, he had as a child been sworn to revenge."

"Thief!" the young man shouted at Peter's prostrate form, over which a doctor worked. "I saved you for last so you would know what was coming and would spend your final days in terror." He spit at the stage.

As I returned to the stage and stood beside Jayne, Lieutenant Washington signaled to his men. Jayne took my hand as they led Christo—Lorenzo—away.

Chapter 49

"No kidding . . . yeah . . . well, let me know if there's any change." Lieutenant Washington put down the receiver and smiled grimly.

"It looks like Grover's going to make it. The bullet passed through without damaging any major arteries or organs. He probably fainted from shock."

Cass, Agatha, and Jayne were sitting on the pale green sofa backstage in our dressing room, while I sat sidesaddle on its left arm. Lieutenant Washington straddled a chair by the makeup table. There was a knock on the door, and I opened it to find Shadow and Phoebe in the hallway.

"Are we intruding?" Shadow asked.

"Not at all. Come in." I stepped aside, and the two women walked into the room.

"Any word on Peter's condition?" Phoebe asked.

"He's going to be fine."

"Will he go to prison?"

I deferred the question to Lieutenant Washington, who shrugged and said, "Probably not."

"But didn't he kill Carlo Verdi?"

"We'll never know for certain," the lieutenant said. "Personally, I doubt it. I've been looking at the old accident report. Not only did the autopsy show Carlo to be legally drunk, but several eyewitnesses saw him driving at an excessive speed shortly before the crash. Carlo's death was probably what it appeared to be at the time—an accident."

"But even if he's not a murderer, Peter's certainly a thief," Shadow said. "Can't he be put in jail for that?"

"No. That's a civil case," the lieutenant said. "Remember that thing a few years back when Art Buchwald sued Paramount, claiming he, not Eddie Murphy, was the real author of *Coming to America?* Same deal. Maria Verdi would have to hire a lawyer and instigate a lawsuit."

"But you managed to find her somewhere, right? Mrs. Verdi?"

"That was Agatha," I said, smiling at my blossoming fuzzy-haired assistant who stood beside Cass.

"You found her?" Phoebe stared at her former secretary with new respect.

"Actually, Mrs. Verdi found me," Agatha admitted. "On Saturday afternoon she left a message on the answering machine at Steve and Jayne's house. When I retrieved the messages, I called her back at her home in Naples, Florida. She was in a difficult position. She loved her son Lorenzo and shared his hatred of Peter, but she just couldn't stand for there to be any more deaths."

"Mrs. Verdi's call broke the case, of course," I explained. "She hadn't seen her son in nearly a decade, but the moment she started reading about 'The Jinx' in her supermarket tabloids, she knew he was behind the deaths."

"You'd better start at the beginning, Steve," Shadow said, getting comfortable in a chair. "We have tons of questions."

"In a way, Mrs. Verdi *is* the beginning. She was intensely proud of her husband, and she knew all about the game he called 'Detective.' She knew Carlo had pitched the idea to an important customer at the Brown Derby. When Carlo was killed, she was pregnant. The money Carlo would have earned from the show would have assured their son a good life. It was why they had come to America. Peter's theft and her husband's death destroyed those dreams."

"But why didn't she go to the cops? Why didn't she sue Peter the moment *The Murder Game* went on the air?" Phoebe questioned.

Jayne answered. "In 1966, Maria Verdi hardly spoke a word of English, and like most newly arrived immigrants, she was terrified of lawyers, police, anyone official. And she had no proof. Carlo had a few scrawled notes, but whether through ignorance or trust, he had not retained a copy of the game outline he had given to Peter."

"I suppose she didn't even understand about copyrights and patents and stuff," Phoebe said sadly.

"She may not have known her legal options, but she understood vendetta as only a Sicilian could," Lieutenant Washington said.

"Some Sicilians," I said.

"Although her son never knew his father, he was raised in the shadow of the great wrong that had been done the family. The mother recited the story of the stolen *Murder Game* as a bedtime tale. While other children Lorenzo's age grew up on *Jack and the Beanstalk,* Mrs. Verdi swore her son to vengeance against their real-life ogre."

"And yet she finally relented," Shadow said.

"Yes," I said. "She married again, a Jewish fellow who ran a hardware store. She learned English, had two more children, and lived a pleasant middle-class life in Florida. Although the anger never completely went away, at least she wasn't inclined to murder over it anymore."

"Too bad Christo couldn't have gotten the message."

"The boy grew up on anger; he was nurtured by it. Programmed from birth for vengeance. When his mother married again, he saw it as a defection from the cause and at seventeen he ran away, drifting almost unconsciously toward the scene of the crime. He cut off all contact with his mother, became a loner."

"How sad," Phoebe said.

"Lorenzo was very bright. He seems to have inherited his father's talent for games and puzzles," Jayne said. "Naturally, that made him decide to seek his revenge in a manner worthy of the game his father had invented."

"So he created the indolent, dull-witted character of Christo. It was the perfect disguise—the last person you'd expect to have the brains and drive to plan such ingenious crimes."

"And Amaretta was the first move of his game."

"Yes. He set out to marry the aging beauty, and since he was remarkably handsome, it wasn't a difficult task. Being Amaretta's husband gave him an inside line to the members of *The Murder Game*. That's all he needed to carry out his executions and cover his tracks."

"Wait a minute," Shadow said. "Christo and Amaretta were married at least a year and a half ago. That was way before there was even a rumor of a *Murder Game* reunion show."

"Amazing," Phoebe said.

"What?"

"The first feelers about reviving the show were put out by Amaretta. She took one of the network chiefs to lunch . . . God, over a year ago. And the whole thing moved forward from there."

"An idea whispered in her ear by Christo, no doubt. A pillow-talk suggestion easily accepted by the slightly desperate, fading star."

"Brilliant," Jayne added.

"Oh, yes, the man was clever," I agreed. "Not only was a reunion show the perfect opportunity to get all the original bunch together, but in Lorenzo's mind, outmaneuvering us in an ultimate *Murder Game* would validate his father's creativity. He certainly played the game more brilliantly than his father had ever imagined it. Because of his single-minded purpose, drilled into him as a child, his confused logic perhaps made him believe that killing four victims so cleverly that the police didn't even mount a serious investigation would have made his father proud. Even Amaretta's death, although ruled a murder, confused us, since it seemed to be born of such a different *modus operandi*."

"But how did he accomplish all the murders?" Shadow asked. "Even with Ernie's help, I just don't see how he physically did it all. I mean, how can you make a garage door come down on someone's head at just the right moment?"

"Let's start with Ernie," I said.

Phoebe, who had been standing since she had entered the room, sunk into a chair at the mention of her brother's name.

"Are you okay, dear?" Jayne asked. Phoebe nodded.

"I tried to help him, but Ernie had a wild streak. I

343

guess I know some of the details already; I just refused to see them. Go ahead with your story, Steve."

"Christo knew he had to have an accomplice. When he met Ernie, he'd found his man. They met when Ernie was working in the mailroom at the network. Christo asked him out for a drink and listened to him complaining about his seven-dollars-an-hour pay. Christo laid out the fortune they could make selling marijuana, cocaine . . . ecstasy to the high rollers at the studio. He had no trouble convincing Ernie how easy and natural it would be. Delivering mail to the network offices, Ernie had access everywhere and a clever way to make the trade—money for drugs. So they became partners. Christo supplied the drugs, Ernie turned the deals."

"But how do you know that?" Shadow asked.

I turned to Lieutenant Washington, who cleared his throat. "Several months ago," he said, "the top brass contacted the LAPD and the Sheriff's Department asking for an investigation. The narcotics division has actually known about Christo's involvement for several weeks. I wish they had told *me*. Unfortunately, different departments of a law enforcement agency generally don't connect."

Washington nodded at me to continue the story. "The undercover operation was able to document a number of meetings between Christo and Ernie," I said. "In fact, they'd even determined that Christo's real name was Lorenzo Verdi and that he had a juvenile drug record in Florida. They were just holding off on the arrest until they'd built a better case. Also, of course, they hoped to get a line on Christo's suppliers."

"So Christo was Ernie's 'rich friend.' But I thought

344

you said it was Peter." Phoebe gave me a skeptical look.

"I was mistaken. Peter was not involved with Ernie at all. All the information I had about that, you know, came from Christo himself. The story about Ernie talking about his friend's yacht was pure fabrication. Christo wanted to send me down a wrong road, and he knew exactly how to do it. He knew that by pointing the finger at Peter, he'd make me move cautiously, Peter being an old friend and all."

"But why drugs?" Phoebe asked. "What did enlisting my brother as a drug pusher have to do with murder?"

"Once Ernie had become his brother-in-crime, so to speak, Christo knew it wouldn't be difficult to talk him into more of the same."

"But murder? That's a big jump from drug dealing, Steve."

"Perhaps, but the money Christo promised Ernie for both spoke the same language to your brother, who was jealous of your success."

"A week before he died, Ernie deposited forty thousand dollars into his account," Lieutenant Washington said. "By that time, Verdi was so sure of himself and his ability to get away with the murders, he paid Ernie by check—signed Lorenzo Verdi."

"Where did Christo get that kind of money?" Shadow asked.

"He's actually a wealthy man," I answered. "He's been running con games on people since he left Florida, and he never lived an extravagant life. Once he married Amaretta, of course, she footed all the bills. I'm sure it was easy for someone so clever to talk someone so desperate out of additional monies from time to time. Regardless of where the money came from, it, plus the camaraderie he offered, bought Ernie's help. Christo's first accident was fairly simple to arrange and contained an element of poetic justice, in that failed brakes were what had killed his father. He sent Ernie to Oasis Village to do a little tinkering with Abe's golf cart. Getting rid of Sylvia was a bit more complicated."

"Did Ernie kill her, too?" Phoebe asked.

"He hasn't confessed, but my guess is Christo did that one himself. An anonymous phone call alluding to Peter's theft of *The Murder Game* concept from an Italian waiter would have whet Sylvia's keen reporter instincts. He would have had no trouble luring her to the pier for further information. The note we found: VERDI. 10 AM UNDER THE PIER. MASTER C. was in Sylvia's handwriting, probably made at the time of the call.

"What about the Master C. part?"

"Christo probably told Sylvia he would tell her everything, including the details of Abe's murder," Jayne said. "Maybe he mentioned the failed master cylinder. Maybe he promised to bring it along as proof of Abe's murder—by Peter."

"The fog that morning was a lucky break for him," I added. "All he had to do was hold Sylvia's head underwater until she drowned."

It took some time to cover everything, and in a few places I could only make an informed guess as to what had happened. With the murder of Susan Fitzgerald, for instance, both Ernie and Christo had been present in the darkened house. Either of them could have pushed the befuddled old woman down the stairs. I guessed it was Christo. Perhaps he hadn't even planned Susan's death for that evening, but he was fast and clever enough to take advantage of the situation when the house was dark and the opportunity presented itself. Revenge was constantly on his mind, and having all the intended victims together in one place certainly would have made him open to any possibility to act it out.

The next murder was Carrow's. I was virtually certain this was Ernie's doing—at the behest of Christo/Lorenzo, of course. Death came not from the door itself, but from Carrow's head supposedly hitting the pavement. If Ernie had been hiding in the garage when Dominic arrived home, he could have easily cracked him over the head with a piece of lumber or a garden rake, placed the limp body under the garage door, and pushed the button on the electronic closer. As for Peter's simultaneous call to Carrow, that was simply coincidence.

"Now we come to a problem," I said. "As everyone began to die off, it would have been highly suspicious if some attempt had not been made against Amaretta and Christo. So we have the shots fired at their car. Ernie would have to have done that. At the time we were confused because it seemed obvious that if someone had *really* wanted to kill Amaretta and Christo, he would have fired as they were leaving my driveway. The shots, therefore, had to be a smoke screen, to draw suspicion away from Christo. The blackmail note sent to Amaretta was likewise an attempt to draw suspicions away from Amaretta's household, and it cleverly muddied the waters for a time."

"But Christo drank the same elixir that poisoned his wife," Shadow objected.

"He only drank a little, and he drank reluctantly, I can assure you. That was a calculated risk, but he believed his general health and youth would pull him through. It was a bold, ingenious move. A very convincing cover."

"Then he was the one who sent the money and poison to my friend Matt!" Shadow said. "Wasn't that a big risk? What if Matt had taken the letter to the police?"

"Christo was smart. He researched your friend thoroughly. Knew he needed the money, knew that he was . . ."

"Weak?"

"Christo had a genius for understanding people's psyche. He figured out how to control Ernie, your friend Matt, even Jayne and me."

"You two?" Lieutenant Washington seemed amazed that I would admit to having been duped.

"He knew our weakness was sleuthing, so he cleverly dropped us just enough clues about Peter's yacht so we'd go out looking for the damned thing. Ernie was a liability by this time, too, so Christo came up with the perfect plan to get rid of the three of us at once."

"But we escaped," Jayne said, "and were able to set up this special show for tonight."

"Hoping, of course, that Christo, thinking Jayne and I were dead, would not be able to resist using the true-life edition of *The Murder Game* to make an attempt on his final victim."

"You used Peter as *bait?*" Phoebe asked.

"Well, we knew Christo was the killer, but we didn't have a lot of proof to take to court. It was very helpful that he revealed himself at the end so obligingly. Of course, Peter wasn't supposed to get hurt; that's why there were cops all over the place."

"Unfortunately, we weren't looking for a woman," Lieutenant Washington muttered.

"And this time Christo didn't plan to get away. Peter would be the last victim, the vendetta would be complete, and the young man would take his bow—on live coast-to-coast television, no less. And that's about the end of it."

"Oh, no you don't," Shadow said. "You haven't told us how you escaped from the yacht."

I smiled and was about to respond, when the dressing room phone rang. I picked it up, and my smile vanished. "Hmm," I said. "I'm listening. . . ."

I held onto the receiver for several minutes while the others watched me, growing more and more curious as I said nothing more. Finally, I dropped the receiver onto its cradle and turned back to the others. My smile had returned.

Jayne looked ready to burst from curiosity. "Well?" she said at last. "Who was it?"

"It was Peter. He phoned from his hospital bed. I guess he's doing okay."

"What nerve! Is he really going to get out of this scot-free?" Phoebe asked.

"Yes and no. He wanted to tell me that he's giving Carlo's widow all his money, even his house in Bel Air. He thinks it's only fair, since he lost the game."

"The game!?" They said it in unison.

"In his own way, he wants to play by the rules."

"But the house in Bel Air is worth millions! Is he really giving that up?"

"That's what he says, and I believe him. He said he'd keep enough for a first-class ticket, one way, to Singapore, and fifty thousand dollars to start over."

"What the hell's in Singapore?" Cass asked. He had been keeping fairly quiet much longer than he was usually able to.

"Opportunity. Peter feels the Pacific Basin is the

place where a guy like him can make a killing these days. I guess he's just looking for a new game to play."

"It looks as if I'll have to find a new game myself," Phoebe said unhappily. "This is certainly the end of the line for *The Murder Game.*"

"I have an idea for a show," Agatha said.

"You do?"

The timid girl started boldly pitching it right then and there. Phoebe gradually brightened as Agatha suggested making a movie-of-the-week out of a murder mystery—this murder mystery, to be exact.

"Maybe it could be a pilot for a series," Phoebe jumped in excitedly. "We could take other unsolved murder cases and play them out. Maybe even use a 900-number for viewers to call in with their solutions! It could be a monster hit!" Optimism runs high in Hollywood when a bright new concept is found.

"Well, I'm ready for a late dinner," I said to Jayne.

"Wait just a minute," Shadow said. "You haven't quite finished your tale. What about you and Jayne on the yacht?"

"Ah," I said. "Yes, that certainly looked foreboding for a while. We and Cass were trapped in a sinking yacht, miles from shore. Thank goodness a school of dolphins came along, and they were all smart students."

"Dolphins?"

"And tuna."

"Steve . . ."

"Dolphins swim with tuna, you see. Why they do so no one knows, but fishermen take advantage of the fact and track dolphins through the high seas, to snare the tuna. And that's what happened. Flipper and his friends unwittingly led a tuna boat our way. In just the nick of time."

"And they rescued you! Thank God!"

"I'll second that," Jayne said. "Come on, Steve, let's go have some dinner. What would you like?"

"Anything but a tuna sandwich, dear. We owe them too much."